Also by Laura May

The One Woman

I See You in My Dreams

I See You in My Dreams

LAURA MAY

Sometimes those dreams are just too real...

Content Warning

Dear Reader,

This book contains scenes that may be uncomfortable or even painful to read for some readers. I care about your well-being, and I believe reading should always be an enjoyable adventure. That's why I decided to compile a short list of topics that can be difficult for someone to read about.

If you are not easily triggered, feel free to skip this section, as it may contain mild spoilers.

Here's a description of what could be found in this book:

- Violence: Some parts of this book depict physical violence.
- Suicide: This topic is included in the book but isn't described in detail.
- Abusive situations: The story contains physical and emotional abuse.

- Steamy sex: There are explicit sexual scenes in this book.

Thank you for choosing this book, and I hope to see you on the other side of the story!

This is a work of fiction. All of the characters, organizations, and events portrayed in this novel are either products of the author's imagination or are used fictitiously.

Published in the United States by Creative James Media.

I SEE YOU IN MY DREAMS. Copyright © 2024 by Laura May. All rights reserved. Printed in the United States of America. For information, address Creative James Media, 9150 Fort Smallwood Road, Pasadena, MD 21122.

www.creativejamesmedia.com

978-1-956183-36-8 (trade paperback)

First U.S. Edition 2024

One

During the past two weeks, I'd been living a double life. One, my usual daily life of a high school student; second, the life of a seventeen-year-old girl from Riga, somewhere in the mid-thirties of the twentieth century.

My life? There was nothing to tell. Her life was pretty much the same but at a different time with peculiar decorations.

Every night when I went to sleep the moment I closed my eyes, I opened them as hers.

The first time it happened was exactly two weeks ago. It was the usual Friday night; I could have said that I was hanging out with my friends at the party, but no, I was at home with my parents. It was a night like many nights before. After we devoured the burgers my dad grilled outside, we watched the latest superhero movie on our new TV which was the size of Monaco. The volume cranked up high to outcry the roar of cicadas who occupied a nearby tree. Three of us were perched on our recliner chairs, the bowl of butter popcorn half finished.

After I kissed my mom good night and shuffled upstairs, I propped up my pillow and opened a book. I was reading *Rebecca* for the first time, and its tale of the darkest web of secrets pulled me in. I wouldn't want to take her place, the infatuation of a young girl with a man old enough to be her father who was as cold as his mansion. Putting the book on my bedside table, I closed my eyes and tried to imagine myself in Manderley, stepping through those dark corridors, a shadow of another woman watching me...

I opened my eyes and stretched in bed, the sun shining through the window. And then I noticed that the window was different; this one was wide with white crossbars, and my bed was not mine. It was narrower, and the sheets were crisp white while my linens were always colorful. And this place smelled differently, not a trace of the artificial cinnamon that filled my room; here, the space was filled with the freshness of a blooming cherry tree.

I rubbed my eyes and noticed the hands—these were not my hands, the fingers were more delicate and longer, the nails cropped short. And when that hand moved the blanket, I realized I was wearing a white nightgown, a huge thing that covered all my body. Wait, this was not my body. I wanted to touch my face, my hair, but I couldn't. This body sat on the bed and looked out the window. The lush greenery with the white buds of a cherry tree filled all the view, the trees swaying in the wind.

I tried to stand, but the body didn't listen, the eyes fixed on the windowpane.

It was a strange dream, but it was a dream. In the back of my mind, I remembered that my name was Cassandra, that I lived in Tallahassee, Florida and that right before I drifted to sleep I was reading *Rebecca*.

Usually, I didn't realize that I was dreaming up to the moment I woke up. Here I was sure, but the world I was seeing was sharp, not blurred like I usually remembered my dreams. And the strangest thing was that I couldn't control the body I was in. As I watched through her eyes, I could feel what she felt, but my thoughts were separate like I was looking from a small chamber hidden somewhere in this girl's mind.

Where was I? I could breathe in the scent of my room, feel the pillow my head was lying on in my real life and at the same time be here. The sound of a faraway highway turned to a background hum in this world. Under her fingertips was the hard wool of a brown blanket; I wanted to trace it, but she sat motionless.

The girl finally stood, the cold floor stinging my feet—wait, her feet—but I could feel it. She put a robe on her shoulders and stepped to the door, finally giving me a chance to look around. The room was small, but the ceiling was high, a writing desk stood in the corner, a vintage fountain pen laid on an unfinished letter, an open book covering the bottom of it. An intricate lamp was set in the far right corner of the table, shaped like a half-moon looking down with a butterfly in the middle, tassels framing it. A small bookshelf stood right by the table, dark covers stacked neatly, leaving no empty space. A wooden chair was hidden under a pile of clothes, a woolen shawl draped on the back of it.

I was in a museum: The interior was like in the movies showing times before WWII. The girl turned the door handle and stepped into the corridor; it was narrow but long, six doors leading to unknown rooms. That same hand opened the door opposite the one we stepped from and turned the key in the lock. It was the bathroom, a huge bathtub took up almost all free space, the shining steel tank stood right by it. There was black and white tile on the floor and white walls, and there was one toilet with a rectangular seat and a sink held by two additional legs. The room was big, but all the appliances were so huge you would need a slender figure to operate here. The girl stood by the sink and turned the handles of the faucet, warming her cold hands. She splashed water on her face and finally lifted her eyes to the mirror on the wall.

My heart skipped a beat—a familiar face looked back. The girl looked like me, but different in her own ways. She was the same age as me, we shared the same hair color—fair brown—her eyes were bigger, but dark blue like mine, her cheekbones more pronounced, the lips fuller than mine, maybe her face was thinner, but if you put me and her side by side, we could be sisters, twins even. She was more beautiful, her features sharp, skin glowing. The girl took one more look in the mirror and splashed her face again making me twitch in my bed.

I opened my eyes, *my* eyes; I was back in my bed in Florida. The darkness outside, familiar sounds of the faraway highway, the sounds of the night. I looked at my hands. These were my hands for sure, a little chubbier than those from the dream. I lifted them, good, I was back to controlling my movements. I swung my legs off the bed and rushed to my bathroom, turning on the light, almost tripping on the pink rug at my sink. I looked at myself, touched my nose, my cheeks. This was my face. But the eyes, that girl had the same eyes. I splashed cold water on my face, like that girl before I woke up.

That was the first time I was in Sophia's body.

Two

During those past two weeks, every time I closed my eyes for the night I was transferred into her daily life. The date and place Sophia always wrote in her journal. Every morning after she woke up and went to the bathroom, she sat by the table in the corner of her room.

She wrote:

May 15, 1930. Riga

In my 2009 it also was May 15, so we were separated by seventy-nine years. After a couple of my nights there, I got the feeling that it might not actually be a dream—I didn't have any control of her movements or her reality. And what mundane dreams those were.

Sophia wasn't leading an exciting life, mostly she stayed at home reading. She was a fan of Agatha Christie—in her time they were freshly printed as they were written ten years before she was reading them. I wanted her to read something other than stories of Hercule Poirot, so I could check if this all was in my imagination or reality. But she kept reading them, and, unfortunately for me, I read that series when I was fifteen. Well, I loved classics.

I tried to Google her, but of course the information on families living in Riga in 1930 was scarce. And I didn't know her last name nor the street she lived on. So I couldn't check if at least those existed or if it was only in my head.

Sophia didn't go out much. There was a park right outside her windows, the one I saw that first time. Every day, after breakfast, she took her book and wandered down the same path through the old trees, landing on the same bench to read.

She was reading in English; books had been shipped to her from England. And as far as I could understand from her short talks with her father, she spoke Latvian, and her chaperone, Elena, spoke Russian. In those dreams, I could understand what they were saying, as I received information partially from Sophia.

One morning, just after I spent the last hour of my sleep listening to Sophia discussing birds in the park with Elena in quick Russian, I jumped from my bed to my laptop and opened YouTube. I tried to find something in Russian; a language learning video would do. I pressed play and my heart sank. I did not understand a word they were saying. The language flowed in an unfamiliar flat line. I sighed.

Sophia's closest friend was Elena, a woman in her mid-thirties with dark auburn hair cut into a stylish bob, wrapped in a three-piece suit. It was as though she wanted her clothes to complement her fierce spirit, always adding a personal touch to the attire. Her kind brown eyes studied Sophia with worry. Elena was always close, ready to plant the smallest smile on the girl's face. Sophia didn't go to any events. Her life was confined to the apartment and the park close to the building.

Every morning, Sophia sat by the desk in a corner, took a black fountain pen and wrote down what she was feeling.

I SEE YOU IN MY DREAMS

May 17, 1930. Riga

I miss my mom. I miss her gentle touch, I miss her smile, I miss our talks. How I wish for her to be back. Tuberculosis took not only her life, but my father's. His cheerfulness died with her, now only a shell left of him. I see how difficult it is for him to look at me, he sees her in my features. I need him, I am grieving too, but I never knew that grieving was such a solitary thing. He tries to protect me, but in truth he has no idea what to do with a daughter of my age.

Every morning her father had breakfast with her, but he rarely took his eyes off the newspaper he was holding, and after wiping his huge mustache with a cloth napkin after coffee, he stood with a grunt and went to his office, closing the door shut for the day like he was closing the door on Sophia's heart.

A few times, Sophia went back to her room and spent a long time looking at a framed black and white portrait of a woman, who smiled joyfully from the photo. Those piercing eyes were like Sophia's, like mine.

I watched her life, and after a week I started getting mad at her inactivity. Why was I watching her boring life? I wanted to scream at her: *Get out of the house! Do something, stop just sitting there!*

These were the first thoughts after I opened my eyes in the bright Tallahassee room. I looked around and froze. My room was what Sophia would have had if she lived in 2009. There was a table in the corner; a laptop sat there in the middle of colorful stationery I was lately a fan of. The chair was ergonomic, a sweatshirt with a swoosh logo draped on the back. Even my bathroom had a familiar setting, except for a huge metal tank. The window in my room looked out over a dense line of trees, dividing my neighborhood from the next one.

And my life—it was the same boring existence as Sophia's. I didn't have many friends. My closest one was Lorraine, a dark-haired comics nerd who stayed indoors as much as I did. I read a lot, and the time Sophia spent reflecting in her diary, I spent on social media. Boys? There were as many boys as in her 1930 life —none.

The one difference was my parents. After twenty years of marriage, they still looked at each other with love. My Dad worked as an accountant at an international freight company; my mom was a manager at a local chain bookstore. We were a happy family, always laughing at Dad's jokes. The three of us were close.

But I had a feeling that if you took one of my parents away from the other, a shell of grief would be left, similar to Sophia's father.

Three

May 23, 1930. Riga

I want to travel, I want to see the world! But Father doesn't go anywhere anymore, even for business his farthest travel is to the city center. I wish to see Paris, London, Berlin ... but there is no way, now at least. I am confined to this apartment, to this neighbourhood, to this life. I want to see something for real, not to read about life. All the time I ask Elena to tell me about Sankt Petersburg. She is from a small town not far from the city and she used to visit it when she was young. At least tomorrow is Saturday and we can go to the center, to the market. I want to see people. I want to see life!

When I opened my eyes, I felt this longing in my bones. I wanted to see life too, but I was too comfortable in my small world. Yesterday, we were offered to go on a school trip to Washington DC and I refused, but now, laying in my bed and glancing at the phone in my hand, I decided to ask my dad if I could go. Honestly, I felt it was not entirely my decision—it was Sophia's desperation that moved me.

I pulled on my pants and a sweatshirt and stumbled downstairs to the kitchen. My Dad, Chris, was sitting with a cup of coffee and a half-eaten bowl of cereal, reading a newspaper. When he saw me, he smiled.

"You're up early," he said.

I took a milk jug from the fridge and pushed a button on a coffee machine.

"Hey, Dad, I wanted to ask you something," I said and scratched my nose. "Yesterday, Ms. Monaghan at school said she's planning a trip to Washington for a weekend. Do you think I could go?"

Dad froze with a cup midway to his mouth. "Are you sure? You hate traveling."

"I don't hate it, I . . ."

Let's be honest, I didn't love traveling, but it was time to give it a chance. At least I could do it, I owed it to the girl who desperately wanted to see the world but who was confined at home with her father and maid.

"I want to go," I ended.

A sly smile tugged my dad's lips. "Oh, I see, is there a boy who's also going?"

I took a steaming cup from the coffee machine and turned to look at Dad who wiggled his eyebrows at me. I snorted.

"No, there isn't."

"Are you sure? Because if there is, that's good, just stay safe."

"No, Dad, there's no boy," I said.

"A girl then? Mom and I are okay either way."

I groaned.

"No, no girl! I just want to see the world."

"You? See the world?" He laughed and glanced at his watch. "Sorry, honey, I need to go to the office, but yes, I'm totally on the see-the-world boat. Talk to Mom."

He kissed my forehead and rushed to the door, kissing Mom at the doorway.

"You want to go to Washington?" Lorraine asked, stopping in the school hall.

I nodded. "Come with me! We never go anywhere. Don't you think we need to see what's out there? We're going to miss the experience of going away for college since we'll be staying with our parents and going to FSU, don't you think we need to start traveling?"

She looked me up and down.

"Is everything okay?" Lorraine asked and touched my forehead. "Where's Cassie? What did you do to her?"

"It's me, I just think I need to go," I said.

I didn't tell anyone about my dreams, that sometimes my thoughts mixed with another person's, that my wishes weren't totally mine anymore.

"You know, there are great comic stores in DC, do you think we could visit?" Lorraine asked after a pause.

"Yes! Would you come?" I asked and looked at her with puppy eyes.

"Even if I don't see your point, okay, let's do it."

I almost squealed and hugged her.

"But no more surprises like this out of the blue," she warned, smiling.

I looked away and thought that Sophia would be proud of me if she knew about my existence, if she knew that she influenced my decisions.

Since I dropped into her life, something started happening in mine. First, I started sleeping much better; almost instantly after I closed my eyes, I opened them eighty years ago. And even after those dreams, I felt refreshed. I saw the old world and its limits, and I wanted to expand mine. Now I was diligent with my bedtime schedule, going to bed every day at the same time. Mom even asked if I was using a sleeping meditation app which helped me sleep.

No, it was curiosity, and, tonight, I would see a little bit more of the old world.

I opened my eyes and my gaze darted to the sky. *Blue.* The sunlight glinting on the wooden windowpane. I felt Sophia's happiness about the weather. She hopped out of bed and stopped by her table to scribble just a few lines in her journal. She almost ran to the bathroom, taking her clothes from the massive wardrobe.

May 24, 1930. Riga
Saturday! Market day, I am so excited!

She took off her nightgown and put on a two-piece undergarment. Sophia looked up to the mirror and froze for a second. She was curvier than me, and those old-fashioned silks covered much more than modern underwear, but still, it looked more appealing than my mostly sports bras. Sophia traced her cleavage, looking at herself in the mirror and bit her lip, a blush spreading on her cheeks. I felt something stirring in the pit of my stomach, her stomach.

She shook her head and put on the rest of her clothes: a blouse, a modest gray skirt and a jacket with a belt, making her hourglass figure almost perfect.

Today, she and Elena were planning to go to the city center for a crafts market. I figured from their talk it happened once every month.

Sophia almost ran to the dining room, kissed her father good morning and perched on a stool by his side.

"Are you sure you don't want to come with us?" she asked.

He looked away from his newspaper and glanced at her hopeful face.

"I am sure. I am too old for all the folly," he said, his eyes lingering on her face, a flash of pain quick as thunder, paling his features as he turned away.

It was difficult to live with a parent, her only parent who could not even look at her. I wanted to scream at this man, grab his elbow and shake him. *Look at her, she needs you!* But all I felt from Sophia was sadness. She was used to it by now.

"I will eat something later," Sophia said and stood.

Her father just nodded.

She quietly closed the door to the dining room and stepped into the kitchen; Elena stood over the sink. Even at home she managed to look stylish, her body wrapped in a dark suit that looked more modern than everything around. An apron shielded the fabric from the splashes from the tap.

"I am ready," Sophia said.

"Give me ten minutes," Elena said, drying the plates with a towel.

Sophia stepped closer to the window, this one facing the wall of a narrow inside yard of the building. The sun was still shining.

"Do you think today there will be a glass maker? I loved the glass figures he was selling the last time," Sophia asked.

"At your age, you need to be going to parties and worry about men, not the silly Saturday markets and glass animals," Elena huffed.

"We've talked about it a million times. There is no chance for me to get into society since my father stopped attending all social events after," Sophia paused, "mother. Don't you think I would love to?"

Elena put the last plate on the shelf and walked to the window.

"I am so sorry," she said and put a hand on Sophia's shoulder, the girl pressing her hand on top.

"I miss her. She would know what to do," she said quietly.

Elena paused, her eyes darkening, but said cheerfully, "I bet the glassman will be there, let's go."

Outside, they turned in the opposite direction of the park. I cheered that finally I would see a city. The buildings were not high, four or five stories, the narrow street leading to the wider boulevard with train rails in the middle. Just a few black cars were waiting at the traffic lights, my eye catching on one. A handsome man sat in the driver's seat, and there was a woman in her thirties, the shining curls pinned on top to the right side of her head. She was beautiful in that old-fashioned way of almost one hundred years ago. They were holding hands.

The tram rumbled to a stop in the middle of the street; it was a boxy loud thing, white on the sides and blue on top. Sophia stepped inside, showing me the interior and people inside: a family with two kids of ten, two women chatting in the corner, their small hats so stylish. A man standing by the entrance looked Sophia up and down, appraising. She looked away—it would not do to be so openly stared at.

The tram drove slowly, wheels banging on the metal, jerking at the stops and showing the city outside. Sophia sat by the window, glancing at the buildings, some dark and grim, others with white icing like cakes, the wide street showing the life of 1930. Life was quieter then; people enjoyed a warm Saturday. The weather was nice, and families poured outside to catch the rare sunshine. A group of women gathered on the bench laughing. A small boy paused to look at the sunbeam. When the tram turned, I felt Sophia smiling at the hustle and bustle of the square that opened to the view. She took Elena by the arm, and when the train stopped, almost everyone was exiting, the smell of sweet cinnamon pastry hitting Sophia's nose. The long rows of crafts, paintings, pottery, embroidery, hats, jewelry were crowded with gaping people. Somewhere in the distance a fast song of an accordion flowed in the air. The stalls were filled with what would be antiques in my time; here, all these things were brand new. Sophia stopped at the booth with stationery, a few shining black typewriters catching her eye. She touched one gently, dragging her finger on the keys.

They spent time trying on hats, choosing a shawl, marveling at paintings of the countryside and gaping at the intricate earrings.

"He is here!" Sophia said to Elena, pointing to the few booths ahead.

There was an old man sitting surrounded by glass statues and vases of all colors and shapes. The sign said, "Venice Glass". Sophia almost ran to the stall. When the man noticed her, a warm smile spread on his wrinkled face.

"Good morning," she said, beaming.

"Good morning to you," the man replied.

Sophia stood looking closely at every glass, animal, vase and lamp showcased. As for me, it was too colorful, too out of fashion, but I knew about the famous Murano glass. I couldn't understand what she found so interesting here. She chatted politely to the man, asking about the intricacies of glass blowing. I found out that he studied in Venice and returned to Riga and that he had a small studio on the outskirts of the city. Sophia was fascinated by the small animals and bought two: a hippo and a horse. I wanted to move to see other goods, but Sophia was not in a rush.

Elena wandered to the closest booth, checking the white ceramic plates with blue paintings of houses. Finally, Sophia joined her.

"I am starving," she whispered in Elena's ear.

The woman smiled and pointed to the direction of the old small houses, the historic center. "I know a place where they bake divine pastries."

And they moved through the crowd, stopping here and there to the end of the market.

Four

I woke up to the sound of a chirping bird; it had perched right in front of my window and had decided that it was a good idea to let me know that the sun had risen.

The green outside caught my gaze as I turned to the side and inhaled deeply. Why was I seeing these dreams? Why did I keep returning there? Why did I see everything through Sophia's eyes?

There was no answer as I was pulled there time and time again.

That old city had magic. Sophia loved her hometown, but when I was looking at the colorful small buildings, the old-fashioned signs through her eyes, I felt longing for those times. When she and Elena walked by a hotel with red flags adorning every window, an elegant car stopped at the entrance and a woman stepped out of the passenger seat, her slender figure hugged by a deep green dress, a fur stole on her shoulder, dark lipstick and the smallest hat held on her dark updo. She screamed of money. Sophia even paused to look at the sight, and I, I swear, my breath hitched in my dream when I looked at the scene. Women knew how to be elegant and sexy, not showing a piece of skin more than necessary. In 2009, fashion was far from the elegance of 1930.

After my extensive googling, I finally found what the car was: It was the Rolls-Royce Phantom I Jonckheere Coupe of 1925. It was the most beautiful car I had ever seen; with that model, you could see where they took the name from. The black cape of the hood gave a mysterious look, and the round door gave it some kind of otherworldly feel.

Lorraine asked me to stay for a sleepover at her house the day before the trip, and I was nervous about how sleeping in other places would influence my dreams of Sophia's life. I packed my bag and drove to her house in the evening, saying goodbye to my parents. I'd be out for three days only.

Lorraine was alone at home, and she opened the door and pulled me into a hug. Her father was a successful entrepreneur and they had moved to a much fancier house two years ago. Her parents loved traveling, bringing the weirdest things from all over the world. The living room was covered in dark wood panels, showcasing the bows, arrows, hats, wooden figures of animals, African paintings.

"My parents are out to the party and will be back home late. Do you want anything?" she said.

I perched on a dark green velvet sofa, looking at the latest updates to their collection.

"No, I'm okay," I said.

Lorraine turned to me, her eyes glinting.

"Dad brought a fancy whiskey from Scotland; do you want to try?"

"I'm not sure I'm a fan of whiskey," I said.

"Let's try," she said, turning to the bar.

This was unlike her. Lorraine usually was not a drinking person.

"Okay," I said slowly.

She quickly poured a dark golden liquid into the glasses and held one out to me. Her hand was slightly shaking. Lorraine sat by my side on the sofa, pulling her long legs closer and drank three huge gulps from the glass.

"Is everything all right?" I asked.

She screwed her nose at the drink and put a hand to her throat.

"That burned," she croaked and took a deep breath. "I need to talk to you."

"Sure."

"Drink," she motioned to my glass, and I took a cautious sip. The liquid burned my tongue, but an instant warmth spread down my veins.

"I wanted to tell you something," Lorraine said, and her eyes went down to her glass, a shaking hand brushed through her blonde hair. "I . . ." she stopped.

"Everything's all right, you can tell me anything. We've known each other since diaper changing times." I put a hand on her elbow and nodded when she finally looked at me.

"I . . ." she breathed out. "I like girls."

I was silent. "And?"

"That's it, that's what I wanted to say." There was fear in her eyes.

I smiled. "I think I knew on some level; you never looked twice at a handsome boy, never shared my comments on sexy movie stars. Wait, why were you so nervous to tell me?"

I looked at my hand still holding her elbow; she saw my blush and laughed.

"No, I'm not in love with you," she said, her usual light turning back on in her eyes, "I just thought that you might think I'm some kind of a freak."

"You? You're definitely a freak, but I'm okay with it." I hugged her. "Though I'm a bit offended that I'm not your type," I said into her hair.

"Nah, you'd be too much for me," Lorraine said, her typical self coming back again.

"Why now? Why did you choose to tell me now?" I asked.

"I was dreading the moment you'd start seeing somebody, sharing those juicy parts, and see how indifferent I was, and, well, since your love life is even worse than mine," she looked mournfully at me.

"Nonexistent," I whispered.

"Yes," she nodded. "I met a girl online, Paula, she's nineteen, and she lives in Mobile. We started talking in a chat related to comics and one thing led to another, we started video chatting, till she said that she likes me, not only like a person, but . . . and she sent me her naked photo, and I, oh my God, I want to meet her so much."

"Are you going to?" I asked.

"She'll visit in two weeks, we're going to see each other for the first time, and I need my friend to talk to," she said. Some kind of glowing happiness lit her features when she was talking about this girl.

I took one more sip of that awful drink and leaned back on the sofa.

"Tell me everything," I said.

And, oh, she smiled.

Lorraine told me what she was feeling, how her emotions were so heightened every moment she talked to Paula, how she started feeling differently in her body, some kind of a newfound sexuality. And I looked at her, the secret smile tugging her lips in all the right places of a story, her new feelings. I was happy for her, but a crippling sadness pulled at me. My life was void of that. I was seventeen, and I'd never liked anyone who could sharpen my need like that. I only knew one person who felt like this, and I was not sure she was even real. Sophia.

And even when I was away from my bed, sleeping over at Lorraine's, I still saw her in my dreams.

Five

The trip to the capital was not as fascinating as I thought it would be. Lots of history, lots of monumental buildings, the widest boulevards. Honestly, I spent more time talking to Lorraine about her and Paula than looking around. I guess the difference between me and Sophia was that I *could* travel, which was why I was taking it for granted.

We had free time after hours of history, which was not bad, just not as exciting. Lorraine suggested that we go to that comic shop she wanted to visit. As we followed a maps app, we saw a little of the real city, not only the parts that were essential to the tour. As we stopped to grab coffee in a stylish loft, a barista in black-rimmed glasses looked vaguely amused by us.

When we stepped into the comics shop, Lorraine immediately went to the cashier to talk about a particular series she was interested in, and I drifted around the rows, seeing familiar names on the covers, not really knowing anything but stories that were turned into movies.

"I want to buy a present for Paula, we were talking about Wolverine Volume 3 issue number 20 when we met online for the very first time, and they have it here!" Lorraine said, her eyes scanning the rows with a manic glint.

"Nerd," I whispered. She just laughed.

After what seemed like hours, we finally went to the register, our hands full of comics. A man in his forties with green hair scanned the magazines, nodding approvingly and making geeky small talk with Lorraine. When he moved to the left, I noticed a small shelf behind his back, a small collection of glass animals standing there: a glass fox, a white rabbit, a howling wolf. My head started to spin; I gripped a stand before me. No one noticed.

"What are these?" I asked, pointing to the shelf.

The man looked at me, noticing for the first time that Lorraine was not alone, as I had shown no interest in the comics.

The man turned, and a goofy smile tugged his lips. He rubbed his forehead.

"This is my collection of vintage glass animals. I collect a lot of things, stamps from the 1960s, comics obviously, these little things."

"Can I get a closer look?" I asked.

He shrugged and gingerly placed a small glass wolf on my palm. The moment it touched my skin, my mind spun in vertigo.

Our hands were different but similar; Sophia was holding a similar glass figure in my dream. The realities glued together in this moment: her life, if it was real, and mine, now.

"Are you okay?" Lorraine asked. "You look pale."

"Yes, I'm okay." I gave the wolf back to the man.

"You look like you saw a ghost," the man joked, and I tried to smile.

It actually felt like I saw a ghost.

Six

As the time went by, I fell into a comfortable pattern of having a dual life, one where I was leading a boring existence of a high school student, void of the drama that usually went with that experience. My grades were okay, my family whole, my free time spent with a book in my hand. No one knew that in the night I traveled almost eighty years back and saw life from different eyes. But Sophia's life was as exciting as mine, she was homeschooled, and all her free time was spent with a book also.

One morning, Elena came to Sophia's room and slipped a book under her pillow.

"Don't show it to anyone," she whispered and winked, closing the door behind her.

Sophia moved her pillow away and saw a blank blue cover, only small black letters on the side binding showing the name: *Lady Chatterley's Lover*.

The name didn't ring any bells for her; I vaguely knew the premise. After all her chores, Sophia retreated to her room and opened the first page. She was a fast reader, and the deeper she dived into the book, the more heat I felt on her cheeks, her breathing got faster, unfamiliar feelings steering somewhere down her core. I felt it all with her.

Her heart beating fast in her ribcage, Sophia stumbled to a bookshelf to find a cover she could use for the book. Finally finding one that fit, she put a shawl around her shoulders, hastily saying to Elena that she would go to the park. Pressing the book to her side, she almost ran outside.

She found a way to her usual bench and perched on the side, the sun warming her skin, hiding her blush; she continued reading. After an hour on that bench, Sophia could feel every part of her body, the fabric pressing against the most intimate parts, the movement of her breasts as she breathed. This was new for her and for me. Rarely had I felt this kind of internal turmoil and usually only after seeing a particular sex scene in a movie.

Sophia held a hand to her lips, trying to hide a smile, still throbbing under the thin dress. She stood and slowly went back home, listening to the birds singing in the trees, the green of a late spring so vivid, the branches swaying under a warm breeze.

Taking one step in front of another on the wide staircase of the building, images from the book still in her mind, she stopped at the noise on her floor.

The door to an empty apartment next to hers stood wide open, boxes by the entrance. She heard voices, and when she carefully stepped over the box to get to her door, a man stepped out of the apartment. He was in his early twenties, tall, a flock of blond hair framed his face; as his green eyes landed on Sophia, two small dimples appeared on his cheeks. His sleeves were pushed up, showing the veins on his arms.

When he saw Sophia, his leg tripped on one of the boxes, sending him into the opposite wall.

"Damn, that was graceful," he mumbled in Russian. "Hello, my name is Daniil."

"Hi, I am Sophia, I live here." She gestured to the brown door.

"Oh, we are going to be neighbors then. My family moved from Moscow."

Sophia nodded, her heart fluttering in her chest.

"Okay then, I should be going," she said and rushed down the corridor.

"I'll see you later," Daniil said, not unlike a question.

She paused, a hand on the handle. "Yes." And she stepped into her apartment.

The sweet smell of strawberry pie hit her nose as she closed the door behind her and pressed her spine to the wooden frame. The boy was handsome, and she had zero experience in talking with the opposite sex, her mind shutting down.

She took a deep breath and followed the clatter in the kitchen.

Elena stood at the stove, her back to the entrance. The white apron was covering a dark burgundy suit.

"We have new neighbors," Sophia said and dropped to the rickety kitchen stool.

"Oh, really?" Elena glanced at her and paused, stirring the soup. "What's with you? Have you been reading a book?" she asked, a sly smile on her lips.

Sophia blushed profoundly. "Where did you find it? I am sure it's banned from the libraries and stores," she hissed.

"Oh, I know the ways. And besides, a girl needs to learn."

"What?" Sophia asked, shocked.

"All you do is stay at home and read, at least you'd know how things work," Elena winked. "And wipe off that horrified expression from your face," she laughed.

They heard steps in the corridor, and Sophia's father stepped inside the kitchen.

"A family moved into the big apartment next door, I just introduced myself. They are from Russia and the man is a wheat trader who needs to spend a year in Latvia. They are a respectable family and the wife seemed lovely. She would be a good addition to your female company. Also, they have a son, he's a bit older than you," he nodded at Sophia. "And well, give them some time to settle and maybe you should go introduce yourself."

"Yes, father," Sophia said, trying to catch his eye, but his gaze was on the floor.

"Good," he said and walked away, a door to his study softly closing.

Elena turned to Sophia, wiggling her brows. "So, there is a son."

Sophia laughed, "I met him in the corridor already."

"And?" Elena was eager.

"He's nice."

"Nice? That's all?"

"Yes," she smiled, hiding her eyes.

"Nice will do," Elena said, turning away to the stove.

The doorbell chimed. Elena reduced the fire under the pot and went to open the door.

Sophia heard a familiar voice making an introduction and asking for matches, shuffling from the corridor and then the clicking of the closing door.

Elena stumbled back into the kitchen. "*This* you call nice? He's like a candy of a man. Have you seen his muscles? Nice," she said. Elena shook her head and turned back to the stove.

Sophia laughed and went to her room, the book still clutched to her chest.

Seven

I couldn't stop thinking about that man from Sophia's life. I daydreamed about him while writing term papers, trying to focus on the task. My heart hitched every time I saw blond boys in the mall, almost circling them to see their faces. It was irrational, I knew. My dreams were a past reality or the imagination of my bored mind. But I couldn't stop going back to the moment when Sophia met him, how his eyes grazed her face. *Hers*, not mine, I kept repeating to myself. I felt that Sophia was mildly interested in him too, but my mind went crazy. I rushed to bed every evening, but I found out that I couldn't go to sleep earlier than eleven, and my dreams came at the same time every day. I couldn't conjure them earlier.

Sophia was much better at this than me. If this man moved next door to my house, I would be running to get matches from them myself. Her days crawled like they used to before the incident. She read in the park; she helped Elena. Only once did Sophia mention him in her journal, saying that the family moved next door, her heart hammering in her ribcage when she was putting the words down.

Lorraine finally met Paula, and the next day I heard all the details.

"The video didn't show her real beauty, you know, when I saw her," Lorraine said, holding a latte in her hands, "it was like my reality shifted, highlighting her, and she was radiant. All day we accidentally grazed our hands, and in the evening, right before she was leaving, she leaned in and kissed me. And damn it was beautiful and hot, she's like the first ray of sun at the sunrise, lighting me from inside."

I looked at Lorraine and squeezed her hand.

"I'm so happy for you," I said. "You make it look so effortless, you know, we always said that relationships were too much work, and now I see you, and I want it too."

Lorraine hugged me and whispered in my ear, "You'll have it. Look at you, you're gorgeous."

"Thanks," I laughed, my mind shifting to those green eyes.

Sophia was walking in the park. Summer heat had finally reached Riga, usually a rainy place turning warm. The short sleeves of her dress allowed her to catch the sun and she stopped by a tree and closed her eyes, the sun drawing rainbow circles under the closed lids.

"I see you like the warmth," a familiar voice made my sleeping heart flutter.

Sophia opened her eyes to see Daniil standing a few feet away. He was wearing a white polo shirt that showed off muscled arms and a broad chest, with light gray pants and a brown belt matching his shoes.

"I do," Sophia said.

He stepped closer, his eyes never leaving her face. "May I walk with you?"

"Yes," she said and started walking, Daniil stepping to her right. "How do you like Riga so far?"

"I didn't see much yet. With all the unpacking and Father dragging me to his meetings, I saw only a few blocks from the car window."

"What kind of meetings? It doesn't seem like you enjoy them."

He ran his fingers through his blond hair and breathed out. "Yes, I hate them. Father thinks that I should be his successor, that I should be his copy. He wants me to take over the business he created, but . . ." he trailed off, looking at the trees.

"But?" Sophia asked, finally studying his face. Those green eyes, I daydreamed about them every day from the moment Sophia saw Daniil in the corridor.

"But I don't want that," he stopped, looking away.

"What do you want?" she asked.

And it was like something lit him; he turned to her and smiled. "Nobody has asked me that."

"I asked," she said.

"I want to go to America, I feel that it is my country, I want to be separate from my father's expectations, I want to build something from scratch, I want to be independent. And staying here, with my family, that would never happen," Daniil ended, looking away again.

She started walking. "Okay, this is a doable dream, first, how's your English?"

He caught up with her, looking at her face. "What?"

"For you to go to America, you need to know English," she explained.

He looked at her open mouthed. She stopped. "What?"

"You are the first person whom I told about America, and you are not telling me that this is a stupid idea, that I will be nothing there."

"Listen, you need to reevaluate your friends if they don't believe in you at all," Sophia laughed. "So, how is your English?"

"Bad, very bad."

"This won't do, how are you supposed to build something in a country if you don't even speak their language?"

"I have a book and try to study every day, but honestly, this is the worst way possible," he said.

"I can teach you," Sophia said in English with a perfect British accent.

"I have no idea what you just said," he laughed.

"I can teach you." This time she said it in Russian.

"Would you do that?"

"Of course, what time of the day are you usually free? I am homeschooled, but usually by five in the evening I am free," she said.

Daniil smiled, and this smile was so sincere, so open, so light, that I was sure my heart in Florida, eighty years forward, started beating faster. Sophia's vitals didn't react like mine did; she was calm, but she enjoyed his company. That I could feel.

"So, at five tomorrow?" he asked.

She nodded, finally smiling back.

Eight

And they started learning every day without days off. At first, they sat in the library of Sophia's apartment, with the door open so Elena could check if they really were studying or doing something else. She rarely checked, but Sophia's father insisted.

Daniil wanted to know the language, and for the first two weeks he stumbled with the grammar, the pronunciation, but he was diligent. I saw that he was a fast learner, the familiar words spilling from his lips. Even though in these dreams I perfectly understood Russian, English was my native language in real life. And with Sophia's perfect British accent, Daniil learned the clear language.

It amazed me that they were actually studying, nothing more. Yes, they laughed, they joked, but that's all. Every day they sat, opened the book, and with Sophia's explanation, they progressed.

As for me, my summer break paled. My vibrant Florida summer, with its hot, sticky days, was boring. All I wanted was to run away in my dreams; I felt alone in my reality, stifled by my days, every day was the same. Lorraine spent all her free time with Paula, and after coming out to her family and them being supportive, Paula almost moved for the summer to Lorraine's house.

My parents saw the shift in me, and they blamed it on my best friend who was distracted by her relationship. But that was not true, even with Lorraine I didn't open up anymore. Because I had a secret. I had a crush on a man from my dreams, and it was stupid. I knew that. So many times I Googled him or Sophia, and I never found anything. It was all too old, and I had no idea if they really existed.

My parents took me on hikes on the weekends, and for the first time after Sophia met Daniil, I realized that I was freer when I was out. That nature allowed me to take my mind off things, it went blank from my daily routine in 2009, from my nights in 1930. I could just be. There, in the middle of the forest, Spanish moss hugging the branches, I could remember myself, who I was. I could admit that I didn't know what I wanted, that I didn't actually know what to study, and in a few months I should be applying to university. I was stressed, stressed that I had no idea what to do with my life, with my time, that I felt lonely. And jumbled in self pity, nature took my thoughts away. I could breathe. And to my surprise, I started taking walks to the nearby trail, long, hourly walks with the phone muted in my pocket. I walked and walked, daily. And the heat, the exercise, took my worries away.

Nine

"I was thinking," Daniil said and scratched his nose, "with all these gerunds and infinitives, what do you think if we take the lesson outside tomorrow? Maybe Jurmala?"

Sophia was looking at the pages of Daniil's handwritten sentences, but at the word Jurmala, she paled and looked up.

"The last time I was there was with my mother; she loved walking by the sea edge, following seagulls."

"I am sorry," Daniil said. "Okay, disregard my suggestion. Here is good. Less distraction," he said.

"No, you know, I would love to go to Jurmala, I like the place. But Father couldn't bring himself to go there, and I . . ."

"Are you sure?" he asked.

She nodded. "Yes."

I felt how Sophia missed her mother, the hidden grief rolling inside.

"Hey," Daniil said, and his hand moved closer to Sophia's, but he stopped and hid it under the table. She didn't notice. I did.

"I want to go, really. Sooner or later I should have faced the place, and making you remember the verb tenses would be a perfect distraction," she smiled.

The next morning, when I opened my eyes in Sophia's world, I felt her heart fluttering, a note of anticipation. Finally, she was melting towards him, because her reserve made me crazy. I tried to memorize every line of Daniil's face, but while Sophia was teaching him, she never looked twice at him.

Today something changed; she wanted to go, and she wanted to go *with* him.

He said he would take everything they needed and for her just to be ready.

Sophia put on a white dress with a high collar and short sleeves, pulled on white gloves and took a small dark blue purse. Her long hair was curled back, a blue headband holding it in place; a smudge of lipstick polished the picture.

When she stopped in front of the mirror, I looked her up and down and liked the result—in 2009 she would be beautiful, the long white dress hugging her figure.

"Oh, wait a minute," Elena said when Sophia peered in the kitchen. "You look stunning," she whispered. "Our neighbor won't be able to learn anything today," she winked. "Good luck!"

"I don't know what you are talking about," Sophia said.

"Of course you don't, enjoy," Elena said, and a warm smile spread on her lips when the doorbell rang.

Daniil froze when he saw her, his eyes pausing on her lips. She laughed.

"Stop staring, I can be pretty when I want, let's go," she said.

He didn't say anything about this, pointing her to lead the way.

They took a train to Jurmala. I had Googled the place, so I roughly knew where they were going. The train was new and painfully loud: the stream of people filling the carriages, the anticipation of a warm summer day by the sea. It was not hot—the climate much colder than I was used to—but in summer, Latvia was warm, comfortable, without the stifling humidity of Florida.

Sophia was looking out of the window, the city changing to the rural area.

"I wanted to ask you something," Daniil said. "Our studies started from the one thing—you asked me what I wanted, and I never asked you what you wanted," he cleared his throat, smiling. "So, Sophia, what do you want? What is your fiercest dream?"

She closed her eyes for a moment, the sun warming her face. "I want to travel. I want to see the world."

"You know, looking like you do, you can be a fashion model, traveling the world for photoshoots," he said.

She burst out laughing, gently pushing him. "Very funny, I was not making jokes when you talked about your America."

"I like the sound of it, *your* America, my America," he said. "Back to you: Traveling seems to be a doable dream."

"When you are a man and a wealthy one," she said.

"It also can work when you are a woman, but right, you need to be wealthy."

"Yes," she smiled sadly. "Unless I marry well, I have no idea how to make enough money sufficient for world travel."

"That's different for women, yes."

And they sat silent, watching the trees out of the window. And I thought, how different it was for women in my time and in hers. How much more independence we had now.

They stepped out of the train, and after a short walk in a pine wood, an endless stretch of beach appeared. It never ended, curving and hiding in view, but still miles and miles of seashore.

Some people were lounging in the sun, some even were swimming in the sea, but it was shallow, and you could see people far off the beach, still barely covered in water. The warm breeze ruffled Sophia's dress.

"Tell me what you see, explain with every detail," she said. "In English."

And he did. She corrected him, and he stumbled, mixed up the words, but still he was doing a good job. She nodded, asked questions, pointed to various things, asking him to describe them, helping with new words. And then she stopped.

Daniil turned and looked at her.

A sharp pain sliced Sophia's chest. She couldn't breathe, her eyes glued to the bench in front of her. I felt her pain, the images of an older woman in my mind, in Sophia's mind. A hand on her shoulder, a smiling face looking at the sky.

"My mother, we used to sit here. Every time we came, she made a point for us to make a 'breath stop' as she called it, and sit here," Sophia gestured to the bench. "I forgot about it."

Sophia's view clouded, tears spilled on her cheeks, I felt it all. The wave of loneliness, the absence in her heart, the torn chunk of her soul. It all was gone, gone with her mother.

Daniil stepped closer. He hesitated, but then he lifted his hand to Sophia's face. Catching the tear with his thumb, she didn't pull away. I felt her lean into his hand, never looking away from the bench. Daniil ran his fingers over her cheek, and closing the distance between them, he hugged her, gently. Sophia sank into him, pressing her head to his chest. I could feel his heart beating fast next to Sophia's ear. His arms closing on her back. They stood like this for a very long time.

I opened my eyes in the darkness of my Florida room, the wet warmth of the night spilling through the window. I was crying, tears rolling down my cheeks, I felt it all—I felt Sophia's pain, her loneliness, and that shimmering hope that was Daniil.

I closed my eyes again to find them walking away from the bench.

During the next week, it became more difficult for Sophia to concentrate on the tasks at hand, her mind wandering to the boy next door. She couldn't read, remembering his arms on her back. She became aware of his eyes, how he studied her, her heart racing every time she saw him. Their hands grazing, meeting when they opened the book, when she corrected his writing. They weren't hiding the attraction as it mounted.

On a summer day in late August, Sophia went out to the park. She grabbed a book, a detective story that tried to catch her attention, but her real life was finally becoming more interesting than the book.

She stood by her usual reading spot, the book forgotten on the bench. She watched a squirrel climbing the tree, deep in her thoughts.

"I knew where to find you," a familiar voice said from behind.

She turned, and Daniil was standing there. He had tanned through the summer, the white of his shirt contrasting with his skin.

Heart skipping a beat, Sophia asked, "What are you doing here?"

"I need to do one thing." And he stepped closer.

He brushed a strand of her hair from her forehead, searching her face. She lifted her hand and reached his jaw, fingers barely touching, brushing his neck, looking up at him. Daniil closed the gap, he bent over and kissed her gently as if she was made of glass. As he restrained himself, pulling her closer, the hidden hunger showing.

But what shocked me, Daniil, and probably Sophia herself, was her response. The wildfire roared in her body as she pressed herself to him, each crevice aligning. Her hand on his chest curled in a fist around his shirt, the connected lips growing hungrier as she gave in, the tongues touching. Her hands went up in his hair, searching. He hugged her closer, shielding her from the outside world.

After minutes or hours, Sophia pulled away, his hands on her shoulders never leaving her.

She took a step back and sat on the bench, looking up at him, and then to the park. Daniil sat close, holding her hand.

"What are you thinking?" he asked.

She shook her head.

He smiled. "You are my kind of enigma. You always hide what you think; it's almost impossible to guess what you are feeling. But your body betrays you."

"What do you mean?"

"You enchanted me the first time I saw you in that dingy corridor. And the more I knew you, the more hold you had over me. How you supported me, how you believed in me. But nothing more, during those months you looked at me like on your project. Till..."

"Till Jurmala," Sophia finished.

"Yes, your eyes didn't reveal anything. But when I touched you, you leaned in, when I hugged you, you stayed in my arms, close. And this week, your hands moved in sync with mine. And just now," he smiled, "I finally saw that I was right, you like me, your body pressing into mine. But now again, you are silent, and I can't read you. What do you feel? Tell me."

She just smiled.

"Let my body tell you," she said and tilted her head, moving closer till her lips touched his and he groaned but pulled her close.

Her hands roamed his body, the neck, shoulders, hands, his chest. Urgency in her movements.

"I need to go," she said quietly, opening her eyes and leaning back. She glanced at her wristwatch and nodded.

He stood and held his hand for her; she took it.

"Will I see you tomorrow?" he asked.

"Are you still interested in English?" she asked, a smile on her lips.

He paused, looking at her as if she was a mystery he couldn't decipher, and slowly brushed a thumb on her lower lip.

I opened my eyes; it was still dark, those feelings brimming over the top woke me. I admired Sophia, how she held herself, while I could feel all that she was feeling. She hid it, but how she wanted to stay in his arms, how he allowed her to dream, to feel that she was cherished. She didn't want to open those gates, because it would be impossible to close them. But his eyes, they woke her up, her senses converging on one point: where he was. She couldn't say much because of what she was feeling.

I closed my eyes to appear much later; it was dark already; Sophia was lying in her bed. The flashes of green eyes in her mind. She was throbbing down her core, the pulse so powerful she needed to take the edge off. Everything was quiet in the house.

Sophia touched her lips, remembering the feel of Daniil's kiss, slowly dragging her fingers down her neck. She imagined his hands on her, his fingers instead of hers. Her body quietly buzzed, wanting more.

And I woke again, breathless, to my morning. What was I doing there? I watched their relationship bloom, their need. But why was I seeing that? I felt connected to Sophia, like we were one. I was so lonely in my life, and she was alone in hers. She was afraid to let Daniil in, but it was only a matter of time, and she wouldn't be alone anymore. I wanted this. I wanted someone in my life. But as my days trickled by, all I found myself wanting was to close my eyes, to run away from my life to the life of eighty years back. With all the lust, the craving, and the touch.

I was confused. My dreams sucked the emotions from *my* life. My days turned into a flatline, while my nights were a rollercoaster of longing. I knew something was very wrong with me when I didn't want to wake up to my life, when I would prefer to stay in the dream.

Ten

He was there for her every day. He came to the lessons. He begged her to walk with him after them. Every time she agreed, they stole kisses in the shade of the trees. Every day, he told her what he dreamed of. He told her about America, how he could see himself there. And she told him about books she read, about her life, her parents, about the cities she wanted to visit.

"What are your top three places?" he asked.

"Let's see, Paris, London and New York."

He looked at her.

"What? The list is as standard as possible," she smiled.

"New York, I wonder if we could go there together." And he rubbed the back of his neck, eyes never leaving her face.

"You would be too busy building your life," she laughed.

He stopped her and wrapped his fingers around her wrists. "I will always find time for you."

She laughed and leaned in, kissing him slowly.

"You don't believe me," he said, inches between their faces.

"I believe *in* you," she whispered, and traced his cheekbone.

Those green eyes piercing her, he breathed out and dropped a head to her shoulder.

"Sophia, you are driving me crazy. I feel you close and miles away at the same time," he grunted, hands on her shoulders.

"I am here," she said quietly.

He pressed her closer before letting her go.

"Tomorrow, a jazz band from New York will perform in a small club in the city center, do you want to go with me?" he asked. "Please say yes."

I felt her excitement, but she simply said: "Yes."

"Yes?" His face was so hopeful.

"Yes," she laughed. "I want to go with you."

"As a couple?" he asked.

"As a couple," she replied, and his smile was brighter than the sun.

I was back to school; summer break ended. My days were back in high school with boring lessons. I shuffled through the corridors as a shadow, I felt like one. Watching other couples was painful —my heart and my body longed for the person I saw in my dreams.

Lorraine was back to being my friend, but we only talked about her and Paula. She dragged me to movies, tried to engage me in conversations, but I knew I was pushing her away, building a wall around me brick by brick, dream by dream. She saw that something was wrong with me, but after asking a couple of times, she dropped it.

I had never felt lonelier in my life. I was enchanted by my dreams, by Sophia's relationship. I was worried about her. Sophia feared this love, she didn't want to show Daniil what she really was feeling. She knew he'd be going away soon; he would pursue his dream, and she sheltered her heart from this break, but every day she grew closer to him, crawling under her armor.

His eyes followed her every move, trying to read her, but failing.

There was something unhealthy about me watching them, feeling them. But I didn't want it to end.

The night Daniil took Sophia to a jazz performance felt different. They couldn't stop touching each other, grazing their hands as they walked down the street.

The concert was so powerful, the music touching Sophia's heart. The crowd around them moved wildly, pressing them together. She felt him holding her close. And those notes, the flow of piano, the noise of the sax, it broke her and made her whole again. The music made her feel alive. In my bed in Florida, I felt it all, a tear trickling from the corner of my eye.

Sophia was happy.

"Thank you," she said to Daniil after they went back outside, after the concert.

"You loved it?" he asked, more like a statement.

She nodded, as he took her hand and they slowly moved back home. It was only a few blocks on foot.

"My parents are away in Moscow, they will be back tomorrow," he said. "Would you like to . . ."

They both knew what he was asking.

"Sorry, I . . ." He was lost for words.

"Yes, I want it."

"Are you sure?"

She slid her hand in his hair, the way he loved. "Yes."

They quietly went up the stairs of their apartment building. It was dark inside. He opened the door and turned on the light.

Their apartment was much bigger, lighter, more stylish than Sophia's. But she didn't notice any of this, her eyes on him.

"Where is your room?" she asked.

He held her hand gently and opened the door down the corridor.

The familiar smell hit her; it was all him. The bookshelf, the table. An image of New York on the wall, the unmade bed.

He closed the door behind him and looked at her, he didn't move. She stepped closer.

"I want you," she whispered.

And he scooped her in his arms, kissing gently, growing hungrier. Sophia unbuttoned his shirt, tracing his skin with her fingers. Daniil kissed her neck, slowly peeling off her blouse. She took his hand and led him to his bed. He laid her there, brushing the edge of her bra.

"Please take it off," she breathed. And he listened, unfastening it, sucking in a sharp breath when her breast was in his palm. He lowered his head and kissed the soft skin, sucking on her nipple. Sophia was melting, all her body aware of him so close, on her. She put a hand to his pants, grazing the hardness. She undid the belt and helped him out of the pants as he dragged her skirt down. He tugged down her underwear while she traced her fingers over his torso. Daniil kissed her stomach, going down, spreading her legs, kissing her there while she couldn't breathe anymore, she moaned, till she couldn't do it either.

"I want you inside," she whispered.

"Have you ever done it?" he asked.

"No."

"Are you sure about now?"

She tugged down his underwear, revealing him, the power of him. Daniil watched her all the time, but when she moved her palm up and down his length, he closed his eyes.

"Yes," she said.

He was gentle, all the movements caring. Sophia craved this

closeness. He brushed a lock of her hair from her forehead, kissing her, slowly pushing in. She gasped, but she didn't feel any pain, only new power over her, over them. He filled the tight space inside her and she dug her fingers into his skin, arching her back. They moved together, the sweat of their bodies mingling, their hands roaming each other. She was plunging in the darkness of sweet pleasure when he pulled out and came on her stomach.

Lowering on his elbow, Daniil pressed his cheek to hers.

"You are mine," he whispered. "You will always be mine."

"Yes," she breathed.

"No!" I bolted upright in my bed. I was hot from seeing everything, from feeling them. I was there with them. But amidst the arousal, there was something sinister in Daniil's voice, possessive, manic. Sophia didn't hear it; she was still on a high.

But I had a feeling that these words meant something different for Daniil, not the sweet love of confirmation, but something darker I could not yet put a finger on.

I couldn't go back to sleep, their bodies in my mind. Sophia was hungry for the touch; while her mind and heart tried to shield themselves from falling in love with Daniil, her body did the opposite. She gave and took from him.

I went downstairs and made myself a cup of chamomile tea. My hands trembling, my body pulsing all the time.

Eleven

Daniil and Sophia went on with their usual life. With lessons and stealing kisses, but there was no way for them to stay together long enough. Sophia's father was home all the time. And an old friend of Daniil's father was visiting—the man lived in New York now.

Every day, Daniil came to Sophia's library and told her about all the new things he found out from the man. She made him tell her everything in English. Every small detail he found out about Brooklyn and life there.

One day, Sophia was walking through a park, taking her usual trail. There was no one around, the golden of the fall playing on the trees.

She heard footsteps, and before she could look back, hands landed on her waist, and warm lips touched her neck.

"Here you are," Daniil whispered. He twirled her around, facing her. His green eyes landed on hers, and as usual he paused, just watching. She smiled, placing a hand to his cheek.

"Let's take a walk," he said and led her off the path to the dense trees. After a few minutes of silence, he stopped under an ancient oak.

"Sophia," he said, his breath catching when she looked at him. "I am leaving."

I felt the blow, right in her chest. She was shielding herself, preparing, but the moment those words reached her, it was like a physical kick. She took a small step back.

He was holding her hand, not loosening his grip.

"I will go back with Maxim, father's friend. Max offered me a job, and I need to take it. I want it."

She nodded, she knew it would end like this sooner or later. All those lessons were for one goal.

"I am happy for you," she said. She tried to put on a brave face, but one small treacherous tear was sliding down her cheek.

He lifted her chin, catching the tear.

"I will come back for you," he said. "I am not leaving you."

And he gently pressed her to the tree, taking one hand and then another over her head, securing her wrists with his fingers.

She was breathing hard, her body pinned to the tree. He moved closer, watching the rise and fall of her chest. The grief mixed with desire; Sophia needed his hands on her.

But he planted a kiss on her neck and moved up to her ear.

"You are mine; do you remember? I will come back for you in a year, a year from the day I leave. And I will take you with me, I will show you the world, we will start with New York," he said, leaning back, finding her eyes. "Please, wait for me," he asked.

"Do you want me there with you?" she asked, a thread of hope she tried to hide, shining in her.

He released her, "Of course. What do you think is going on between us?"

"I am teaching you lessons," she said, and he snorted.

"Oh wow," he said. "Is that really what you think?"

She stood silent, hiding her eyes.

"The moment I met you, I couldn't stop thinking about

you. I stay as close as possible, and I see how you fight it. But it's time for you to face it," he said.

"But you are leaving, and you always meant to," she whispered.

"I always meant to leave, yes, but you are going with me," he said simply. "You want to see the world; I will give it to you. I just need a year to stand firmly on my feet there, and I will come back for you. Will you wait for me?"

And he dropped to his knees, pressing his forehead to her stomach, wrapping his hands around her hips. She lowered her trembling fingers in his thick blond hair, the shiver coming down his spine.

"I will wait for you," she said.

And he groaned, rising, finding her lips, kissing for the last time.

"When do you leave?" she asked.

"In three days," he murmured in her hair.

And they stood silent, heartbeats blending, no beginning of one person, no end of another. One.

When Sophia reached her room later that day, she almost couldn't breathe anymore. She collapsed on her bed, silent sobs escaping her. She knew it would end like this, and even though he said he would come back for her, she didn't allow herself to hope. He was leaving for New York! The place of possibilities, the place of fashion and money. And with his looks there would be no shortage of girls around him. All of them more glamorous, more knowledgeable than her.

And Sophia would go back to her old life, to being alone, to being invisible. She knew how it would feel, the gaping hole in her chest where Daniil had carved a place. At least she already had an experience with loss, her mother, being here and fading away in just a few months' time.

As silent tears ran down her cheeks, she finally allowed herself the thought. Daniil was her first love. Of course he was, with all his presence, his laugh, his touch. And now he was going away. She stood by the window, looking out to a dark park, shaking breaths masking the sound of a breaking young heart.

A soft knock on her door pulled her back to reality. Elena peered inside, worry on her face.

"There is Daniil at the door, he says he needs to see you, now," Elena said. "Go quietly so your father won't hear, be quick."

Sophia nodded and moved past Elena. The woman wrapped her hands around Sophia.

"I've heard about Daniil, that he is leaving. I am so sorry," she whispered.

"Yes," was all Sophia could say.

When she quietly closed the apartment door behind her, Daniil reached her in two strides, pressing her close to him, lifting her chin and finding her lips. He kissed her, salt of her tears a bitter reminder between their tongues, and she broke in his arms. His smell was engulfing her, his warmth, and she knew soon there would be only void.

He pulled away a little, still holding her inches away.

"It hurts that you don't believe me," he said. "You don't believe that I would come back, that I am not leaving you."

"How can you be so sure?" she asked, her voice wet. "Now you are here, but there, in a big new world everything is different. You will meet new people, new women, you will leave Latvia in the past. And that's the right thing to do."

"You still don't see it," he whispered, a hurt written on his face. "I love you."

"Stop." She was angry. "Don't you dare say these words to

me when there won't be a trace of you in a week. Don't toss your love in my hands and run."

Something unfamiliar glinted in his eyes, a coldness that was there and gone.

"I will come back in a year, and you will say the reciprocal words to me then. Because I know it, I see it, that you love me. I see it in your eyes, in your anger," he wrapped his hands around her again, making her dizzy. "I feel it in the rhythm of your heart. Sophia, you are mine."

And as she found his lips, her hands clinging to him, she whispered. "I am."

In a few days, he was gone. Only his promises were left. The empty chair in her library, the solitude of her walks, and against all her rational judgment, she hoped that he would hold true to his words, and they would see each other in a year.

Daniil didn't leave her anything to remember of him, but she knew he had her photo framed and hidden in his bag.

He said he wouldn't be writing letters. He had a year to prepare a life for them both. He said that in a year everything would change but for one thing—she still would be his.

"Forever," he said, looking directly into her eyes. Those green eyes were the color of the old oak under which he said that he was leaving.

And Sophia knew, whatever the future held for her, one thing wouldn't change. She was his; he owned her from head to toe, every breath she took was his. And she was okay with it, the hole he left, filled with this magic, this hope, making it just bearable, just.

Twelve

I remembered how to breathe, taking deep breaths. Daniil left Sophia, but against all logic I believed him. I saw truth in his eyes: He would come back for her.

Something changed in my last dream, the tether knitting me to Sophia shifted. I felt it the moment Daniil last kissed her, and I had no idea what it meant.

I found out the reason the next night. The time in my dreams now reformed, I lived it differently. For Sophia the days went by as usual, but I was dropped in at different times, one morning, one evening—all these times Sophia was alone. She studied, she read, she walked. A thread of sadness surrounded her, but life settled in the usual flow. The moment she laughed with Elena, the happiness spreading again in her chest, I felt it, just to be pulled away and dropped the next day.

In a week, I got used to this roller coaster of a time; it leaped in big strides during the night.

And as Sophia's life paled, wrapped in waiting, my life started to bloom again. As I was not pulled into my nights anymore, the days started having more appeal. Mom took me shopping. She chatted away happily, wrapping her hands around my shoulders, beaming, because I was beaming back.

The next day in school Lorraine burst into tears.

"Hey, what's happened?" I asked.

She sniffed and smiled at me. "You're back."

"What do you mean?" I knew perfectly well what she meant.

"It was like you were gone. Like a shadow. Was it depression?" Lorraine winced. "You scared me. And I didn't know how to help. You shut me out, it was like talking to a stone wall. And all this time, you were like a faded copy of yourself, uninterested in anything. Like you faked your life."

She threw her hands around me, tugging me into a hug.

When I saw Sophia's life my life withered away. Like dry petals the days of my existence paled compared to the intensity of her time. Lorraine was right, nothing in my life attracted me, caught my attention when I saw Sophia and Daniil.

"I'm happy you're back," Lorraine sniffled.

And it scared me too. I knew it was only temporary before Daniil returned into my dreams, pulling me under again, sucking me into the world that didn't exist.

I stopped taking walks, worked more on my application essays, and researched universities with my parents. I felt this small circle of people around, staying close, supporting me. It was easy when I allowed them, welcoming their care.

The nights started to resemble the dreams of before, before I was dropped into Sophia's life. Her days jumbled in my sleep, but after those nights I felt more refreshed and focused than ever. But sometimes I woke up breathless, replaying that one night Sophia spent with Daniil, him on top of her, their bodies connected in sweet madness. After those nights I felt lost, like something I wanted was impossible. Because that someone didn't even exist.

"You have that haunted look again," Lorraine said the first

morning after that dream. "Like from before, when you were away in your world."

I shrugged. "I had a bad night," I just said.

She pressed her lips together.

I shifted my focus to my life again. I started to notice the people around me, I started watching movies, reading books. But I knew this all was not over; there would be more. I stopped questioning my connection to 1930; it was what it was. Maybe someday I would tell somebody, but I knew no one would believe that it felt like a separate life, not just a dream.

Sophia was not patiently waiting for Daniil; she buried the hope in a small chamber and closed the door. She knew she would need to find a job soon, so she mastered the art of speed typing; secretary positions opened every day. Her fingers hurt from the constant drum on the typewriter. But she had a goal, albeit small but her own, which didn't include her father, Daniil, or any outside help.

I admired her determination, and it inspired me to move my life. We both worked; I applied to universities, she perfected typing and started learning Spanish. We read, we lived, cherishing the small group of people we had around.

In my three months, the year in her time was coming to an end. She was telling herself that he wouldn't come, that it was a sweet infatuation, but that they were older now—she had to think about herself. But laying in the dark hours in her bed, I felt what she was feeling. Sometimes she was so nervous she couldn't take another breath. There still was no news of Daniil. His family moved away from the apartment down the corridor a few months ago, going back to Moscow.

In my life, I became jumpy, trying to take my mind off the day when a year would pass. I hadn't met Daniil, but he had the same hold on my life as Sophia's.

Thirteen

And that day came. I opened my eyes in Sophia's room. She listened, but everything was quiet in her apartment. She slowly lowered her feet to the cold floor and took a shuddering breath. It was Sunday, no plans whatsoever. She put on one of her favorite dresses and had breakfast with her father, now an even more distant man. But soon she lurked in the kitchen to chat with Elena. This year they grew closer. Elena met a nice man; he owned a small grocery shop a few streets down, and he was courting her. She played a cold queen, but we both knew soon she would melt towards him. Sophia was looking at their slow relationship and a little fire of shame burned in her chest about how fast she became close with Daniil. How her hunger led her, the body needed skin on skin.

The memories of that one night shifted to something else—she dreamed about him, scolding herself every morning after. Even now she was so soft towards him.

Still the doorbell was silent. No one came. Sophia jumped at the smallest sound, but she couldn't take it anymore. She grabbed her Spanish textbook and went to the park. She tried to read, to memorize new words, but her thoughts were all over the place, curling in the deep shade of the trees. Sophia couldn't sit; clutching the book, she stormed down the green path. She didn't hear the steps behind her, but familiar hands landed on her waist, and she inhaled sharply.

"Where are you running?" Daniil asked.

She turned slowly, and he was there. His features had sharpened in a year, the blond hair brushed back. He was wearing a dark coat, a white shirt, and a tie. The fine cut screamed of money.

His green eyes searched her face. "You look even more beautiful."

"You came," she whispered.

"Of course I did." And he held out a hand for her. She looked at it and placed her hand in his. He gently pulled her closer, eyes never leaving her face. A soft moan escaped Sophia when he found her lips, when their tongues met.

"You are mine; you are still mine," he whispered in her hair, pressing her close.

"I am," she said. And she was delirious in that moment, his body wrapped around hers, holding her.

"I am taking you with me," he said, a statement.

And when she didn't say anything, he released her and took a step back, slowly going on one knee. Green eyes tracking every change in her expression.

"I want to make it official. I want you to be mine in every way possible. Marry me." And he opened a small blue box, a golden ring with a huge clear stone inside. It glinted in the sunlight, catching the green of the trees and multiplying it.

Sophia was fighting for breath, her life changing right here, right now. But when she looked into those green eyes, she felt herself under that tree, a need of this man rolling in waves in her veins.

"Yes," she whispered and as she watched the ring settling on her finger all she heard in her mind was *mine, mine, mine*.

He took her hand and led the shortest way out of the park, the energy crackling between them. Both silent.

"I have a suite in the hotel." He gestured to the white building when they emerged from the park gates.

They went into the hotel lobby, a quiet place with style. The round glass chandelier glistened, reflecting warm light on the walls, a collection of oil paintings decorated the paneling. The faint smell of perfume covered everything. In the elevator, they didn't look away from each other, oblivious to the operator by their side.

In the room, their bodies crashed. She ripped his shirt, gliding her fingertips over his stomach. It had become much harder in a year, a visible cut of the muscles. He unbuttoned her dress; it fell to their feet; her undergarments landed on the floor seconds later. They couldn't catch a breath when he propped her on the sofa, his lips on her breasts. When he went down on her, she broke into the smallest pieces under his tongue and was formed again. Her body trembled with pleasure.

"Take me," Sophia whispered, "take me."

A crazed glint in his eyes showed her that was what he needed. He took her, nothing on her but the ring with a huge stone. She moaned as her legs hugged his hips, she felt him crushing inside her when they rocked. She cried his name as she was falling into the sweet delirium. Nothing else mattered, she was his.

Sophia lay in his arms, her head in the crook of his neck. She breathed in his scent, a faint smell of expensive cologne, but all the rest was him, familiar.

"I missed you, Sophia," he said in the quiet of the room. "Every day I was thinking about you. You'll love it there; I have everything ready."

She dragged her fingers on his arms, the coiled muscles now where the soft flesh used to be. He had changed, became harder on edges, but the way he held Sophia was almost reverent.

Sophia propped herself up on her elbows and looked at him. Their naked bodies were touching, his hand resting on her waist.

"Tell me everything," she asked. "What are you doing there? Are you still working with Max? Where do you live?"

"I stopped working with Max a month after I went there; he helped me settle and I am immensely thankful for that. He knew people. Basically I became a bodyguard of a person who worked for another very influential person. One thing led to another, and I proved myself to be more valuable than a bodyguard. I could count and talk. They used it. I would say now I am working as an assistant to that important person."

"What does he do?" she asked.

He was silent for a few moments. "It's difficult to explain. He manages different businesses. I would say some of them are related to banking."

"This is a vague description," she said.

"You will see everything yourself soon," he smiled. "I live in an apartment on Park Avenue, not far from Central Park. I have a maid and a cook, so don't worry about the household."

"What will I be doing there?" she asked softly.

He looked at her, those green eyes shining in the dark.

"You will be mine." That was all he said.

And in their weird dynamic, it was enough for Sophia. I felt that she accepted her part, something warm rolling inside her.

"Was it difficult for you at the beginning? You were completely alone," she asked.

"I am not proud of a few things I've done, but I was doing it all for us. I had a promise to keep. And you will be living like a queen," he said, and her breath hitched.

He pulled her closer, their lips meeting. His hands roamed her body. Gently, he cupped her breast, catching her nipple between his fingers. She lowered her hand down his stomach to find him hard, she moved her hand up and down and he growled.

"Where is that box?" she asked. Daniil had a pack of condoms, a shining small box. Sophia knew what it meant: It meant freedom to her. She should not be worrying about pregnancy, and it was a crazy sensation.

She opened the box and slipped the condom on. She kissed his neck, his ribs, and then she climbed on him, lowering herself with a delicious moan. Sophia rolled her hips, slowly riding him. His eyes never leaving her, he devoured the view in front of him. It slid over her lips, between her breasts, down her stomach. And it gave her power. His hands moved with her, guiding her.

"You are so beautiful," he said, his voice cracking.

And as she moved on top of him, Sophia was drowning in that green. And then her body shuddered, falling, her hair spilling on his chest. And he was trembling under her, hands around her back, holding her close, pressing her.

"I love you," she whispered.

Fourteen

I opened my eyes, gasping for air. It was back again, they were together. All that ache, all that pull, the sex, they were mad about each other. But there was something off. Sophia craved his body; she felt her power over him, and she was high on it.

Did she really love him? There was lust, yes, but love? Sophia thought she loved him, she tricked herself into believing that. But hidden somewhere deep was a thought she was not facing, and probably would not ever face: He was her ticket out of her old life.

My body was trembling as if it was me who rode him just a minute ago. I felt aware of every inch of my skin. But I knew what it meant for me: I would lose myself again in them. I would fight, but these dreams were too powerful. And I wouldn't leave Sophia now.

I knew I could; I had discovered that melatonin pills erased all dreams, putting me in a slumber. But no, I had to see how it unfolds.

The next few days I struggled to get a grip on my reality, on school. I smiled at my parents, talked to Lorraine, just to discover myself crazed in the night. Their relationship was like fire, it burned holes in my life, sucked all the air from my lungs.

I found it extremely difficult to concentrate on my lessons, my thoughts scattering away. Lorraine dragged me to the college football game when she saw I was withdrawing again. I cheered when she cheered, a smile plastered to my face. The fake enthusiasm convinced her, just barely.

Having a barbeque with my parents proved to be torture. Again, I started fading, almost regretting waking up in the morning, rushing to bed at night.

They told Sophia's father and Elena about their plans to get married in America. Elena cried and hugged Sophia, her father blessed Daniil, never actually catching her eye. They left Riga in a few days. Nothing hurt in Sophia's chest while she looked at the streets from a cab window. She was ready to leave it a long time ago. Her heartbeat fast, imagining the new places they would see.

And he showed her the world as he promised. They spent a week in Paris and a week in London, before boarding a ship to America.

The time in my dreams jumbled again, bending, speeding. I was dropped into different scenes: Sophia laughing in the cafe with a view of Eiffel Tower, the steam of a small ship on the Seine, the madness of their bodies in a hotel room, the protective arm on her shoulder in a London crowd, and those green eyes always watching.

They had a beautiful spacious room on the ship, evidence of how rich he had become. And Sophia was happy, he gave her the world, and would give much more in their new home.

When New York loomed on the vast blue horizon, she felt a tingle in her chest. She would live here, not in the confinement of a Riga apartment and the park nearby. And all because of him. She kissed him, a radiant smile on her lips as he enveloped her in his arms.

"Here everyone calls me Daniel, Danny," he said.

She looked at him, a slick gray suit, blond hair smartly combed back, a heavy-set jaw.

"Yes, it makes sense, Daniel," she said.

They were shedding their past like a pair of gloves. They wanted to forget where they came from. Sophia hoped she would blend easily here. And looking at her now it was easy to imagine: in the fine silks of the latest Paris fashion, and many more dresses in their baggage. And the lace of London undergarments, which Daniel loved to strip her from, slowly.

She felt natural in all of it, as though Sophia was hiding all her life just to make the glorious entrance now.

When she saw the tall apartment building they would live in, she smiled. It was taller than all other buildings, containing setbacks and crowned with a tower on top.

"It's called Ritz Tower," he said.

Sophia took Daniel's hand in hers, slightly squeezing, her eyes never leaving the tan brick wall.

They left all their bags with the usher and slowly climbed up in the elevator.

"Are you ready?" Daniel asked, and opened the door for her.

She gasped. The apartment was light, a fireplace in the middle of the living room. A couch with numerous armchairs stood along the perimeter, intricate rugs decorated the floor, paintings on the walls.

"Welcome home," he murmured from behind, grazing her neck with his lips. Slowly tracing her waist, moving up, undoing the upper button, brushing her collarbone. Her heart was hammering already, and then he released her.

"It's not a big apartment, but it is a good start," he said. "We have two bedrooms, my office, a room for yours, or whatever you wish to do with it. Let me show you around."

And he took her hand and led her to the kitchen. It was shining white; a covered dish with a casserole standing on the countertop. Sophia raised an eyebrow.

"We have a cook, remember?" he laughed. "His name is Roberto, and a maid, Eva. They are often around, but today I asked them to prepare everything for us and leave. You will meet them soon."

He opened a door to his office, dark wood panels covered the walls. A massive table stood in the middle of the room, a dark leather chair, a safe in the corner.

The next room was a guest room with a bathroom. The door down the corridor led to her office, which was empty, pastel walls so inviting.

And for the last he saved their bedroom. It had an enormous bed in the middle of cream-colored walls with paintings of a forest. An adjoining bathroom, the size of half a living room, the clawed bathtub. And the dressing room, as big as her room back home.

She stepped closer to the window. A view of the city took Sophia's breath away, she felt on top of the world.

"This is amazing," she whispered.

He hugged her from behind, she leaned back, pressing herself in his arms. His hand found the next button of her dress, flicking it open, and the next. His fingers found her breast, she felt the hardness of him through his pants. He was kissing her neck, hands on her chest, while she watched New York outside. He pulled her to the bed, shedding her clothes, till she lay naked on the white sheets. He lowered his lips to her nipple and sucked, sliding his hand between her legs. She was rocking on top of the world, when he entered her and found her lips. He was breathing hard, while she forgot how to breathe. He bit her bottom lip, and they both felt her blood on their tongues. They were trembling, a mess of hot lust.

"You are mine, and only mine," he growled as his body rocked.

And she was.

Fifteen

That day, I wondered what Daniel was doing to get rich so fast, in the span of a year to be able to afford such an apartment. And I was mad at Sophia for not asking enough. She dived into this new life never knowing the details. And to me it all looked suspiciously like a golden cage. With Daniel's obsession over her and her body, it could tip into a dangerous path any minute.

"Is everything okay?" Lorraine asked me. I was staring for too long out the cafeteria window.

"Yes, why?"

"Again, you have this vacant look, like you aren't here. What's happening?" she asked.

"I'm okay, honestly."

Lorraine shook her head. "I'm not sure that's true. You know, there's a therapy line where you can text with a therapist, it's much cheaper than the usual therapy, but I think you should try it. You live somewhere in your head; you're losing your focus a lot. Cassie, I think you need help."

"I'm fine," I said through gritted teeth.

Of course I wasn't, my mind was splitting in two, my life

intertwined with the life of the 1930s. I was here, but also, I was there. The dreams creeping into my daily life, the worry. At home, I was constantly researching the topics of dreams, so many theories of why we dream, and nothing hit home with my case. It was not a dream; it was another life.

"My friends will visit today; they need to catch me up on the latest news. You are free to listen in my office, I don't want to keep any secrets from you. But," and his eyes glinted, "nothing you hear here must ever leave those pretty lips of yours," and he leaned in to kiss her.

"Of course," she said. That was the first morning of them being in New York. The time difference woke them up early, a steaming breakfast already waiting at the table. A small balding man in his sixties smiled at Sophia and shook her hand. Roberto.

The food melted in her mouth. It was so good, completely on another level from the one she was used to in Riga. Soon after they finished eating, the doorbell rang. She heard steps rushing in the corridor as someone opened the door. Daniel squeezed her hand and they moved to greet the guests.

There were three men standing in the doorway, handing their coats to an elderly woman. She glanced at Sophia and her eyes widened.

"Miss." She bowed slightly at her and retreated with the coats.

The men wore shining, stylish, expensive suits and hats; they were smiling, but a steel glint reflected in each of them.

"Daniel, finally you're back," the tall man with a crooked smile said. "And look who you brought." His eyes landed on Sophia.

"Let's go to the office." Daniel gestured to them.

When they entered the room, he walked Sophia to the

closest armchair by his side. Two men sat in front of the table, one stood by the window.

"Sophia, this is Robert, James and John," Daniel pointed to each of them, the men nodded. "So, boys, tell me everything. Is everything calm?"

"With all due respect, I'm not sure that Sophia should be bored with details," James, a man with wide shoulders, said.

"With all due respect, Sophia can know everything, and listen to whatever she wants," Daniel said, a hint of anger in his voice.

James nodded, and the man with the crooked smile, Robert, the one standing by the window looked curiously at Sophia. She almost cringed under that gaze but held her chin high.

"Okay. Everything's quiet for us, but two distilling clubs of Antonelli were raided last week. Rumors say that he couldn't reach an agreement with a new officer."

"Did *we* reach that agreement?" Daniel asked.

"We did, but this one is a greedy bastard, he costs a lot to maintain a good relationship. And now he's only looking into the moonshine. But I assume his mug would be in casinos in no time, and he'd want more."

"We need to investigate his connections with the police. Is he standing firm or just climbing the career ladder? We can help him to get a generous pension. What about little Charlie?" Daniel asked.

John glanced at Sophia, as if not sure how much he could say.

"You can say everything," Daniel said, reading that gaze.

And the stream of unfamiliar names flowed. Sophia tried to follow, but too many nicknames and code names of places were thrown between the men. A heated discussion started about the date of an event, Sophia could not catch the details and what the event was. A thick folder landed on Daniel's table. He opened it and leafed through the pages, a silence in the room. Then he nodded and they discussed distribution channels.

After an hour, the men stood, each one shook hands with Daniel, touched the brims of their hats and nodded at Sophia. And they were gone.

Daniel was silent for a moment, the pair of green eyes studying her face.

"So, you are into the moonshine business and casinos," she said quietly.

"Yes, my dear. Does it bother you?"

"The only thing that bothers me is that it's not safe," she said.

"It's safe as long as you are in agreement with the important people. And it's my job: for everything to move smoothly, I negotiate."

"What about banking? You said the person you are working for is in banking," she said, and he laughed.

"One of the teams in our little association is working with banks. They rob them." Those green eyes caught every reaction, every move.

Sophia took a shaking breath.

"Don't worry, they don't operate here, and you won't be meeting them."

She nodded. "Okay."

"You are with me now, and you can go deep into details, or you can stay away from all this business. It's your choice, and I trust your silence," he said.

"I want to do something," Sophia said.

"Every day, I want you by my side. I work from here, and you can work from your office, but I need you to stay close. So, I know you are also good with numbers, do you want to dive into bookkeeping? With training you could help old Ben, he's been grumbling about the workload for ages now."

"Yes, yes, I want to do it."

"Okay, you'll start tomorrow. I'll make arrangements with him. I agree that it's important for women to do some work; household duties are for maids. And I can't understand men who agree for their wives to just go shopping every day and climb the walls from boredom."

I opened my eyes to the chirping of a bird on my window. These were some progressive thoughts coming from Daniel; he appeared to be quite an early feminist. But all he was doing was illegal: casinos, distilleries, bank robbery. That explained how he got rich so fast. But I watched enough gangster movies to know the danger, and the short life of this business. I tried to decipher if Sophia was really fine with all this; but did she have any choice? She was in a foreign city, alone except for Daniel. I felt like she forbade herself to dwell on ethics and the legality of all the things she was drawn into.

A small man in his forties entered the room; he had an eagle nose and lively eyes which immediately bored into Sophia.

"So, you're *the* girl," he mumbled.

Sophia stood and shook his hand. Daniel was away today on some business, and he said that Ben would meet her in her office at ten in the morning. The mahogany table and leather chairs appeared in the room during the evening of their first day in New York.

"I'm not happy that they made me a babysitter, and I don't believe a woman is capable of bookkeeping. So let's try, you'll see that it's not for you and I'll retreat to my office, and you'll go to the hair salon or department store or beauty shop or wherever the women go."

"Test me," Sophia said and circled the table to sit on the chair by Ben's side.

He grumbled but sat, pulling a long list of numbers from his bag.

"These of course aren't real numbers. I sketched a simple task for you," Ben said, pushing the papers in front of her.

He explained what should be done and said that she had a week to complete it. She looked at it, frowning.

"I can do it in fifteen minutes," she said. "Please go to the kitchen, Roberto or Eva will make you a cup of coffee. Meanwhile, I will complete those."

Ben groaned standing up.

"As you wish. Coffee sounds good." And he pointed again to the list, explaining again.

"I got it," Sophia cut him off mid-sentence.

When he was out of the room, Sophia looked at the sheet in her hands. It was easy. The man didn't want to do anything with her as he said himself. She would prove him wrong.

She bent over the numbers; they flowed to a different row, multiplying, dividing. In less than ten minutes, she finished, gave herself one more minute to check, and she marched to the kitchen. Ben was talking to Roberto, a cup of coffee in his hands.

"Ready," she said and stretched out the list.

Ben's eyes slid up and down the paper, nodding. He furrowed his brow.

"Good," he mumbled.

"Give me more," Sophia demanded.

He gave her another list, with the task slightly more complex than the previous. Sophia retreated to her office; ten minutes later, she stood in the kitchen again.

Ben took the paper. Nodded again.

"Let's make it more difficult," he said and added more papers, rows and rows of numbers. This time he didn't explain anything, he just said what should be done.

Sophia withdrew to her room, her mind already on the task.

Fifteen minutes later, she walked into the kitchen.

Ben was talking to Roberto about the wines of California.

"Do you need help, Sophia?" Ben teased.

"Ready." And she gave him the papers. It took him longer to check it this time.

"Bloody Maria," he whispered and looked up at her. "You may not be a lost cause after all."

Ben nodded to Roberto and stood from the stool.

"We have work to do," he said and shuffled to her office, his eyes never leaving the list in his hands.

He tested Sophia till the evening, giving her tasks. When he saw she paused on something, he explained what to do next; she nodded and proceeded.

When it was dark outside, someone knocked on the door.

"Come in," Sophia said, her eyes never leaving the paper in front of her.

Daniel entered the room. Ben put a finger to his lips, gesturing for silence and lifted his palm. His eyes were on Sophia's paper. He bent a thumb, Sophia added a few lines to the paper, a pointing finger, more lines, middle finger, more, and till the pinkie went down, she said: "Done."

The man grinned and took a sheet in his hand. Daniel stood silently by the door, watching them, a mischievous smile on his lips. There were a few beats of silence as Ben scanned the paper.

"Correct," he said and looked at Sophia. "Finally, a person with brains. Honestly, I never thought it could be a woman, but we'll work together nicely." Ben turned to Daniel. "She's smart, sharp." And he tapped his temple.

Daniel smiled broadly. "Oh, I know."

Ben picked up his bag and shook Daniel's hand.

"Sophia, tomorrow, here, same time." And he bowed to her; it was a bit mocking, but a kind smile played on his lips.

Daniel crossed the room when Ben closed the door and perched on the side of the table.

"So, what do you think?" he asked.

"I want more," she said. "I could actually hear my mind working today, and it's quite pleasant to see his approval."

"Yes, Ben is one of the best at his job, but he doesn't really like women, he thinks they are all about looks, fancy dolls for men."

"Poor woman, his wife," Sophia said.

"Oh no, he likes his partners to be male, and slightly younger," Daniel said, and Sophia gasped. "He is safe to work with. Do you think I would have left you with a normal man for a day in a closed room? He is loyal, he likes to get his share, and he is perfect at what he does. And he unfroze toward you," Daniel said and caught a strand of her hair between his fingers.

Sixteen

The days melted into weeks. Sometimes I felt I was losing my grip on my reality, the days in school mixing with the imaginary days in New York.

My parents tried to pull me out of the house every weekend, taking me camping, or fishing. Secretly hoping to erase that distant look from my face. And with each trip I realized I could fake happiness more and more. I asked questions when they needed to be asked. I played my role.

I played in my life; I was not living it.

Sometimes on weekends, Daniel showed Sophia the city. They strolled down the Brooklyn Bridge, went to a couple Broadway shows. A few times they went to a fancy club. I enjoyed watching the New York elite in those dreams. The dresses exposed the skin, hugged beautiful women, men in tuxedos, the jazz songs flowing through the dance floor, the bodies swaying to the rhythm. Every time, Sophia was left at the table, while Daniel negotiated a new deal by the bar or in a corner booth, only men sitting there, puffing their cigars.

Daniel never left Sophia alone in this club; when he went away to talk about business, one of the guys Daniel worked with always appeared by her side. They guarded her. No one could talk to Sophia; these human ghosts attracted curious looks but closed her in.

Sophia didn't like going to this club; she felt stifled. The women competing on their appearances and the men who they clinged to. Everyone assessed each other, trying to understand the status and the size of their wallets. She agreed to go there only because of the music. Daniel didn't dance, and she couldn't dance alone. But the melody touched her heart every time.

Once, a song about lost love was playing, couples slowly spinning on the dance floor. Sophia sat at her table, Daniel gone, two of his friends sitting on the opposite side of the table, discussing something in low voices.

The melody was so beautiful, she wished it would never end. Her shoulders moved slightly to the rhythm. She looked at Daniel sitting with a huge man at the booth and back to the dance floor just to find black eyes on her. He was a tall man with black raven hair with a slight wave in the fringe that framed his face and high cheekbones. A woman was dancing with him, her head on his chest. Sophia had seen this girl here a couple of times already. She was a usual, hunting for men.

Those dark eyes were glued to Sophia's face, and she couldn't look away. There was something mysterious about him, magnetic, and the music just faded away while she was lost in his eyes.

He nodded slightly when the last few notes of the melody flowed, and the woman stood on tiptoes to whisper something in his ear.

Sophia looked down at her hands, a slight blush warming her cheeks. When the much faster song started, she lifted her eyes up. There was no trace of that man.

Weeks turned into months. And again in my dreams, I was experiencing time differently, in one night I could see weeks. It helped. When her time rushed, my time slowed. A slip of a true laugh, a sliver of a smile that was not fake. Calling Lorraine. Watching a movie that held my interest. The dystopian book that caught my attention. Playing boarding games with Mom and Dad.

It was almost the usual life of a teenager. Almost.

Sophia was working with Ben, sometimes he came to her office, but mostly a boy brought all the papers every morning. She buried herself in the work. Daniel often disappeared for days, always coming back and murmuring in her hair how he missed her, leading her to the bedroom. Her body always responded to his touch, but she was not hungry anymore.

She asked where he went, the replies always the same: He went to a country club out of the city with his boss. On the weekends when she was alone, Sophia went to explore the city. New York was crawling under her skin. She found places where she enjoyed her morning coffee, favorite trees in Central Park, busy roads, watching walls of concrete from the cab window.

But when she saw a whole city stretching before her when she stood at the top of the Empire State Building, Sophia realized that she was in love with New York; they had a perfect romance. The city enveloped her, the noise of it in her ears murmuring that she was not alone, that it was her home, like too many before her and millions after.

Sophia settled into her life. It was very different from the time they spent in Paris and London, the romantic story ending when she stepped out of the ship onto American land. They both had work to do, and she knew that she was contributing a great deal now, seeing all the documents and numbers that went through her and Ben. And she was okay with it.

She wanted to see the world, to get out of the city she loved but which was too small, which reminded her of a mother who loved her, which held the shell of a father. The small buildings, the old center, it was all nice, but Sophia wanted more. And Daniel gave it to her, he gave her the world, she was looking at it when the wind ruffled her hair while she stood on top of the Empire State Building, a small smile playing on her lips. Daniel never promised her a love story, and she was not the one craving it. He came back for her, he gave her a new home, a new job, a new world, and she was immensely grateful for it.

She replayed a conversation from yesterday in her head.

"How do you want to get married?" Daniel asked. They were having breakfast in the kitchen of their apartment. "Do you want it to be posh with lots of people? We will be the highlight of the news section that day, you know," he said, taking a sip of coffee. "Or do you want it to be a quiet ceremony?"

Sophia looked up from her toast.

"Quiet, I wish there would be only two of us. No news coverage for sure," she smiled.

He nodded, green eyes on her, as always.

"Honeymoon?" he asked.

"Do we have time for it? There is that big lot of whiskey coming and a string of events in a casino. You have to be there, and I need to help Ben to straighten the paperwork."

"Business, always business, I love that about you," Daniel said, a smile never reaching his eyes while he brushed her cheek, while he unbuttoned her blouse exposing a sliver of skin, while his fingers gently caressed the soft skin of her breast through the fabric.

"When do you want to marry?" he asked.

Her heart hammered in her ribcage while he played with her body. He loved touching her.

"Let's do it after the casino events," she said.

He stood and moved behind the stool she was sitting on. He pulled up her skirt, lowering her undergarments. His practiced strokes of fingers against her flaming flesh pulled her to the top, fast.

"I love it when you lose control, when you moan like that," he whispered from behind.

And he left the room, leaving her just a moment after she shuddered. Sophia slowly buttoned her blouse, straightened her skirt, and moved to her office. A piece of paper lay folded on her table. She took it with shaking hands, her body still trembling.

You are mine.

Three words were like blood on white paper. And she knew it was the truth.

Seventeen

New York of the 1930s fascinated me. I filled my days with a part-time job and studies. I plastered on a smile and worked at the coffee joint. The time spent working certainly took away all the questions from my parents and Lorraine; I was working, I was busy, I had a legitimate excuse why I came home exhausted. It had only been half a year since I first landed into Sophia's life, and more than two years passed in her time.

The work allowed me to daydream. I could memorize an order of a Strawberry Matcha Latte while my thoughts were on the streets of Manhattan.

Sophia was content with the cage she lived in. The cage gave her relative freedom: She had her own money which she earned and had a separate bank account. She roamed the city; she felt the power of it, when the sunset light ignited the buildings. But she was alone. Daniel never promised her love or even company, and she never asked for it. But so often he was not even there, just to come back and take what he thought was his. And her body, it was the price to pay for this new life.

Sophia read finance books or detective novels. No romantic stories anymore, those were for the girl who was left behind. She discussed with Ben how markets were working—the man was a hoarder of knowledge who loved talking—and he shared everything he knew in heaps of lengthy talks. She dug deep into terms I had no idea existed.

That morning, Ben came into her office to discuss the details of the latest records. He was always in a rush.

"We have two days to finish it," he said, "and then the taxation period starts. Did you read that book I gave you?"

"Finishing it," she said.

"Good, make sure to note the percentages and categories, we'll need it soon. Okay, I should get going," he said standing up.

She nodded and led him to the door, gave him his coat because Eva was away today, and turned the lock behind him. Muffled voices were coming from Daniel's office. Lots of people came to see him. She rarely met any of his visitors, staying in her office, deep in her work.

Sophia took a coffee can from the cupboard in the kitchen, and her hand was around the cup when a doorbell rang, once, twice, three times. Someone was banging on the door.

She rushed to open it, familiar voices mumbling for her to hurry.

Robert and James were at the doorway. James's face was white as a sheet, he was barely holding himself together, all his weight was supported by Robert. James's hand was bundled in some kind of dark blanket, wet stains visible on it.

"Where is he?" Robert barked once inside.

"In the office," Sophia said, quickly closing the door behind them.

Robert was practically carrying the half-conscious James.

Daniel stepped out of his office and saw the two men, his jaw hardening.

"Is he here?" Robert asked.

"Yes, go to the kitchen. Sophia, help them."

Robert lowered James into the chair in the kitchen, holding him in place. Sweat was dripping down James's forehead, he was mumbling something, his eyes glassy. The scene was so out of place in the serene light room.

Daniel entered, and after him stepped a tall man, dark eyes only for a moment meeting Sophia's as he turned to James. She remembered the man instantly: raven hair, the music flowing. He was the one from the club. She had only a moment to register it before he stepped to James.

"What the hell happened?" Daniel asked Robert.

"He was driving the boys from the bank, all was quiet, it was a small place on the outskirts of the city. The guard decided to be brave and ran out to shoot at the car. The boys only got scratches; the man met a bullet with his eye. But James here, caught one with his hand."

"Did anyone follow you?" Daniel asked.

"No, they switched cars and laid low. The doc was not in his office, the nurse told us that he's here. When one of the boys found me, little Jamesy was almost unconscious. I had to bring him to the doctor. Daniel, there was no tail, I'm sure."

Daniel nodded while the man opened his brown bag, syringes and scalpels were attached to the walls of the bag. So he was the Doc.

"I need alcohol, strong," he said, his voice low.

Sophia bolted to a bar by the fridge and fished out the bottle. Even though it was illegal to store spirits now, Daniel didn't care.

She gave the bottle to the man, their fingers touching slightly. He lifted his eyes to her and immediately looked away.

He put the bottle to James's dry lips and motioned for Robert to hold him. He took the syringe, quickly filling it with the transparent liquid from the small vial and pushed the needle in James's shoulder.

"Drink."

James took a few gulps of golden liquid.

"More," Doc said, and he obliged.

Doc gingerly touched James's hand above the elbow, putting the blanket on the marble countertop. James screamed when Doc started unfolding the cloth, his eyes rolling in his sockets. His eyelids dropped and didn't open again.

"Good, he's out," Doc said.

He continued to unfold the blanket. A mass of flesh was where the palm should be, and everything red, red. Sophia gripped the countertop but stood watching.

The man with the raven hair disinfected the scalpel and sliced the skin.

"God," Daniel muttered and left the room. Sophia stepped closer to the window, looking out. She heard noises of metallic pieces landing on the countertop.

"I need more light," the man said, and Sophia went to the living room to bring more lamps.

It took an hour for the man to take out all the metal from James' hand, a few more hours to try to save what could be saved. The long needle penetrated the skin, blood was everywhere, but the hand was stitched back, and a layer of white clean bandages covered the wound.

Daniel came back and stood by the door. The silence filled the kitchen.

"He needs to rest," the man said and looked at Daniel.

"Sure, he can stay in the guest room for a couple of days. I already rang Eva; she will be here soon. She used to be a nurse, so she can help."

"Good," the man nodded.

They scooped up unconscious James and brought him to the guest room.

Robert took a swig of whiskey on his way out, his eyes haunted. He shook Doc's hand.

"You're our savior, as always," Robert muttered.

The tall man cleaned the kitchen counter and all his instruments from the blood and stepped to the door.

"I didn't get a chance to introduce myself," he said, looking at Sophia. "My name is William."

"Sophia."

"I know," he smiled and closed the door behind him.

Daniel stood in the kitchen, staring at a place where only an hour ago was a pile of raw meat instead of a hand.

"I need to work," he said and strode to his office, a motionless mask on his face.

Sophia also had work to do, but she couldn't leave the kitchen. Only now a small understanding of what they were doing came to her. It was dangerous. The numbers from her papers took the form of reality, the blood, violence, robbery.

She took a sip of whiskey, the liquid burning her throat, she took another one, bigger. The warmth spread down her veins. She slowly walked to her office, closing the door behind. She sat in her armchair and took a sheet of paper in her hand, a pen, and continued working. She had a lot of work to do.

※

A week later, Daniel took her again to the club. She was wearing a dark blue dress, her back completely exposed, a heavy bracelet on her wrist—the latest gift from Daniel.

They entered the hall and sat at their table, Robert was there, his hand wrapped tightly around a young woman, a couple of men who visited Daniel almost weekly, and William, with a chirping girl with an impressive bosom fit tight in her red dress by his side.

Daniel motioned for Robert and his men to go with him—

again, that big man in a suit was puffing a cigar in the corner booth.

"Will, please look after Sophia," Daniel asked and turned away.

The girl in the red dress went to the ladies' room, leaving only two of them.

Those dark eyes the color of the night landed on Sophia's face.

"How do you like New York?" he asked.

"I love it, the rhythm of the city matches mine," she said. "Are you from New York?"

"All people here are from New York." He put *are* in the air quotes, smiling. "But no one actually is, we all came here, or our parents. My family's from Warsaw."

"Riga," she said.

"What do you think about this club?" he asked.

She noticed that not only his eyes were the night: They were the starry night. Stars glowed in the dark of his irises when he looked at her.

Sophia leaned closer. "I hate it here."

Will snorted.

"I hate these half-naked women who jump on men, who almost flash everything they have, nothing is secret. I hate how hungry the men are, how they touch those women, just to see them here next week with completely different women sitting in their laps. I hate that I am always left here alone, Daniel goes to sort out his business, leaving me here with his random pals. You are actually the first person who talked to me. One thing I love here is . . ."

"Music," he ended.

"Yes."

"You know, some of these men here are actually bastards with wives and kids at home. But some are lonely, and these girls, even for the night, help to fill the void."

"Oh, I am sure, with a bust like your companion she definitely would fill the void," Sophia laughed. "Speak of the devil," she muttered as the girl in the red dress came back and brushed Will's neck.

He caught her hand and tugged her lower to whisper in her ear. She nodded, a disappointed look on her face. The girl looked Sophia up and down and turned away, marching to the bar.

"She didn't like what you just said," Sophia laughed.

"Oh, yes, I said I wasn't in the mood today," he said and lit the cigarette.

Sophia noticed his long fingers. "So, you are a doctor."

"And you're an accountant."

"I am." She was proud of how he referred to her, not Daniel's girl or fiancé, not Daniel's anything.

"Do you miss home?"

She brushed a lock of her hair away. "Not really, I always wanted to escape it. I miss my maid though, after my mother died, she became much closer than just a maid, a friend. But we correspond. When I was leaving, she had just found her peace, her love; she isn't alone anymore. What about you?"

"Almost all my family's here now, sisters, cousins, parents, grandparents, all here. Do I miss Warsaw? We left when I was young, so I remember the city, but for me it was more about the people, and everyone is here now. So, smooth transition."

"It's a good profession you chose, you help people," Sophia said.

"Not really, I could have worked in the hospital, there you really help people. Here, I save or try saving men who got shot, stubbed, beaten because of the business we're all in. I don't fool myself with a high-minded cause, I'm here for the money. They pay much more than I could ever make in the hospital. Nothing noble."

He took a cigarette to his lips, watching her.

"It's a choice," he added. "The one I make every day, but the same as you actually."

"No," she shook her head. "The difference is that I don't have a choice."

A cold palm landed on her shoulders, sending shivers through her spine.

"We need to go," Daniel told Sophia.

She stood, he was already moving to the exit.

"Goodbye, Doctor."

Will watched her a little longer than necessary.

"Good night," he said.

Eighteen

"Your name?" I asked a man in a gray suit, his black hair combed back, holding a marker and a paper cup in my hands.

"William," he replied, not looking at me.

I wrote his name on the cup, smiling to myself. He resembled Will from my dreams. Was it the hair? Definitely not the eyes, this man had blue eyes. His movements were sharp, as he kept glancing at the clock impatiently.

I hurried with his order, still smiling.

Daniel became irritated, and Sophia often heard angry shouts from his office. He regularly left for days, which was okay with Sophia; she loved the quiet of the apartment.

One morning, Daniel marched into her office.

"We will go to a party this weekend. It is my boss' birthday and he invited us to his house outside of the city," he said and put a card on her table. "Call this place and arrange a time when you could come. I already talked to them, it's a boutique, the owner's name is Franchesca, they buy dresses directly from Paris."

"What is wrong with the dresses I have?" Sophia asked.

Daniel flashed his eyes—a hint of annoyance and it's gone. "This is different, you need to look your best there. Also, they will help with your hair on the day we are leaving. Just do it, okay?" he tried to sound gentler.

"Okay."

"You are my beauty, Sophia, but we need to highlight it," he dragged his thumb on her neck and turned to walk away.

When he left the room, Sophia caught herself wishing that he was gone on one of his trips again.

※

When she entered the shop, a tall woman in her forties met her; she scanned Sophia's appearance, but her face betrayed nothing.

"We have a few dresses for you to try on," she gestured to the changing room.

The woman, Franchesca, showed her four dresses, each one of the softest silks. Sophia put the first one on, the color of peach, one shoulder exposed, the other one hidden under the fabric.

"No, no, definitely not your color," Franchesca said.

The next one was black.

"Not bad but go on."

The next was silver, beautifully hugging her body.

Franchesca motioned to the last one: dark green. The dress didn't expose a lot of skin, but her shoulders were bare, the dress high on her neck. It made her look taller, slimmer but highlighted all the good parts.

"Yes," the woman said.

Sophia would have preferred any other dress; this one was the color of Daniel's eyes, the exact hew. And she suspected that

Franchesca knew about it. That's why when Sophia suggested the black one, but the woman refused.

They chose her shoes and purse. And Franchesca called for two girls who worked in the shop. One girl looked as though she stepped from the latest fashion magazine: She was stunning, full lips like the petals of rose, the hair of finest silk, but there was something wrong with the way she looked at Sophia, some kind of hatred she didn't want to hide. The other girl was also pretty but in the plain way, far from the beauty queen standing by her side. Unlike her companion, she looked kindly at Sophia.

"What do you think about her hair?" she asked.

The three of them stepped closer, trying on different hairstyles. Sophia hated it, how their fingers drifted between her strands of hair, but stood there. Finally, they agreed on the style —hair gathered at the nape of the neck, exposing the shoulders.

"I will come to your place on Saturday and help you with your hair," the beautiful one said, Shirley.

"I want it to be Mary," Sophia said, pointing to another girl. "I liked her suggestions."

Shirley wanted to argue, but Franchesca agreed. "Okay, Mary'll come at 9 AM with the dress and makeup."

When Sophia finally left the store, she breathed in slowly, hailing a cab and making her way back to the apartment.

The look on Shirley's face haunted me for hours after that dream as I was walking absentmindedly through the Walmart rows, clutching the grocery list I was trusted with.

When Sophia was at this boutique, I felt like she was amongst the snakes. Franchesca didn't try to hide her resentment; Shirley simply glowered. Mary, on the contrary, tried to brighten the mood, her touches soft, her comments kind. She looked with her big eyes at Sophia, wonder there, and a glint of pity I couldn't understand.

The dress they chose was stunning, that's why Sophia didn't push for another one. It was their job to make Sophia glow, and they did their job. I had a feeling Sophia wouldn't agree on Shirley coming to fix her hair, even if Franchesca insisted. I felt the waves of distrust emanating from Sophia towards her.

I got used to following Sophia's life and was proud of her. Daniel and Sophia didn't hurry with the wedding, and I felt like she saved as much money as she could, just in case. There was no closeness between them now. Was there ever?

Maybe when Daniil was just a boy from Russia in a foreign city, and the girl believed in his dreams, maybe there was a connection then. All that came next was lust.

And now I saw it. Daniel was sucked into the illegal life of the Great Depression, dragging Sophia with him. I watched them, my life quieting around me.

I got accepted to FSU, no surprise there. I would continue living with my parents, my day would change, but my nights would stay the same.

❦

Mary did a great job on Sophia's hair and make-up. Sophia liked the softness of the girl; she didn't talk much, but she was kind. I wondered how she was working with those snakes.

When all was finished and Sophia looked up in the mirror, she saw herself, powerful. Big crimson lips, dark eyes. The green dress hugged her hips, showing a thin waist, hiding her cleavage, but beautifully enfolding her chest. Her nails were the same color as her lips. She held herself high, the power of authority emanating from her.

When Daniel entered the room, his eyes widened. He stepped closer, a hand on her waist, moving lower.

"I would have ripped this dress off you, just to see what's under it," he whispered in her ear. "Maybe later I will do it, you look stunning."

The comment didn't stir anything in Sophia. She just nodded.

Nineteen

A black Ford took them to the party. The trip took hours it seemed, but Sophia had never traveled outside the city limit and her eyes were glued to the window. The car slowed before the big house; the fleet of shining cars already parked outside. The Victorian mansion glowed in the dark, bright light emanating from the windows. A dark garden and miles of immaculate lawn stretched towards the back.

Daniel took her hand, and they stepped inside. The man she saw every time in the club in the corner booth met them, a perfect wife by his side. They were in their forties, the style and elegance from the woman mixed with the boredom in her eyes.

The man hugged Daniel.

"Happy birthday, Alexander," Daniel said. "Thanks for having us."

Alexander released Daniel and looked at Sophia. He had such small eyes for such a big man, and those eyes slid down her breasts, her waist, going up again to her face. Sophia was glad her dress hid everything under the fabric, even though it hugged her tightly.

"This is Sophia," Daniel said.

The man kissed Sophia's hand, a wet smack, eyes on her lips.

"Hello, Sophia. I see why you brought her all the way from Riga," Alexander said, winking at Daniel. I felt shivers crawling down Sophia's arms.

But a new pair of guests just arrived, and Alexander and his wife turned to them. Daniel took Sophia's hand and led her further.

"Alexander helped me to stand firmly on my feet. I used to be a bodyguard for his second, Donald, and the rest is history."

"Is Donald here tonight?" Sophia asked.

"No, he got shot five months ago," Daniel said and shook hands with another man who stood by the table.

Waiters slid between people, offering various canapés. There was a bar in the corner of the hall.

"Isn't it dangerous to drink so openly?" Sophia asked quietly.

Daniel snorted. "Alexander has the police in his pocket. He is the most powerful man in New York, don't worry, dear."

Nothing warm was in that *dear*.

Twice, Alexander joined them, finding Daniel in the crowd. Sophia saw how Daniel was proud of being here, how he puffed up being so close to the mighty Alexander. As the evening went on, more drinks were served, men talked more and more about business, about money. Wives gathered in another part of the room, talking about kids, vacation homes, and competing for whose husband had more money.

Alexander's wife would have won there, but she said that she wasn't feeling well and retreated upstairs soon after the party started. Sophia hated each second, the poshness and meaninglessness of it all. It was not so different from the club, just on a different level. Grander.

When she heard a conversation between two men, their eyes glassy from the alcohol, she couldn't take it anymore. One man was saying how his French maid moaned when he took her, how her little breasts bounced when she jumped on top of him. Earlier that day Sophia saw this man with his wife, dark circles under her eyes, and later, she was talking about their kids, and how the smallest one was not sleeping well because of his teeth coming in.

Daniel was somewhere in the crowd of men, Alexander's hand on his shoulder, all of them laughing loudly. Sophia took a glass of water and stepped outside; the warm evening muted all the noise from the inside. The long balcony was deserted, everyone was inside.

She looked into the dark sky, big nothingness where she wanted to drown.

"Beautiful, right?" Will was standing by her side. She didn't hear him coming close, a dark shadow.

"Sky?" she asked.

"Yes," he said. "Party's awful." There was a smile in his voice.

Sophia turned to him. "If you hate it so much, why are you here?"

"It's part of my job."

"Why aren't you there?" Sophia asked and pointed to a group of men, all of them laughing wildly.

"Oh, I'm not that important, and not that close. They run to me only when blood is gushing from their bodies, other than that I stay away."

"And are they okay with it?"

"Yes, I do my job well, the blood stops running out and everyone's happy. The less I know the better. I just patch them up and a month later one of them is on my table again."

Sophia nodded and looked at the sky again.

"Do you know why this place is even worse than the club?" she asked.

"Many things, but why?"

"Music," Sophia said, "There is no music to disguise their voices."

"Yes," he said simply and looked up with her. They stood in silence, only booming laughter came from the hall, but it got lost in this darkness.

Will moved slightly and touched her arm, a swift brush on her wrist and he was gone, disappearing into the crowd inside. Sophia's heart picked up the pace and she looked inside, but no one was watching the balcony, the place she stood was hidden by the wall. No one saw, and she tried to calm herself looking up at the sky. But her heart didn't want to slow, and a few moments later she found herself smiling.

Twenty

Weeks went by. Every day, Sophia buried herself in numbers. Day and night alternated. I had two months before my university started, and I actually enjoyed working at the coffee shop. People knew me, I knew them. I worked, I read, I talked, I had a double life. I finally mastered the art of pretending, participating just enough that no one frowned at me, laughing in the right places.

Lorraine took me to the movies every Friday, both of us enjoying our guilty pleasure afterwards—fried chicken sandwiches from a fast food chain restaurant. Life was good, even if sometimes I faked it.

Sophia hadn't seen Will since that party, and she tried to forget that touch. She kept saying to herself that it was nothing. And my heart broke for her: There was no way in the world Daniel would let her go. He thought of her as his beautiful doll, as his property. Daniel wanted to marry and get over with the official stuff, but Sophia had postponed it a few times already, saying that they were busy with other events. And he agreed, just to disappear for a few days saying he had plans with Alexander. And Sophia breathed more freely every time.

One morning after her usual walk in Central Park, Sophia turned into an alley. She was smiling, the sun warmed her face, the coffee she had in a nearby cafe pumped her step. Every morning, she had a few hours to herself before the papers from Ben came.

The ornaments of their residential building were looming in the distance, just two more blocks and she would be in the quiet of her office. A black car stopped in front of her with a screech, the doors were thrown open and two men stepped on the sidewalk and grabbed her elbows. There was no one close. She screamed, and people from far away saw the commotion, but there was no chance they would reach her in time.

Sophia struggled, her nails scraping their bare necks, but a third man stepped from the car, there was something in his hand. He pressed cloth to Sophia's mouth and nose, and everything went dark.

She opened her eyes in a gray windowless room. It was bare, just a lightbulb hanging from the ceiling. Dark stains marked the floor, an acrid smell hitting her nose. Water dripped from the ceiling in the corner. Sophia was chained to a metal stool; she tried to free her hands, but nothing moved, a metal scraping her wrists.

With a crazed eye, she looked around; there was nothing in this room. She noticed red splashes on the wall behind her, the blood. It was everywhere. A soft sob escaped her lips.

There was a movement behind the door, and it opened. The man with the cloth stepped in. He closed the door and the lock clicked; someone locked the door from the other side.

The man laughed. "They think you will try to sneak," he snorted. "But you are not going anywhere, are you?"

He was wearing a simple brown shirt with rolled sleeves and

black pants with suspenders. His head was cleanly shaven, his hands big.

"We are just going to talk, me and you," he said and slapped Sophia's face. Her head rolled to the side from the impact, her teeth clacked, blood filled her mouth. She turned to him, shock and fear beating in her veins.

The man grunted. "Oh, I need to remember that you are not a man, I will be gentler next time, lassie. Usually from a punch like this nothing happens, but your lip cracked." He looked at his palm, the bright splotches of red on it. The man licked his hand, catching the blood on his tongue.

"Your blood is sweet, you know? Like you are." He looked at her with cold eyes. "But don't worry, we are here to talk and to emphasize some points. Those beautiful lips of yours will heal. I am not here to ruin you."

"What do you want?" she growled, amazingly the fear didn't show in her voice.

"Finally, my monologue grows into dialogue."

He paced the room from wall to wall. "I need you to take a message to Daniel, he sticks his nose in the business of ours. When you tell him he will know what I am talking about. He needs to stop or consequences will be worse." The man stopped in front of her and punched Sophia in the ribs, all breath rushing out of her lungs.

"You hear," he tapped his ear, "nothing is broken. Just breathe, lass."

The firework pain in her side receded, and she could breathe again. The man proceeded to pace.

"I am not sure even Alexander knows about Daniel's plans, and if he doesn't, then we are making him a big favor, saving his sorry ass. But if they are both in it," and he stopped again, moved closer and grabbed her arm, "remember those words, Sophia, you need to tell them exactly like this," he was squeezing his fingers around her wrist, she could feel her bones crutching under the pressure. "If they don't stop, there will be a war."

The man released his grip, and Sophia looked at her arm. It was purple.

"And do you know an interesting thing about war?" he asked, his voice calm.

She was silent. He turned and smashed his fist into her stomach. She couldn't breathe again.

"Answer me, Sophia, it's a dialogue, remember? And you see, I am gentle, I am caressing you, as I said, my job is not to break you. I will ask again; do you know what's interesting about war?"

"No," she croaked.

The man was again close, his face inches from her. She could smell the sweat and cheap alcohol on him. "People die, Sophia."

And he smashed his palm across her cheekbone. Her vision clouded.

The man stepped back, admiring her.

"Finally, tears. I was afraid I was not expressing myself enough." He caught one of her tears with his thumb and licked it.

"Even your tears are sweet," he laughed, a steel cold sound.

Sophia was trembling, her face hurt, her stomach and ribs on fire.

"He wouldn't care, you know," she whispered.

"Come again, dear?"

"He would not care about me, he would not listen to me, I am nothing to him," she said, looking at the man.

"Oh, no, here you are wrong. That beautiful face of yours will heal in a matter of weeks, I am not a monster to destroy such beauty if I am not forced, and nobody forces me now," he gestured to the room. "We watched you; you know. Among his many girls you are chosen, he . . ." the man trailed off, studying her face. "Wait, you don't know about the other girls, do you?"

The man squatted in front of her and smiled, a cruel grin on his face. He crossed his arms and looked at her.

"Now it's going to hurt differently, here," and he pointed to her heart. "Let me tell you a story of our friend Daniel. I am sure you are familiar with his career path, slick as a fox he is, but his love life is as adventurous. The first year he came to America, God bless this country, and when he was finding his footing with Alexander, every night you could find him in the club, every time with a new girl by his side. Each of these girls left with him for the night, and the rest is history. Till he met Shirley, you know Shirley, you met her at Francesca's. Dazzling thing she is, right? Anyway, Daniel fancied her, and he stopped the kaleidoscope of girls and ended the days with her. Numerous nights in hotels, and as we keep tabs on our friends, we knew that they were not drinking tea there. *Yes, Daniel, yes, yes,* she screamed. Don't look at me like this, Sophia, I have read the report." He scratched his nose. "But he never took her to his apartment, and abruptly he broke up with her, oh how she cried, and a few days later he was gone to Riga."

Sophia could barely breathe, the bile choking her.

"If I knew you would have this reaction, I wouldn't have touched you in the first place." Something like distorted amusement played his features. "So, let's continue. Daniel gets back to New York with the purest creature in tow. That's you, lass. And everyone knows that you are his fiancé, and people talk that the love era of Daniel has ended, that he has finally settled. And it was like this for a couple of months, till he came back to the club. One night I walked into the restroom, just to find it occupied. One of the club girls was bent over and Daniel took her from behind, his hand on her breast, she liked it. Oh, Sophia, you paled, is everything alright?"

He dragged a thumb on her sore lower lip, there was blood on his finger. "Let's add you more color," and he drew this finger on her cheek. She felt blood smearing on her skin.

"But now Daniel is back to his old habits. Where does he say he goes when he leaves for days?"

Sophia was silent, she just stared at the floor.

"Answer me," the man growled and bent her pinkie, a sharp pain slicing the fog.

"To Alexander," she whispered.

"Oh, he visits Alexander often, that's true. But mostly Shirley is wrapped around him on these days. And when Alexander's wife is away in Europe back to her numerous lovers, Alexander arranges secret parties at his home, you don't want to know what happens there. You need to be better in your duties as a future wife, you know. But it's Daniel, one woman won't be enough for him."

He stood and leaned against the wall.

"So we had a conundrum, who could deliver the message to our dear Daniel. But since you live with him, and he wants to marry you, and he went all his way to Latvia to get you, we thought you'd be a better courier. I didn't know we would have so much fun together, me and you."

He looked her up and down. "Your eyes are blazing, Sophia. And with the blood all over your face you look like a warrior. It's anger, is it? Shirley would be so boring, she would cry and beg, but you, I admire you. And now is the time for you to go home."

"No," she said, her voice rasping.

"No?" he laughed. "Do you want to stay here?"

"Don't take me to him," she whispered.

The man's eyes darkened. "No, no, Sophia, you need to deliver the message, can you hear me? That's the point of our little meeting here." His hand went to her neck, squeezing. "Tell him what I said," he was blocking the air, she started wheezing, "and then do whatever you want with the knowledge I revealed to you today. Because if he doesn't get the message, next time he will read it on your dead body." Her mind clouded again, but the man loosened the grip.

"Do we agree on the matter?" he asked lightly, as the air rushed back to her throat.

She nodded.

"Say it, lass."

"Yes, I will deliver your message!" she screamed.

"Good girl. Okay, it was nice meeting you. The boys will drop you by your home." He knocked on the door. It opened and the room was silent.

Her body started trembling, but not from the pain; red fury flashed in her mind. Bastard.

Two men walked in the room, they put a bag over her head and helped her stand. But she couldn't, the sharp pain sliced her side, even though the man said her ribs weren't broken, she was sure they were. A man scooped her in his arms.

"We are taking you home," he said.

He brought her to the car. They drove for what felt like hours. Finally, they pulled off the bag, revealing that they were close to Sophia's home.

She looked down at her hands in her lap, the pinkie bent in the wrong direction, pulsing wildly.

The car stopped in front of the building entrance.

"Say that Thom Foley sends best regards," one of the men growled in her ear.

Another man helped her out of the car. This time she tried to stand, bending in half. The man motioned for the concierge, an elderly man, always so polite, smiling. His eyes widened in horror when he looked at Sophia.

"Get her in her apartment," the man barked to the concierge and disappeared back into the car, which slowly was moving away.

Sophia almost fell into the concierge's arms. He tried to take all her weight from her legs, and she noticed the horrified expressions on the faces of passersby. The man grunted, but he scooped her in his arms carefully, trying not to cause any more pain and went in, hiding her from the looks of distress from the people outside.

"Everything's going to be alright, Miss Sophia," he whispered.

In front of the apartment door, he helped her to stand and rang once, twice. Eva opened the door and Sophia saw how her expression changed from surprise to dread.

"Help me to the couch, please," Sophia asked the man, her voice gaining power. "Eva, call Daniel, please."

The man placed her on the couch, the sweat glistening on his forehead.

"Thank you very much," Sophia said, but he was already retreating to the door.

Moments later, Daniel stepped out of his office; he stopped, his hand going up to his mouth. Those green eyes going to her face and down her body.

"Eva, I need a doctor, please get Will, and please take the rest of the day off," Sophia said, strength flowing back to her at the sight of him. When the woman didn't move, Sophia raised her voice, "Now."

Finally, Eva bolted to the door and closed it behind. The apartment plunged into eerie silence.

Sophia propped herself on the pillow, looking at Daniel.

"So, Daniil, Thom Foley sends best wishes." She felt a ping of satisfaction at the fear distorting his features. "And he says for you to stop sticking your nose into their business," and as she searched his face, she said, "I see that you know what he was talking about, because if you don't stop there would be a war, and people die in war."

Son of a bitch, she thought.

Daniel moved closer, his hands going to her good hand.

"Don't you dare touch me," Sophia snarled, and his hand jerked as if from fire.

"What did he do to you?" he whispered.

"Oh, don't worry, we just had a talk."

"Did Thom himself do it?" Daniel asked.

"The man didn't say his name, the one who so gently explained his message was clean shaven, eyes set wide, calling me lass."

Daniel dropped to the floor by the sofa.

"It's him, and he is a monster, Sophia."

"Really?" she snorted.

"He dismembers people. No one leaves him whole; he cuts and chops human flesh."

"He liked me then, you see, no pieces cut from me." She tried to smile, but pain was rolling back to her limbs, adrenaline wearing off.

"Did they touch you, you know, violate you?" he asked.

"No, they didn't. I was only a good punching bag while he talked, making sure I remembered the message. He only fancied my face, my hands, my ribs, and wait, there was definitely a blow to the stomach."

She tried to smile; her lips caked with blood.

"So, Daniil," she switched to his old Russian name; there was no Daniel anymore, that glamor of a name washed off with the truth she found out today. "If you want to live, you don't want to meet Thom, and if you don't want to meet him, do as he said, leave whatever it is you are doing."

And she dropped her head to the pillow, breathing hard. He moved his hand to her shoulder.

"Don't," she growled again.

And like this they stayed. She lay there, her ribs crushed into the insides of her stomach, the pinkie definitely broken, her throat rasping from every breath, still she couldn't take a usual breath since Thom squeezed her neck.

And Daniel didn't do anything, frozen in his thoughts, shocked by Sophia's appearance.

Finally, the bell rang, and Daniel went to open the door.

William stepped into the room and when he saw Sophia, a flash of such profound pain was in his eyes, she wasn't sure she saw it there, or if it was a play of her ill imagination.

Will rushed to her, falling to his knees. He traced his fingers on her neck, barely touching, her cheeks, examining her purple wrist twice the size of another one, and her finger.

"She met Thom Foley," Daniel said.

Will's hand froze, his eyes darkened.

"She what?" He turned to Daniel.

"Thom used her to send me a message," Daniel said quietly, looking at the floor.

"Oh my God," Will said standing. "You should have seen this coming. Why didn't you give her security? And with your new plan with Alexander you should have known they will take the weakest link," he was shouting at Daniel. "I guess your mind was elsewhere." His black eyes bore into Daniel, who said nothing in return.

Sophia sobbed; her body started shaking.

"I'll take her to my office, she'll be there till she heals," Will said, standing up and marching to the bathroom. When he emerged, he was holding a big white towel soaked in warm water.

He dropped by Sophia's side and gently touched her cheeks, removing the blood. She flinched.

"I'm so sorry," Will said, his touch becoming even lighter.

Sophia saw the towel become pink in a matter of seconds.

Will gingerly scooped Sophia into his arms, the dark pain slicing her ribs. She cried out but held onto him with her good hand. Will stepped to the door, motioning for Daniel to open it.

The three of them were quiet in the elevator. Daniel went to hail the cab while Will stood with Sophia inside. When the cab stopped in front of the entry, Will slipped inside, barely moving Sophia in his hands.

She saw how Daniel was left standing on the sidewalk, his

eyes wide, following the cab. Eventually, he disappeared from view.

Will looked out of the window, the slideshow of New York. From time to time, he looked down at Sophia, murmuring, "You're safe now."

She dropped her head to his chest, inhaling the scent of his cologne. He smelled like a forest, like leather, like sandalwood.

When the cab stopped, Will stepped from the car, still holding her close. She didn't look around, she closed her eyes, she breathed.

Once inside, Sophia allowed herself to watch as he opened the door to a room. It was sterile, the room furnished with an iron bed, tiles, and numerous jars with medicine. It was his working office—the hospital room. But Will stopped at the entrance and turned around into the corridor. A few doors down, he opened another door; this was his room. A huge bookcase took up the wall. He lowered Sophia to his bed.

"You'll be more comfortable here," he whispered. "I need to look at your wounds. Tell me where it hurts."

"Ribs," Sophia said. "He said they are not broken, but they hurt."

"I need to take off your blouse, are you okay with it or do you want me to call a nurse?" he asked.

"I don't care," she said and started unbuttoning it with a good hand.

He helped her out of the silk blue blouse which was covered in blood now. Sophia lay in front of him in her bra and skirt, and even with the pain screaming in her head she felt shy.

"Crazy psychopath," William said when he looked at her ribs.

Both sides of her body were dark purple, the middle of her stomach had a blue mark of a punch. Will ran his fingers through the ribs, making Sophia wince.

"He's a monster, but he knows what he's doing. Thom didn't break any bones; the stomach looks worse than it is."

Will's hands went up her neck.

"Why was he choking you?"

"He wanted me to remember the message."

"I'm so sorry they dragged you into all of this," he said, examining her wrist. "The wrist isn't broken, the pinkie also, but he dislocated it. I'm sorry, Sophia, but it needs to be done." And he pulled her finger fast, sending a blast of pain through her. She cried, her throat rasping. And it was gone.

"That's it, you're a brave girl," he said, but her vision clouded in tears.

He lifted his hand to examine her face, his fingers flying over her cheekbones.

"Nothing is broken, thank God. He wanted it to look worse than it is, it all will heal in a matter of weeks."

Finally, he met her eyes.

"Sophia, I need to know if they touched you." His eyes were dark, voice low.

"No," she shook her head, "He didn't, the lowest point where he punched me was the center of my belly." She pointed to a blue circle on her skin.

"I thought so," he nodded. "I'll bring salve now; it will help with the bruises."

He stood. "There is no swelling, which's good." But he froze, looked down at her, and his face fell.

"Damn, I'm so sorry, I keep pointing out how he knows what he is doing, how he made it look worse than it is, like you got lucky, but I keep ignoring the fact that they took you in the first place, how you must have been scared. I will get you up and running in no time. Trust me. I just wish you could forget today. I wish you were back to your usual life."

"Who is he?" she asked.

"Thom?" he asked, and she nodded. "He is a famous New

York butcher, he cuts people in half when they are alive, he distorts bodies. Oh, oh, you don't need to know that."

"No," Sophia said angrily, "No more secrets. And even when he was beating me, he gave me something, he told me . . . Doesn't matter."

Will looked at her for a long moment before going outside.

She lay there, looking around, listening to her own rasping breaths. The pillow smelled of Will—again, that smell of sandalwood. Sophia closed her eyes, just to see *him* at the edge of her mind.

She bolted upright, the ribs screaming.

Will rushed into the room. "What happened?"

"I saw him." She was choking. Will carefully lowered her back, brushed a strand from her forehead.

"He's not here," he whispered and held her hand while her breath calmed. "I brought you fresh clothes, this is mine, but it's clean." He pointed to a white shirt and pajama pants. "Tomorrow, Eva will bring yours, but I thought you might want to change now. Do you need help?"

"No. Thank you," she said, and he stepped out of the room. It took her fifteen minutes to change; she almost fainted from the pain a couple of times, the sweat on her forehead. "Ready," she said.

He walked in and smiled. "It suits you."

Sophia clutched a fist to her stomach. The throbbing got worse while she moved.

Will came closer and, with practiced strokes, first bandaged her wrist, her finger, then put an ointment on her ribs and bandaged them too. He gently rubbed an herbal salve into her neck, her cheekbones, and cleaned the wound on her lip.

"You need to rest," he said.

"I can't, I see him," she said. But one thing she didn't tell Will was that *him* was not Thom, it was Daniel.

"I thought so." He pulled out a syringe. "Aren't you afraid of these?"

She shook her head.

"Of course you aren't." He smiled and moved her shirt sleeve, revealing her shoulder. The needle plunged in her skin, and a few moments later, the warm sensation spread down her body, her eyelids getting heavy.

"Good night, Sophia," Will murmured from somewhere far away.

I opened my eyes to find my face wet, the damp pillowcase under my cheek. I was crying when Thom was beating Sophia. I could still feel the phantom pain in my own ribs, my face. My lip was not cracked, but it was pulsing like Sophia's.

How could he? I assumed there was something wrong with Daniel, with his constant chant of possessing Sophia, of his absence. And now, she was alone in a big city, betrayed, hurt and lost.

Twenty-One

Sophia woke to a bird chirping on the tree outside, and for a short moment she thought she was back home in Riga, and all this life of casinos, moonshine, illegal drugs was not real, her room, Elena, father, was all that mattered.

Till it wasn't.

The doorbell rang somewhere inside the apartment, and Will went to open it. She heard a familiar voice and her blood stopped cold. *Him.*

"I want to see her, how is she?" Daniel said.

"She is sleeping, I gave her a dose of morphine," Will said. "Let me check on her, please wait here."

She heard footsteps and the door to her room opened.

"I don't want to see him, please don't let him inside," she whispered.

William looked at her silently, then nodded.

"Say that I don't want him to see me like this." And she pointed to her face.

"That's a lie, is it?" Will asked, his black eyes on her face.

Sophia took a deep breath. "Yes."

"Okay." He went out of the room.

"Daniel, she's still groggy from the drug. And she says she doesn't want you to see her with bruises on her face."

She knew that was a lame excuse, but Daniel grunted. "Okay, it makes sense."

And a few minutes later, he left.

Sophia moved in her bed; the pain dulled but still something sharp sliced her ribcage. Will entered the room and rushed to her when he saw she was clutching her side.

"I'm okay, this was just unexpected," she said.

"Daniel brought your clothes." He put a bag on the floor.

"I want to use the bathroom," Sophia asked, and he helped her out of bed and led her to the adjoined room.

"I can manage myself here, thanks," she laughed.

Will shook his head, the raven hair falling to his eyes, his cheeks blushing.

"Yes, sure, I'll wait outside."

It took her forever, but when she looked in the mirror over the sink she saw that her features were the same, not disfigured or puffy, just dark purple crowned her cheeks. The neck was worse; you could actually see fingerprints where Thom squeezed the air from her. It was difficult to move, every step caused pain in her abdomen and ribs.

When she opened the door, Will stood at the bookcase, an open book in his hand.

"Can I use a bathtub?" Sophia asked quietly.

"Sure." He took her by both hands to lead back to the bed. "Please wait here while I prepare it."

"Thanks," she murmured, her head spinning from the exertion already.

While he was inside, she studied his bookshelf. Lots of books about medicine, the latest detective novels, and many books on psychology, the one he had been reading was by Freud.

"Ready," Will said and took her hands again to lead her inside, guiding.

"I can walk by myself," she said but didn't pull away.

"Can you?" he asked, a smile in his voice.

The sweet smell filled the bathroom, the steam clogged her vision, the bathtub was filled with bubbles.

"I put the bag with your clothes here." Will pointed to it. "I'll be outside, call me if you need me."

And he turned to walk away. Sophia held his hand a moment longer, making him look up at her.

"Thank you, Will." And she released his hand.

"It's nothing," he said and closed the door behind him.

When the hot water hit her skin, she groaned, the feeling was so pleasant, her limbs relaxed in the warmth, the tremble going away. It was as though the sweet bubbles made her dark thoughts disappear, even for a short time. She closed her eyes and saw the night sky; she smiled.

Sophia found a fluffy towel on the side of the bathtub and gently dried herself, avoiding the blue on her skin. She looked at the bag of clothes and familiar disdain filled her again when she saw the nightgowns Eva packed. She remembered Daniel's hands on her when she was wearing one of those, his fingers tracing the skin under the fabric.

She put on Will's pajama pants again and his shirt. When she opened the door, the steam from the bathroom burst in the room. Will was sitting on the bed, reading the same book.

He turned his head to her, and his eyes crinkled, the stars shining in the dark. Her wet hair was gathered at the top of her head.

"I'll get you more of my clothes," he laughed.

"Hope you don't mind," she said.

"You can have all of it, it suits you much better." Again, that smile, like a moon shining in the dark night.

He stood from the bed and helped her to get in, the bottles of ointment already on the nightstand. He bandaged her ribs, wrist and finger again. Her eyes were already closing, the warmth of the bath still on her skin.

He drew the blanket to her shoulders.

"Get some rest," he whispered and a few moments later, the door clicked.

The walls were gray, splotches of blood on them, dark stains on the floor. The bed with white sheets was in the middle of the room, and Sophia was chained to it. Her hands could not move, steel slicing her wrists. Daniel stood above her, and Shirley stood behind him, wearing Sophia's nightgown. She was kissing his neck, her hand on his pants. Daniel lowered his face to Sophia and brought his hand to her neck; he started squeezing.

"You are mine, Sophia, I own you," he said, while Shirley laughed and laughed and laughed.

"No!" Sophia was screaming. "No, no!"

The warm hand found her fingers; another landed on her forehead.

"Everything's okay, Sophia, you're safe." It was Will, and the warm light of the streetlamp filled the room.

She was breathing hard, still feeling the hand on her throat. The violent tremble shook her. Will moved closer, his hands on her shoulders, and she dropped her head to his chest. She inhaled the sandalwood and listened to his heart. Her breath calmed as she tried to match his. She was clutching his shirt, while he hugged her closer, his hand in her hair.

He rocked her slightly, till she was silent in his arms, till sleep took a hold of her again.

"You're safe," he whispered when he laid her back on the pillow. She dreamed he kissed her forehead before leaving the room, or maybe it was not a dream.

Will's warmth, his protection, it all leaked into my life. How could I feel so cared for, so secured and shielded when I never even met him? I searched for the feeling in the faces of people I knew and people I didn't, this balmy heat of safety that lived in my chest now. Even when I was awake, even when I kept reminding myself that I was not Sophia, I felt Will's invisible presence in my life.

Twenty-Two

"Good morning," Will said, placing a tray with steaming coffee to her side.

She opened her eyes, and he was standing there, his eyes dark as night on her face. He lowered himself, touched her cheek with his fingers, and for a moment, Sophia's heart started beating faster, but he moved to the side, examining the bruises on her face. The featherlight touch on her skin, on her neck.

"I'm sorry for last night, and thank you," Sophia said when he took her bandaged hand in his. The dislocated finger didn't hurt anymore, and the swelling on her wrist was subsiding.

"It's okay."

"Can I ask you something?" Sophia said quietly.

He nodded.

"Can I stay here for now? I can't go home," she said.

He gingerly placed her hand back on the white sheet and looked at her.

"Why?" he asked, the brow furrowed.

"Please," she said.

"I need more than that. Tell me, Sophia."

She stayed silent.

"You can trust me," he said, "please."

"When Thom was talking to me, he told me about Daniel and Shirley and other girls. I had no idea," her voice was trembling. "There is no love between us, not now, and I am not sure it was ever there. No light, no warmth. He thinks that he owns me, and I . . . I just can't go back."

Will ran his hand through his raven hair and let out a long breath.

"I'm sorry, Sophia."

"So, in a way, I am glad I had that meeting with Thom. Now, I need time to get better. I have money, the amount should be enough for me to go away, to run."

Something changed in Will's expression for a moment; the hurt was there and gone. He moved his hand to hers, just a twitch, but stopped and rested it awkwardly on his lap.

"You can stay here as long as you want, I'm going to tell Daniel that your ribs are actually broken, that you need constant medical assistance. But, Sophia, please let me help you, please don't run out on me."

She wanted to move her hand to find his fingers—his face was so raw with an expression she couldn't read—but she didn't.

"Okay, I still need to come up with the plan. Thank you, Will," she said. "Can I call Ben and ask for work? He probably is going crazy there without my help. The boy can bring the papers here."

He laughed. "I didn't know you were such a workaholic. The phone is in the corridor, but don't sound cheerful. Remember, you have your ribs broken. Do you need help to stand?"

Wincing, she moved into an upright position. The pain was there, but it was not skull crushing anymore.

Later that day, a boy from Ben brought her papers with a note.

Sophia, get better! It said.

She plunged into the numbers, her mind getting into working mode, no more thoughts about her life, the pain, the betrayal.

It was almost dark outside when the bell rang, there was a commotion in the corridor, voices, a cry and a whimper. Men were talking.

"He got shot when he was transferring money, his partner got lucky, not a scratch, but Sam here caught a bullet with his shoulder," an unfamiliar voice said.

"Bring him in," Will said.

"So much blood, so much blood, it hurts, the bullet is inside, it's tearing my shoulder apart, help, help me," another voice slurred, mumbling, begging.

She heard a cry from this man when he was placed on the iron bed.

"I'll take it from here," Will said.

There was a yelp from the wounded man.

"The pain will go away soon," Will said.

Sophia heard the clatter of an instrument. And quiet.

"I've got the bullet," Will said.

And more silence. "It caught nothing major, he's lucky."

And more silence.

"He'll stay here for the night; I will clean the wound. You can go. Arthur, thanks for bringing him in."

Arthur mumbled something Sophia didn't catch. And when he was at the door, "Thanks, Doc."

Sophia heard the click of the lock and steps when Will went back to Sam again. She heard him working, and she looked back to her papers, drowning in numbers.

Hours later, she heard Will walking past her door.

"Will?"

He paused and opened the door. He was tired, blood on his white shirt, but he smiled when he saw her.

"How is he?"

"He'll be fine, he has a risky job. He's going to sleep like the dead till tomorrow."

"You are a good man, Will."

He nodded, "Good night, Sophia."

"You can't hide from me; I will always find you. I will always take what's mine, and you are mine, Sophia."

Daniel was standing in front of her, his face changing to Thom's and back. He punched her stomach.

"Can you hear me? You are mine from the moment you gave yourself to me back in Riga, remember how you trembled in my arms?"

And he slapped her.

"I," a punch, "own," one more, "you."

"No," the blood was filling her mouth.

He took her pinkie and twisted, and she screamed, opening her eyes in the dark room.

Will was rushing to her bed, finding her, pressing her close.

"You're fine, you are safe, it's just a dream," he was rocking her, while a scream still echoed in her throat.

"I hate him." She was crying.

Strong arms around her grounded her; this was reality, that was just a dream.

"Please don't disappear, Sophia," Will said quietly.

She said nothing, only inhaled the sandalwood, and slowly relaxed. Her fingers found his, a warm touch as they entwined.

"I can't lose you," he whispered.

These last words didn't leave me until long after I opened my eyes in my room. They stayed with me as I drove to work, as I smiled at the customers, as I listened to Lorraine, and as finally I went to bed again. Closing my eyes I saw night, the stars, and heard these words again, as though whispered in my ear. *I can't lose you.*

Twenty-Three

Sophia woke up to a bell ringing, her heart hammering. *It's him*, she thought. But when Will opened the door, she heard a panicked voice of a woman.

"Where's Sam? I came as fast as I could, I was visiting my parents when I received a call. How is he?" A fear mixed in her voice.

"He's here, he's fine. Please, calm down."

Sophia heard the door opening and the woman cried when she saw Sam.

"My love, how are you feeling?"

Later that day, Sam left with this woman. According to bits and pieces Sophia heard the woman was a nurse, and she would take care of him at home, change his bandages.

"I'll visit him in a few days. If you see anything wrong, call me immediately," Will said to them when they were leaving.

"Thank you for saving him, thank you so much," the woman voiced.

And the quiet filled the apartment again. Sophia lowered her eyes to the papers in her hand and tried to focus. She didn't want to think about the first words of that woman when she saw that her husband was hurt. *My love*. So much hope was there, not a look of fear, coldness, mixed with a hint of revolt when Daniel saw her for the first time after she was beaten.

The shrill sound of a phone blew up the silence. She heard Will's footsteps, and he picked up.

"Hello?"

Silence.

"She is getting better but not so fast, she barely moves. Yes."

Silence.

"Daniel, it will take time, I don't know, weeks."

Silence.

"Okay, bye."

Long exhale. And he knocked on her door.

"Come in," Sophia said quietly.

"I assume you heard who called," he said, his eyes so sad.

"Yes, what did he want?"

"He asked how you are, and how much longer you should be here. And he called from the hotel, he said that he won't be staying home for a couple of days and that I could find him in the Plaza if needed."

It didn't hurt as much as she thought it would.

"He is with Shirley, right?" she asked.

He nodded.

"Good," she said and when he furrowed his eyebrow, she explained. "I need his attention to shift from me so that when I am gone he won't be searching that hard, that Shirley will take my place and I will be free."

"I hope it'll work," he said. "How are you feeling?"

"Give me a few days and I will be as good as new," she said, smiling.

When Will saw her smile, something warm played on his face, and he looked pleased.

The rest of the day she spent working. When Ben realized that she wasn't hurt enough to do the job, he sent the delivery boy with more papers. In the evening, she took a hot bath and plunged under the covers, grunting. The pain in her ribs was fading.

Will knocked at her door.

"I just want to take a book," he said when he came in.

He looked at the bookcase, scanning the names. When he found the one, he turned to Sophia, her head on the pillow, wet hair after the bath glistening.

"Please stay," she whispered. "Could you read here?"

Will just nodded and sat on the bed, her knees touching his hips. Sophia lay there and listened to his breathing, her mind drifting away. She felt a touch to her cheek, and a small kiss to her forehead. There were no nightmares that night.

Twenty-Four

Days passed and Sophia got stronger, the purple subsiding from her cheeks. Her neck didn't hold fingerprints anymore. Will read by her side in the evenings, both of them quiet.

One morning, she felt that she could move easily, that the pain wasn't crushing her anymore. Sophia went to a bathroom and looked at her reflection; she was almost back to her old self, but her eyes glistened somewhat differently, lighter.

Her bra was killing her these past days. It rubbed her ribs, but she couldn't take it off, because Will was around all the time. She looked at her reflection and laughed as her bra landed on the floor, and she put the shirt back. The fabric didn't hide anything; her nipples were visible. She shrugged, light playing in her eyes.

Sophia stepped outside her room and into the kitchen, her bare feet touching the tile. She heard Will moving in the guest room. No one questioned why she was staying in his bedroom, not even Daniel.

She found coffee and brewed two cups, placing them on the table and perched herself on the countertop.

Will walked into the kitchen and when his eyes landed on Sophia, he dropped the book he was holding. It landed with a thud.

"I can see you," he said. "This shirt isn't doing a good job of covering . . . you."

"Oh, I know," she said and smiled when his eyes lowered to her breasts again. "Does it make you uncomfortable?"

"I wouldn't say that is the right word." And he swallowed.

"Good, I made you a coffee." And she slid off the countertop and to the table.

Will took a step closer to her, he grinned when he saw her lips parting, he moved his face even closer, the sandalwood enveloping Sophia. But he put his lips to her ear.

"Don't tease me, Sophia," he whispered.

He moved back, sat on the chair and made a gulp of coffee, all the time watching her.

"Is everything okay? You're breathing hard," he said, a smile playing on his face, showing dimples.

The next day, Sophia woke to sweet music flowing from the kitchen. She rushed to the bathroom and splashed cold water on her face, looked in the mirror and walked to the kitchen. A small portable gramophone was sitting in the middle of the table, slow jazz filled the space.

Will stood with a cup of coffee, but when he saw her, he placed it back on the counter and stretched his arm to her.

"Dance with me," he asked.

And she stepped into his arms. Sophia was wearing one of Will's shirts and his pajama pants; he was wearing the same, they both were barefoot. Her hands went to his neck, his arms gingerly on her waist. And as the music poured in waves around, inches of space between them melted, she was falling into his arms, he was pressing her gently into him. Moments later, Sophia put her head on his chest, her body merging with his. They swung slowly. His chin on top of her head.

When the last note played, he said, "I want to go with you."

He took her hand and they sat at the kitchen table. Sophia's heart was beating wildly.

"The world is dangerous, especially for a young woman. Let me protect you. At least till you settle somewhere. You'll be traveling with a big sum of money, people will talk. But with me, they wouldn't look twice. I can pretend to be your brother, or . . ." he paused. He looked so vulnerable, and his black eyes landed on her hand, so small in his. He brushed her knuckles with his thumb.

"But your life is here," she whispered.

"This all is useless, I patch up men who mostly deserve what they get, they do dark things, Sophia. I'm tired of this wheel; I want to break free. And I know they won't let me go; I know too much. So I want to disappear, to work somewhere in the hospital where I can save people who need saving. I was a coward, but as I see you so determined, I want this."

"Why do you want to be chained to the weakest link?" she asked.

The words hit him as though she slapped him. He had called her the weakest link back in Daniel's apartment.

"I knew you would remember it. I meant that everyone in the group has security, a guard, they don't move solo, even Daniel always leaves the house with someone. And you, he allowed you to just walk around alone," he said, the veins in his neck pulsing. "I'm so sorry, that's all I meant, that you were alone without any protection. You won't be anymore, if you allow me to go."

"Okay," she said.

"Okay?" he said, hope shimmering in his features.

She nodded. "I would love us both to go together. We will be runaways."

And they started to form the plan. She would sneak to the bank to withdraw her share of money, no one should see her, because according to the legend she was still immobile with broken ribs in her bed. Will would do the same. They would drive to the west coast; no specific destination was set, they would choose between Los Angeles or San Francisco. They both had impressive amounts of money saved. Dirty money, but it would help them settle.

"I will go to the bank tomorrow," Sophia said.

They decided to make the move in four days.

"They'll search for us, so we need to move fast. Daniel won't be happy with you running away," Will said.

"I don't care about his happiness, he's a bastard and a cheat, I don't want to have anything to do with him," Sophia scowled. "I hate him."

Will looked her in the eyes and smiled. "Let's dance."

And he lowered the needle, this time much faster jazz filling the room.

They both laughed as they danced.

There was something so warm about William, his dark tall figure like a protective shadow around Sophia. Those eyes, I couldn't stop thinking about them when I was working in a coffee shop. I felt how cautious Sophia tried to be, but she found herself by his side all the time. She leaned into him, and Will opened his arms to meet her.

This tender feeling bloomed between them, his kindness and attention, her hope. I watched as she was waking up for the first time in New York, the real Sophia, not the one confined to a cage. Something so warm stirred in her chest every time their eyes met. I felt for the first time since I landed in those dreams that she trusted someone, that power grew inside her, calmer, steadier: She was falling in love with him.

Twenty-Five

It was dark already. That day, Sophia went to the bank and returned with a bag of bills. This was enough for her to live in a foreign city for a couple of years.

Tomorrow, Will would go to the bank. They would leave everything behind. They would run.

Her quiet footsteps died in the hall. She opened the door to a guest room where he was staying. It was bare, the room without character, so unlike his bedroom. When she saw he was reading on the bed, she walked in.

Sophia took his book from him, marking the page, and set it on the nightstand.

"I'm afraid," she whispered.

The stars in his eyes blazed. "I know, but I am going to protect you. Come here."

And she lay in the crook of his arm, feeling the warmth, his closeness. She turned her head up, and there were inches between them. Her palm was on his chest, and she felt his heart raced under her touch. She moved her hand to his face, tracing his nose, cheekbone, a stubble under her fingertips, his lips. And then Sophia lowered her lips to his, a feather-like touch at first, the movement growing, the closeness pulsing. Will placed a hand to the nape of her neck, drawing her closer, his fingers lost in her hair. They kissed till there was no air between them, tongues grazing, lips crushing. And then Sophia looked into his eyes, the vastness of starry night.

"I remember the first time I saw you in the club. I thought you were not real, so beautiful, so alone, proud. And I remember the sadness when I saw who you were seating with—you would never be with me," he said.

"You saved me, you are saving me every moment. I'm free," she whispered, "and I'm with you." And she found his lips again.

Sophia opened her eyes in the morning to the sweet memories of his lips, but the place by her side was empty.

There was a note at the nightstand. "Gone to the bank."

She closed her eyes and remembered last night. Will didn't lower his hands below her shoulders, but his lips on her neck made her tremble. Something shifted when she was with him, something warm bloomed between them.

Sophia looked at the piece of paper and wondered what he was doing at that same moment.

She walked into the kitchen and started preparing sandwiches. Ten minutes later, the key slid into the lock of the front door, and it opened.

Will found her in the kitchen, face flushed, two bags of money in his hands. He dropped them to the floor, crossed the space between them, and found her lips. He was here, he was close, she brought her hand to his hair, and he hugged her.

"I need to talk to you, Sophia," he said, letting her go, taking a step back. "I don't know what you see in me, why you are looking at me like this. I wanted to be with you from the moment I first saw you, and even in my wildest dreams I could not imagine this look in your eyes, it's trust, it looks like . . ." he paused, took a deep breath, "you care."

Her cheeks pinked, but she didn't say anything.

"But I don't want you to think that you owe me anything, that you're obliged to do anything because I'm going with you. I just can't stand the thought of you being away, and it's such a selfish thought. But you don't need to be like this if you don't want it. I'll keep my distance, and if you don't want me in your life I will disappear once I see you settled safely. I don't want you to think that you don't have a choice here. If you don't want *us*, I will step away, just say so."

There was a mixture of fear and pain in his features, but his eyes had such immense hope when he looked at her, it caught her breath.

"Will, I would never be with you if I didn't want it. You saved me when I was hurt, when my body was broken, you showed me what kindness is. With you I can breathe, with you I am strong, and," her breath hitched in her throat, "damn, I was always awful with words. I want to be with you, and what you see in my eyes, trust it, it's true. I have never felt what I am feeling towards you."

He stepped closer and lifted his hands to her face, a thumb grazing her cheek. The stars were shining so bright in his eyes as he lowered his face to her, and their lips met.

They decided to run tonight. They would take just a small suitcase of clothes and necessities, all the rest they would buy on the road.

Sophia finalized all the paperwork for Ben and left it in the corridor with a note. Just one word was scribbled on the small piece of paper, *Goodbye*.

Her heart beat fast the whole day: when she packed her clothes, when she dressed in one suit she had, when she covered the top of the bag with money with fabric.

It was dark when she stepped into the kitchen. Will was there, standing and looking out in the black of the night. She stood silently and watched his broad back, the back of his head; he felt her gaze and turned around, giving her the widest smile.

She stepped closer and unfastened the few upper buttons of his shirt, sliding her hand inside.

And she saw that raw hunger when he swept her in his hands and placed her on the countertop. When his hands entwined around her waist, they were both breathing hard. Their lips crashed, when her shaking fingers worked on his shirt, when his face was lost in her hair when he kissed her collarbone.

They didn't notice the click of the back door, lost to each other.

"Well, well, well, looks like I was right," the cold voice sounded in the kitchen entrance.

Daniel stood there. Will turned around, but a banging sound crushed the space around them, and a red dot grew on Will's chest, spreading fast. His legs buckled and he went down slowly, like in a dream.

Sophia gasped trying to hold him, catching him when he was falling, falling with him, softening the impact.

"No, no, god, no," she was whispering, "Will, stay with me, listen to me."

The huge tears choked her. She looked at his chest, the blood gushing in the place so close to his heart, the place where just moments ago her fingers touched the skin. The light from his eyes was fading, the stars disappearing.

"Please," she kissed his lips, his cheek.

"I'll find you," Will breathed, and the stars in his eyes dimmed, forever.

"I love you," Sophia whispered in his ear. But there was nothing, he was gone.

She pressed her face to his chest, wet blood on the shirt and screamed, an animal raw sound scraping her throat. The pain was so strong, as though it was a bullet in her chest. He was gone, and she knew what she needed to do.

She brushed a lock of the dark hair from his forehead and stood, looking at Daniel.

"Did you think I was not keeping tabs on your bank account? The moment you withdrew money I received a call from the bank. I set boys to look out for you, and it was easy to figure it out when the next day William withdrew his share. Sophia, wash that blood from your hands and face and let's go home," he said.

Sophia looked at the gleaming revolver in his hand, such a beautiful thing of shining metal, but it brought so much pain, such devastation.

"Home?" she laughed, her voice breaking. "I have no home."

"Stop with this nonsense, you had your little affair. I understand, everyone needs a distraction, and I forgive you, Sophia, now, let's go."

"Oh, yes, distraction, I know everything about your distractions, one of its names is Shirley," she spat.

Nothing changed in Daniel's hard gaze, those green eyes choked her close to where Thom's hand had been on her neck.

"I hate you," Sophia growled. "I wish I'd never met you. One good thing, one beautiful person came from me meeting you, and you killed him. Will was my light, and you pierced his heart with a bullet." She looked back at the beautiful face, so serene on the tile, the puddle of blood growing bigger. Sophia wanted to kneel beside him and wail, because everything was dark now, but she had a job to do.

"Don't lie to me, Sophia," Daniel barked. "Would you wish

to stay in Riga? To rot in that apartment with your father? All you dreamed of was to get away."

"Yes, I wish I would have stayed there, I would have built myself, I would have a job, my own money, my own place, and I would be free, free from you," she spat.

"You gave yourself to me, do you remember the night after the jazz concert? You practically jumped in my hands, begged for me to take you. And I did it, and you liked it, don't deny it, and the most important thing was that *I* liked it. Oh, you were good, you are still good, the best I would say."

"I was young!" she cried, "So young, and we were never close, Daniil, all that was there was lust. The sweaty crushing of two bodies."

"You made me feel special, even after I tried all these women in the first year here, you were the best. The look on your face when I am inside, how you breathe, how you gasp, it fills my heart every time."

"You don't have a heart," Sophia said quietly. "I believed in you, that is why you think I'm special. I believed in a boy from Moscow who was delirious about America, who couldn't say two words in English, and who everybody laughed off when he talked about his plans. I was the first to believe in you."

"And look who they were laughing at, who I became, how rich I am, how powerful, I wish I could wipe the smiles off their faces now. And I will, they will see."

Sophia was shaking her head, her hand twitched, she wanted to sit by Will, to take his hand, to entwine her fingers with his.

"You are nothing but a criminal, and I am not far from you. Helping Ben with counting all that blood money, the profits, I am as good as you."

"Yes, and finally you understand it," Daniel said. "You're like me, that's why I chose you to build a family, I need a son to grow an empire."

"Family?" she choked. "Kids? I would never bring anyone

into this world, it's dark, it hurts, it destroys. Bring a kid into a world that dies every day? And where his own father contributes to the world's destruction. How many people died because of the drugs you're selling? How many families are broken from the alcohol you're making? How many souls are lost in casinos? You are catching them in your spider web, eating them from the inside, all this time taking money from them. And we all were helping this bloodlust grow, this machine to work. And I wanted to escape, to escape this pain we were causing, and I saw the light. We still could make it right, we still could break free from the web," she looked at Will, "but I was mistaken."

"Sophia, don't be a hypocrite. You loved living with money, you loved living in a beautiful apartment in one of the most expensive buildings in New York, you loved being on top of the world, you loved those dresses."

"No," Sophia said looking into those green, cold eyes. "*You* loved all these things; I just was there with you. And I hate that I was blind, that I didn't want to face the truth earlier, how dirty our souls became, all that money I saw on papers, drugs bringing in the most income. And I closed my eyes to what it meant. I looked only at the numbers, but what I didn't want to see was that I was looking at the spread of death on the streets of New York, and that I was contributing to it. I was not strong enough to fight, I was a coward."

Sophia stepped closer to Daniel. She took his face in her hands, smearing the blood, leaning in as though to kiss him, but with the fast flick of her hand she took the gun from him and pointed it at her heart.

"I quit," she whispered.

And fired.

The world went black.

I screamed into the night, my heart beating fast as though a bullet went into my chest. I heard my parents rushing through the corridor, opening the door to my room. Dad was breathing hard, and Mom dashed to my bed, finding my face.

I was looking wildly at her, not seeing, the echo of thunderous pain in my body.

"I'm fine," I said, rasping, "just a bad dream. Please make me a cup of tea downstairs, I'll be there in a minute."

Dad nodded and hurried downstairs. Mom stopped at the threshold and looked back at me, her brows knitted.

"I'm okay," I repeated. "Just a nightmare."

I needed a minute to myself.

When she left, I started crying silently, hiding my face in my pillow. Sophia gave up, Will was dead, they both were dead.

I never dreamed of Sophia again.

Twenty-Six

TEN YEARS LATER

Months after Sophia shot herself, I stumbled, dazed in my life, and it was the worst time possible. I was starting university, I needed to make new friends, but all I felt was a ghost of pain in my chest. All the power I had I used on education, trying to stay afloat with all the knowledge teachers were cramming into my blurry brain. And after time passed, I got a grip on uni life.

I started going to parties. I had two boyfriends during those years, I had sex for the first time, and it was far from the one I experienced in Sophia's body. It was flat, clammy, but I had it again and again, and then with another guy. On the outside, I was leading the life a student was supposed to have. The usual girl who talked about boys, who had a trusting support system of parents and friends. Who sometimes dreamed of people who were long gone.

I dreamed of Sophia looking at herself in the mirror, I dreamed of Daniel and his cold eyes, I dreamed of numbers, I dreamed of Central Park, I dreamed of Riga, but most of all I dreamed of stars, of those black eyes, of that beautiful face, the pale strong hands, those lips touching Sophia's, that love.

As the time went by, the dreams faded also. I was beginning to forget the faces of all of them. But even though those dreams stopped, I felt everything was unfinished. I was choking in Tallahassee. And when I graduated from FSU, I shocked my parents that I wanted to move to New York.

"I just want to see the world," I said. "And don't worry, I'll visit often, and if I don't like it there, I'll just come back."

They were proud of me.

Lorraine almost cried when I announced my plans, she told me that I was brave, and that she would always be here waiting for me. She was living with Paula now, they made it work throughout high school and university, the relationship growing and solidifying. I loved them, and watching those two made me believe that someday I would find something similar for me. That light, that warmth, that trust. So after university, I landed an internship in a New York digital marketing firm and stayed there.

I rented a tiny, renovated apartment the size of my room back home, but I was living alone, and I loved this place. New York was pulsing all around.

I found the building where Sophia and Daniel lived, the Ritz Tower, now lost between taller skyscrapers. I stood there, looking up, trying to find the window where they once stood. The road in front of the building was filled with modern cars, but I could see the old ones, the one that took Sophia and Daniel to a club, another that dumped her after she was beaten, the ghost of a concierge helping her. It was surreal, the building still there, old, extravagant, impossibly expensive. I peered inside the hall, and it was exactly like my dreams, which made my knees buckle, scraping my hands over the limestone.

I didn't know much about New York before my dreams, and when I moved here and started to recognize places from almost one hundred years ago, I had a strong feeling of deja vu walking the same streets Sophia walked. I realized once again that those were not just dreams.

Somehow in my sleep, I had opened a window to another time, to another person.

Did I feel lonely those first months in New York? No. I had heard the stories of the city's rhythm swallowing you, the high prices, the constant running. But it clicked for me.

I ravenously explored the city, finding familiar bits and pieces. I didn't mind running. I loved my cupboard apartment. I felt free.

A marketing company hired five interns with me, all young people with shining eyes, mostly fresh out of universities and colleges. Three of us stayed working there: me, Jane and Noah.

We were new to the city and almost the same age, and these two became my closest people in the whole of New York, no, scratch that, in the whole world. We were finding our way in the concrete maze of a city and in our lives.

Jane was a tall smiling person with a pixie haircut, always with a book in her hand. She was from a small town in Maryland who always dreamed of a life in a big city. She was a creative ideas generator. Noah was the most stylish, smart, on top of the latest technologies, and so gay. The three of us became inseparable from the first day in the company.

Jane and I even lived within a five minute walking distance, and six months later, Noah moved into the building across the street from mine. We joked that we could watch each other from the window like in *Friends*. Thankfully, his windows were blocked from me by stairs, because Noah loved walking naked in his apartment. His parents were rich, but he wanted to build a life of his own.

And my life was perfect, even when the city was far from the shining New York of the 1930s, even with all the trash bags on the streets and millions of people: I felt at home. And even when sometimes I stopped dead in the middle of the street when I saw a lock of raven hair, or when the stranger in the street had the same piercing green eyes, I moved on.

Everything changed with nine simple words.

"Do you want to go to a gallery opening?"

Noah asked me and Jane during our lunch on a warm May day. Three of us were sitting on the grass in Central Park, takeout boxes in our hands.

"Again?" Jane groaned.

"I met this guy," Noah said.

"Oh my god, you change them like a pair of gloves," I exclaimed.

"Socks I'd say, I have my one and only favorite pair of gloves," Noah said. "And yes, unlike you two, I have a vivid sex life, and you need to get rid of that pink toy you ordered online." He nodded at me, my cheeks growing red.

"How do you know?" I asked.

Noah shrugged. "You forgot to hide it when I was at your place the last time."

Jane sniggered.

"Oh, don't you gloat, I know you have the same one," Noah said.

Jane narrowed her eyes. "How do you even know that?"

"I know everything."

"That toy does wonders, sometimes I think to hell with all the dating when they're making such a great sex toys now." She was looking directly at Noah, no shame in her voice, while my cheeks still burned.

"You're impossible, you need to stop reading those dirty books, and get a life, both of you," Noah said. "Anyway, I met this guy, he's impossibly cute, and he's a manager at the gallery.

He invited me to the new collection opening on Thursday evening and there'll be free champagne."

"I'm in. I don't have any plans anyway," I said.

Jane looked at us. "You two or my pink friend?"

"That is insulting," I laughed.

"Okay, I'll go," she said.

The gallery was a bright spot on the street, the high glass windows opened to a view of the commotion inside. The people were smartly dressed, each one nursing a glass of champagne. The waiters moved silently around, the soft ambient music playing in the background.

"Wow," Jane whispered. "Is it by someone famous?"

The gallery was divided into two sections with a veil. One section was a collection of beautiful nature and landscape paintings, while the other was of dark abstracts. The creator showed the difference between the outside and inside worlds when he moved to his parents' house in West Virginia while battling drug addiction.

A tall thin man saw Noah and went to kiss him on the cheek.

"I'm so glad you came," the man said, a hint of longing in his eyes when he scanned Noah in his black suit. Damn, the man attracted handsome men.

Jane rolled her eyes and went to the first painting. Three paintings down her eyes were shining.

"I want to talk to the artist," she said and marched to the group of people standing in the corner.

I watched the collection alone. The beautiful green fields on his canvases were lifelike, but something unsettling crawled on the edge of each painting. And with each painting it pressed on you, till you crossed the veil to see depressing gray colors smeared on the canvases. All paintings were made with oil paint, but in the first section of landscapes, the images were painted in a realistic way. Here, so much paint was used on each canvas, the strokes of gray created volume on each one. And it grew darker and darker with each painting, till on one there were three red dots in the right bottom corner. And the next one had a splash of blood red in the middle, making my heart burn as I remembered the pool of blood growing bigger on the tile of the kitchen. The painting made my head spin.

"You know, the artist tried to harm himself while creating the collection. He became a fan of his little blade, as he said himself, and this one shows the culmination," the voice said.

I tried to look away from the painting and saw a tall man, his blond hair in a crew cut, wearing an expensive dark suit. The gray eyes were scanning my face.

"May I say that you looked surreal standing in this black dress in this ominous room with the blood on the wall. You looked transfixed. Sorry I disturbed you," he said.

"It's okay," I said, the images fading from my mind. I looked closely at the man's face; he was handsome, power emanating from him, but something unsettling played in his eyes.

"My name's Jason," he said.

"Cassandra." I shook his hand, a small jolt of electricity crackling between our fingers.

He took an empty glass from me and expertly took two more from the waiter's tray. A full glass appeared in my hand in a matter of seconds.

"So, Cassandra, what does such a tender creature do in this macabre gallery?"

I felt my heart gaining speed when Jason lowered his eyes to my neck and back to my eyes.

"My friend's a friend of the gallery manager," I said.

"And my friend loves this artist; he hunts his newest collections to buy the grandest. I'm sure he'll buy this one." Jason pointed to a blood canvas in front of us.

"Isn't it too depressing to have this one hanging on the wall at home?" I asked.

"He thinks they aren't depressing, they're manifestations of life that even after the darkest events people are reborn like phoenixes."

"Oh wow, does he see it in this one?" I laughed and turned to the canvas. "I see pain here."

"Look at the artist, he was feeling all this," Jason looked around, "and look how he's glowing now."

The man was talking excitedly in the corner of the gallery—Jane was one of the people who listened to him open-mouthed.

"I see your point. But I wouldn't put any of these in my apartment. There's something dark even in the brightest fields."

"Like in all of us," Jason said quietly, and I turned to him. He was looking at the canvas, and I wondered how it would feel to touch his marble features with my fingertips.

"I'd like to take you out for coffee some time," he said.

"Here you are," Jane said, a warm hand landing on my shoulder. "You should listen to how he talks; with his story you could feel even more looking at the paintings." She looked at me and then at Jason. "Oh, I'm sorry."

"It's Jason," I said, and they shook hands.

"I should get going," Jason said and fished his card from the pocket and gave it to me. "Cassandra, please call me. I hope you'll accept my invitation."

His eyes locked with mine for a moment, and he bowed slightly to me and Jane and disappeared into the crowd.

"He was undressing you with his eyes," Jane murmured in my ear.

I laughed.

"Are you going to call him?" she asked. "You must call him. Damn, he's hot, like a Hugo Boss ad. Who is he?"

I looked at the card, "Jason Montello, a criminal tax attorney."

Jane whistled. "You're going to be filthy rich," she said. "And his body, oh my god."

I knew that I would call him, not because of his looks, not because of who he was, but because he looked at me in that way—there was something familiar I couldn't put my finger on.

Twenty-Seven

I texted Jason six days later. My fingers itched to pick up the phone and send a message that first night, but according to imaginary dating rules everyone was supposed to follow, I needed to wait. And then a whirlwind of work happened, and six days just flew by.

Finally, I sent a message saying that I would like to accept the coffee invitation. Immediately, he called back.

"Cassandra," he breathed, "please don't keep me waiting this long next time. I was waiting for your call, and you never did. I tried to find you online, but then I realized I knew nothing about you."

I was beaming, my heart thunderous in my chest. We agreed to meet for coffee the next day: Saturday.

That evening, we were drinking wine at Noah's. His apartment was a little bigger than our closet-sized ones. Jane lay on the sofa, I sat on a huge pillow on the floor, my head propped on a sofa, Noah was sitting on a similar pillow, a cheese plate between us.

"I texted Jason," I said quietly.

"Finally!" Jane said.

"Wait, who's Jason?" Noah asked.

"It's this god of a man who Cassie met at the gallery opening. You could cut tension between them with the knife, and Cassie waited almost a week to text him."

"Good girl, you need to keep them waiting," Noah winked. "Have you Googled him?"

I shook my head. He grabbed an iPad and tossed it in my hands. I opened an incognito tab and typed his name. The first result was a business website, followed by professionally set social media.

Noah peered over my shoulder and almost squealed.

"He's gorgeous, I wonder how his body looks without that suit," Noah said.

"That thought kept me going for the last six days," I laughed.

We started discussing what I should wear on the next date. The decision landed on white leather sneakers, a floral dress, and a jacket.

"Hair down, definitely," Jane said.

The next morning, I entered the coffee shop we agreed on. Jason was sitting in the corner looking at his phone, brow furrowed.

But when he looked up and our gazes met, he smiled. I sat opposite him on a vintage chair, and he still was looking at me.

"You're so beautiful, Cassandra," he said instead of greeting me.

I blushed but I couldn't take my eyes off him, something magnetic pulled me. He was casually dressed, wearing gray pants with a leather belt and a blue linen shirt.

"What can I get you?"

"Latte, please."

He nodded and stood, still looking at me.

"Sorry, I keep staring," he said and shook his head, stepping to the counter.

I saw how the face of the barista changed when she took the order, how she smiled at Jason, how she looked him up and down, the broad shoulders, the muscled arms under the shirt. But his eyes went back to me.

He returned to the table.

"I want to know everything about you," he said, placing a cup in front of me and sitting back in the chair.

"There's not much, I grew up in Tallahassee, graduated from FSU, and came here for an internship with a marketing company. I'm still there, I work with famous brands on growing their social media presence. I live in the smallest apartment, but it's lovely, and it's within walking distance to Central Park and my work," I blurted everything out in one breath. "What about you?"

"I was born and grew up here in Harlem. I went to NYU School of Law and have practiced since I graduated. I have my own small team now. I never really traveled, something in New York glued me to the place. I don't have siblings. I love swimming and go to the pool four times a week," he said and took a sip of his flat white.

Jason told me about his family; I told him about Tallahassee. He was four years older than me, loved good food and worked a lot; even by New York standards he was always busy. Two hours flew by as we sat in that coffee shop, the world around us muted.

"Do you want to take a walk in Central Park?" he asked.

"Sounds great."

We walked side by side, our arms grazing. I described my childhood, how I struggled to stay afloat. He talked about his father who never appreciated his achievements, saying that Jason could do better, that he failed.

His fingers touched mine, and a few steps later, he took my hand in his, our fingers intertwining. The warmest butterflies woke up in my stomach every time Jason turned to look at me, his gray eyes searching my face.

He slowed down in a quiet alley; no one was around as he stood in front of me. The massive stone hid us from the bigger pass, but I didn't care a bit where we were when he traced my jaw with his fingers. I leaned into the touch. Jason lowered his face and in a few slow moments found my lips with his. And then there was fire, his hand went to my neck as I was drowning in him. I pressed my body to his, not a drop of modesty in me.

I didn't care that it was the first date. I wanted it, I burned from the inside as our tongues met. I forgot how to breathe as we stood in the shade of an old tree, its branches hiding us, leaves whispering.

"I wanted to do this from the moment I looked at you," he whispered in my hair.

If he wanted to undress me right here, I would have allowed him. But I needed to take a moment to remember where I was, who I was. I pressed my forehead to his chest, and he closed his arms around me.

I barely disentangled myself from him that afternoon. He walked me to my home, and we stood kissing on the sidewalk, the world around us still running, his lips on mine. The ache between my legs was so strong that I needed to force myself not to invite him in. I wanted these fingers to peel off my dress, I wanted his hands on my breasts, him inside me.

I had never felt this kind of lust before, burning.

I put a hand on his chest to distance myself a little, my head was spinning.

"I need to go," I murmured.

"Okay," he looked at me, his lips raw. "I want to see you again, soon."

Oh, how I wanted it too.

"You have my number," I said and took a step to the stairs, his hand still holding mine. "Bye, Jason."

He released my hand, and without looking back I disappeared into the building. If I looked back I knew I would be in his arms again, and I was on the brink of no control. I went up to my apartment and closed the door.

I took a few steps and fell on the sofa. My body was buzzing, I felt how my bra hugged my breasts, I felt the fabric pressing between my legs. I wanted to take it all off, to be naked, to be with him, on top of him.

I called Jane, and twenty minutes later, she was sitting with me on that sofa, a bottle of Cava in her hands.

"You know, it was like the movies, like books, maybe even stronger. Nothing else mattered but us, our bodies, our lips. I honestly forgot how to breathe for a few minutes. My head was spinning," I said.

Jane took a sip from her glass.

"It's like the story from that indie erotica website I'm subscribed to. They see each other in the fashionable art gallery, he's an alpha male of course, and the moment he sees her he wants her, and he gets what he wants," Jane said. "Cheesy, and I'd have chosen a different scenario for myself from that website, but oh my god, Cassie, you're going to have so much sex soon."

"I didn't know I was this kind of a girl. I didn't know it existed in real life," I said. Only in dreams, I remembered Sophia and Daniel, and a chill went down my spine. I pushed the thought away; this was different.

"Maybe now you'll stop judging me," she said.

"What do you mean?"

"Me and Robert."

Robert was Jane's friend who nobody had met, and they met once a week for recreational sex as she called it. Nothing more, no strings attached.

"I never judged you!"

"Oh, you did," Jane said. "You said what was the point of having a sex-only partner, what about closeness, and now look at you," she laughed. "You got what you criticized. And I'm so happy for you," Jane raised her glass, a warm smile on her lips. "For the merits of recreational sex."

And I clinked her glass.

Later that night, Noah joined us, saying that he would prefer to be in the bed of that guy from the gallery, but the man needed to go to his sister's birthday at their parents' house.

"And can you imagine, he wanted me to go with him!" Noah said, pouring himself a glass of Cava.

"Did you want to go?" I asked.

Noah laughed, "Of course not."

"You sound fake, you wanted to go, didn't you? But you're afraid of commitment," I said.

He looked at me and Jane.

"I like him," he said and lowered his gaze. "But is it time to settle? I'm still so young and there's so many men around I want to try, if you know what I mean," and he winked.

"We know, Noah. But do you really like him?"

"I feel so good when I'm with him, protected, cherished. He listens to me; he makes me warm here." He pointed to his chest.

"Noah's falling in love," Jane sang, which earned her a pillow flying to her head.

"And I don't want to lose him, but I'm so afraid to make a move. I want him to know how I feel, but I'm paralyzed," he ended.

"Talk to him, just talk to him," I said, and Jane nodded.

Noah looked up at us and smiled, so blinding.

"Maybe I am falling in love," he said and laughed, the tinkle of a sound, as though he couldn't believe himself.

Twenty-Eight

Jason sent me a message that he wanted to see me, but that he would have an extremely busy week; there would be a hearing on Thursday, and he needed to get ready.

He called me on Monday morning.

"I have an invitation to a fundraising event on Friday evening, would you join me?" he asked, his voice rasping.

I needed to ask what the event was to play hard to get.

"Yes," I said, to hell with all games.

"The dress code is formal, I'll pick you up at 7 PM," he paused. "I miss you, but I have so much work these few days. Soon it'll be over, just a few days and I'll see you."

Warmth spilled down my core. "See you soon," I whispered.

After the call, I messaged in a group chat to Noah and Jane.

"SOS. I need a formal dress for a fundraising event for Friday evening, help me!"

Noah was good at shopping; he knew places where he found designer clothes with huge discounts, and he was on the pulse of the latest fashion trends.

So, on Friday evening, I was standing in my apartment in a cream-colored long dress with a deep cut up to my hip, long sleeves, and beautiful V-cleavage. My hair was in light waves, and I wore round earrings and heels so high that they made my legs unbearably long.

Jane and Noah left work at five just to help me dress. And now that I was standing in the doorway, Noah held his hand to his mouth, Jane smiled.

"You're so beautiful," he said.

And I felt beautiful, I felt like a queen. I had never worn something so delicate, so feminine—I felt like a celebrity on a red carpet.

My phone pinged. Jason had texted that he was downstairs already.

"Wish me luck," I said and stepped outside.

"Go get it, girl," Jane replied.

When I opened the door to the street, there was a black shiny Mercedes sedan, and Jason was standing by the passenger door, wearing a black suit that fit him perfectly. The moment his eyes landed on me, something changed in his face, the smile tugging his lips, and hunger, such a wild yearning in his eyes.

"You're gorgeous," he said and opened the door of the car. He held my hand when I lowered myself to the seat.

The soft smell of the new car hit me, the interior of brown leather, light music playing. Jason sat in the driver's seat and looked at me.

He brushed the lock from my cheek and leaned in to kiss me, I felt his hand move down my neck to my shoulder. He groaned.

"I hate that we need to go to the event, I'd want you just for me tonight, I would just look at you, I would just have you," he said, his eyes locked on mine, a thumb on my lower lip.

I felt fire running beneath my skin, in his presence I lost my mind, I felt that thirst that I needed him.

He put his hands on the wheel and maneuvered out of the parking space and into the heart of the city.

The event was held in one of the most expensive New York

restaurants. The dark walls were decorated with modern art, waiters in delicate black masks drifted noiselessly between the crowd. The soft song of the piano filled the space.

I spent the evening by Jason's side, his hand on my waist. I noticed how people looked at me, women eyeing me enviously when they saw his hand around me. Men looked me up and down, a new glint to their eyes. The crowd was expensive looking, the bids during the event were the sum of my yearly salary, the trips to Paris went down twenty times more than the usual price.

Jason talked to smartly dressed men but never released me from his hold. And, finally, hours later, we made it to the exit. We stopped on the sidewalk while the valet was retrieving the car.

"You were the jewel of the evening. Did you see how everyone looked at you?" he said, his eyes searching my face. "Can I take you to my place? There's no way I'm letting you go now."

I nodded. I didn't care about how fast it all was going, I wanted him.

In the car, he placed a palm on my leg, slowly tracing it up, a hot trail left after his touch. I moved closer and his hand stopped on my translucent panties, he ran his fingers on the inside of my thigh, and a soft moan escaped my lips.

His gray eyes flicked from the road to me, and I saw a raw emotion of need. He placed his hand back on the wheel and took a deep breath.

"You can't imagine what you're doing to me, Cassandra."

I crossed my legs and looked out of the window, trying to calm the fire.

The Mercedes veered into the underground parking and Jason slipped out of the car to open the door for me. I took his hand, and his eyes fell to my cleavage.

He led me to the elevator, and while we climbed up, he

traced the fabric so close to my breast. I was breathing hard. There were only a few doors on the landing, and he opened the one to the left.

His flat was spacious and light, New York lights shimmering out of the floor-to-ceiling windows. He took my hand and led me straight to the bedroom.

Jason lowered the shoulder of my dress, revealing a white lace bra. He kissed me when he lowered a bra strap, when his fingers touched the soft skin of my breast, when his hand moved between my legs, when he rubbed the soft fabric, when he moved it aside. I was still standing in my heels, him pressed to my hip, so hard, while his hand circled the most sensual part of my body. I was on the brink when he lowered me to his huge white bed and propped open my legs, when he tugged my underwear, when he lowered himself between my legs, when he kissed my thigh. I was still partially dressed, the dress on my waist, my breasts revealed, my fingers in his hair while his tongue devoured me. I begged as I never did before, the thunderous tremble shaking my body. He found my lips when I fumbled with his belt, he shuddered when I ran a hand up and down his length, and in a moment, he was inside.

That's when I lost myself. There was no me anymore, only primal need.

Afterwards, he fell to my side, breathing hard. He circled the swell of my breast with his finger, the soft touch on the darker skin.

And I wanted more. He helped me out of my dress, the scraps of white fabric falling to the floor.

I tugged on his shirt, revealing strong arms, muscled shoulders. He pushed his pants down, and there he lay in front of me, naked. I roamed his body with my fingers, climbing on top of him, my knees hugging his hips. I lowered my lips to his torso, I kissed his ribs, I barely touched his collarbone with my lips, my breasts pressed to his blazing skin. And I felt it all. I sat upright, and there was a growl from him when I took his hand, when I put his finger in my mouth, when I licked my tongue around it.

He was hard again, rubbing my thigh. Jason kept his eyes on me all the time. And then I slid him inside. I was burning as I moved, it wasn't me, it was wildness. I rode him in a delirious rhythm, his hands on my hips, guiding me. I touched him, I touched myself. And when something bright exploded inside me, I fell into his arms, both of us shaking.

It was hard to move my limbs, so he hugged me, and I pressed my back to him. Jason planted a kiss on my neck, and ran his fingers down my breasts, my thighs and rested his palm on my hip. But I was slipping away already.

He disentangled himself and disappeared into the bathroom for a couple of minutes. Then he came back and pressed me into the same position, lowering his face to my shoulder.

"I love how you smell, you smell of sex, you smell of me," he murmured. "Sleep, Cassandra."

And I did.

Twenty-Nine

In the morning, I looked around, our bodies covered in white sheets. The room was elegant with dark furniture, one wall painted dark green, and a huge TV mounted on the wall.

I closed my eyes and remembered the last night, the blush spreading down my cheeks. It was not me. I never was so crazy, it was as though Jason triggered something in me, a wild streak. And I could feel the thirst again at the back of my throat; my mind and my body wanted different things.

Quietly, I stood from the bed and tiptoed into the bathroom. A shower was separated with a glass, and I stepped inside, the hot water running down my body. I found his shower gel, and now I smelled even more like him. I washed my hair and dried it with a clean towel he had left on the sink.

I wrapped the towel around my body, the wet cascades of my hair falling to my left shoulder.

When I stepped back to the bedroom, Jason was not there, noise coming from deep in the apartment. The floor was warm to my bare soles.

I found him in the kitchen wearing white briefs, his back to me.

"Coffee?" he asked.

"Yes, please," I said as I leaned on the counter.

I saw his muscles work when he pulled cups from the cabinet, and then he turned, a cup in his hand. And I froze, the chill gripping my heart, because it was not his gray eyes looking at me, but the piercing green. I knew this color. I saw it in my dreams, many times towering above me when I looked through Sophia's eyes; that green was the last thing she saw before the bullet struck her heart.

These eyes were hidden behind the black rimmed glasses. But still, they studied me, registering the shock on my face.

He laughed.

"That's why I wear colored eye lenses, to avoid this kind of reaction. The green of my eyes is too bright, and I think gray suits me more." He took a step closer, a cup of coffee still in his hand.

I took it, looking at him all the time. *It's stupid, just a coincidence,* I told myself while taking a sip. The bitterness of coffee burned my mouth. Good, I needed it.

And when I saw the time on his clock I gasped. I had agreed to go to brunch with Jane and Noah today, and I still had two hours, but I needed a minute to myself.

"I need to go," I said, placing an empty cup on the counter.

Jason pulled me towards him.

"I thought we'd have more time," he murmured in my ear. "I'd love to see you without this towel."

And a familiar tingle moved in my core.

"Sorry, but I have plans with the guys," I said, but my body was already responding to his hand lowering down my waist.

"Okay, I'll drive you back," he said, a smile on his lips when he saw how I reacted to his touch.

The green eyes landed on my lips.

"If you keep biting your lips like this, I won't be able to let you go," he growled.

I was biting my lip, and I was breathing hard. Because I was drowning in this green, I wanted his hands on me, that thirst again at the back of my throat. And only he could quench it.

I turned back and walked into the bedroom, his gaze between my shoulder blades.

The pool of white was on the chair; Jason had placed my dress there.

"I can give you my hoodie and pants, but I have no idea what to do with the heels. You need to bring spare clothes here next time," he said, calmly standing in the doorway.

He disappeared into the walk-in closet and emerged with a white hoodie and sport pants.

"These are the smallest I have," he said.

"Thank you," I took the clothes from him. There was no way I would be dressing back into that dress now.

He nodded and walked away, leaving me to change.

The sight was hideous. The sportswear was too big, but it was half of the problem. I looked at my bare feet and clutched the hills.

Jason emerged from the bathroom, glasses gone, the gray eyes assessing me, and then he smiled.

"You look gorgeous, I didn't know my hoodie would accompany the heels so perfectly." He hugged me, planting a kiss on the top of my head. And I leaned into him, trying to forget the silly fear of green eyes. Those were just dreams of non-existent people, I told myself. And I almost believed my own lie.

He drove me back, one hand on the steering wheel, one on my knee.

"I want to see you tonight," he said when the car stopped in front of my building. "Let me take you out for dinner."

Careful, my mind whispered. Green eyes or no, I had never experienced or felt what I felt the night before. It was like my body was discovered, and I wanted more, that greed of pleasure.

I put my fingers in his hair, I traced his brow, his cheekbone.

He found my hand and pressed fingers to his lips. The eyes never leaving my face.

We agreed that he would pick me up at seven, and I awkwardly stepped out of the car, the transparent plastic bag with my dress in my hand. The heels and big sport pants looked ridiculous; thankfully, there were not many people to see this sight, as it was still early for Saturday.

I waved at him and went inside.

When I climbed up to my apartment, I almost forgot about the green eyes, so bright, piercing. My hair smelled of him and the clean clothes he gave me also held his scent. I fell back on my bed and closed my eyes.

The images of last night were rushing into my mind, my skin prickling. I felt like a character from a movie; a sophisticated young woman who had found herself a lover, and she enjoyed herself in his arms. Was it me?

I put on jeans and a light jacket, lifted my hair in a bun and went to meet Noah and Jane.

"Somebody had sex last night," Jane said as soon as she saw me. "You have that glow, and your lip's ruined."

I rubbed my neck, looking a bit guilty.

"Yes, well, I know it's too soon, we only met," I mumbled.

"Oh, did you see yourself yesterday? I'd have shagged you myself if I was a man," Jane said, "and don't wait for judgment from me."

Noah reached us and we walked to a nice airy place a few blocks down.

"Why are you so sulky today?" I asked Noah.

He grunted. "Do you remember this guy from the gallery?"

"The love of your life?" I smiled.

He blushed, even the tips of his ears turned red. "I'm joking," I said hastily, but he didn't deny it, which made me pause.

"He's going away for a week, he needs to be in Miami for an art event, and I . . ." he rubbed his forehead, "damn, I'm needy."

I took his hand, "It's okay. The week will be gone in a blink."

"He suggested that I fly there for the weekend, to spend time with him," Noah said.

"And what did you say?" Jane asked.

"I refused. I don't want him to think that I don't have a life of my own, that when he asks I would run to his lap."

Jane groaned. "You have an extremely distorted image of relationships in your head. You're playing hard to get like in those wonky romantic movies of the 2000s."

"Oh, don't lecture me, you spend your life in books, and look at Miss Minx who still can't breathe properly after the night," he snapped.

Jane lowered her gaze.

"I'm sorry, Jane," Noah said after a quiet moment. "I didn't mean to be rude. All three of us don't have and never had normal functional relationships. And I don't judge you about Robert, I never did. But I want this to work, and I have no idea how to do it properly. I don't want to ruin it with my own swooning."

"Do you want to be with him?" I asked.

He nodded.

"Then stop overthinking it! Forget all the rules you know and follow your heart. Do you want to spend a weekend in Miami with him?"

"I do," he said.

Jane took his phone, which was lying face down on the table and thrust it in his hand.

"Call him."

A small smile was growing bigger and wider on Noah's face, shining. He stood, the chair scraping.

"I'll call him." He turned to the exit, dazed.

We looked at him through the huge restaurant windows.

Noah stood sideways; his hand clutched in a fist. But the moment he started talking, his features relaxed, he laughed, he beamed.

A few minutes later, he returned to us.

"He sounded happy when I told him I'd like to go," he said. "Thanks, guys." He looked at us.

The waiter brought salmon bagels and three cups of cappuccino.

"When are you going to see Jason again?" Jane asked.

"Tonight," I blushed.

"Naughty," Noah said.

I took a shaky breath. "This is crazy, I was crazy, it was as though another person switched with me. I realized I don't know my body too well."

"Look at the two of you," Jane said, taking a sip of cappuccino. "I need to call Robert tonight to stay in shape."

Thirty

A face looked at me from the mirror; it was my face, but a new glint was there, a reflection of someone else, a woman I knew ten years ago. I was wearing jeans, a white shirt with a burgundy jacket, and a clutch with a leopard print. Casual but smart. My hair was up in a stylish messy bun again.

The phone pinged, saying that Jason was outside.

I inhaled and threw a last glance at my reflection, and just for a blink it was not me, it was Sophia. I shook my head and closed the door behind me.

Jason was waiting on the sidewalk. When I stepped closer, he leaned in to kiss me.

"You look dazzling," he whispered in my ear, sending pleasant shivers down my core.

We took a cab to the restaurant with a dark interior and not so many tables, mostly couples.

"What kind of wine do you like?" Jason asked.

"Rosé, I'm not really an expert. We tried to learn the wine, but after sampling brut, Noah, Jane and I went back to rosé."

He nodded. "Challenge accepted, now I think it's my duty to open the wine world for you."

When the waiter appeared by our side, they talked about a type and year, and minutes later, two glasses were filled in front of me.

Jason lifted his glass. "Cheers."

I took a sip from the first one, the sourness tingling my tongue.

"Too dry for me," I said.

"Try the other one."

And this one was much lighter, the sweet notes mixed with a floral scent.

"I like it," I said, taking one more sip.

"It reminds me of you," Jason said. "If you were wine, you would be this one."

He leaned back on the chair and studied my face.

"I had a difficult week with all the court process and thank god it ended. We won for now, and meeting you was such a timely gift," he said.

"What was the process about?"

Jason ran a hand through his hair, his jaw working.

"It was for my big client; he needs my help a lot."

"Taxes?"

"Yes. And his cases take extremely careful handling, and he pays well. But this week the reward from him was dimmed by a woman in white."

I felt a warm shiver as he moved closer and took my hand in his.

"Cassandra, I want you in my life."

"Yes," I whispered. I had never met a man who emanated so much power around him, the grace, the possessiveness. And I wanted his attention on me, I wanted to be needed.

Later, in the cab and after many more glasses of wine, we headed to Jason's apartment again. I looked out of the window, the New York Saturday night life at its peak. Jason opened his arm, and I scooted over.

He put a hand on my thigh and ran his fingers over the zipper, making his way down, and I felt a pressure between my legs, the raw fabric of jeans rubbing my skin. I closed my eyes, I tried not to move, but my body was responding already.

The wine in my veins, his smell engulfing me, the warmth of his arms around me, the sweet need building inside, soaking me.

"You're making me hungry," he whispered in my ear, and I looked up at him.

I placed a hand on his bulging pants; he was hard. I ran my fingers down, and I saw how his eyelashes trembled, how he closed his eyes for a moment.

And I removed my hand, sat straight and looked outside. A small smile playing on my lips.

He growled, crossing his arms, but I felt his gaze on me. I was breathing hard, my heart pumping that liquid desire down my veins.

The cab stopped at Jason's building, and he gentlemanly took my hand while I stepped out of the car. We crossed the hall and silently waited for the elevator.

In the elevator, he pressed me to the wall, kissing hard. His hand was under my shirt in a second.

"Don't play with me, Cassandra. Sometimes I can't control myself," he growled in my ear.

But I didn't care, I was moving against him.

"Take me," I whispered, and it unhinged something inside him.

I saw the fire in his eyes. But the elevator doors slid open, and I saw his hands shaking when he opened the door to his apartment.

I closed it behind me, but Jason stood a few feet away, looking at me.

I pressed my back to the door, burning under his gaze.

"Say it again," he whispered.

"Take me," I said, my voice rasping.

In a second, Jason was by my side, he slipped me out of my jacket, the shirt landing on the floor. He was kissing my neck, his hands on my bra, the soft silk between me and his skin. My nipple was hard, and he circled the fabric around it. My hand moved to remove the bra, but he found my wrist, and in a second, pinned my hands above my head.

I could not move when he traced a finger on my elbow, on my shoulder, my lips, I bit his fingertip lightly, and I saw a wet trace as he dragged it on my chest.

"Please," I whimpered.

That hand moved back and unhooked my bra, the silk scraps hanging loosely around me. He lowered his lips to my breasts, and he kissed, he licked, he sucked. My legs were not holding me anymore, I felt every inch of my skin ablaze, I was burning from the inside.

Jason scooped me into his arms and brought me into the kitchen. He propped a pillow under my back when he laid me on the marble kitchen table. The chill of the surface only heightened my senses. In a moment, my jeans dropped to the floor, my panties following them.

He towered over me, flicking his finger over my burning flesh. I moaned.

In a daze, I watched him kneeling in front of me, the hot waves rolling inside when he ran his tongue over my clit.

"Please," I whispered again.

My fingers were lost in his fair hair, I could not control myself when he fed on me, I was breaking, I was falling. I screamed when the hot white wall hit me. There was not enough air in the room when he stood, when with shaking hands I lowered his pants, and he was inside me, moving, bringing me back to the brink. Till I shattered again, his body falling on top, propped on the elbow.

The sweet opium spread down my veins, and I knew I would be coming for more and more, my new drug was the man who now was breathing hard, who pressed me to the table.

"You're mine," he whispered.

And my reality shattered. I had heard it all before.

But I didn't care, no one touched me like this, no one evoked such thunder. And even if it was poisonous, I would take it.

Again.

And again.

Thirty-One

My days blurred. I was working, I was meeting with Jane and Noah, but during the nights, I took my shot. A few nights a week I stayed at Jason's, sometimes he came to my flat to see me after work.

We were both greedy, I needed his hands on me, his tongue, the length of him filling me whole, he was crazed by my presence. It was a fever we couldn't shake, burning us alive.

"You look thinner," Jane said.

Three months had passed since the day I met Jason. We were eating lunch, the three of us huddled in the cooling waves of air conditioning in the small cafe minutes from our office.

"And you have dark circles under your eyes," Noah said.

"I don't sleep well," I murmured.

"Don't you think your relationship with Jason is a little unhealthy? Where is it going anyway?" Jane asked.

I dropped my hands to the table, palms up. "I don't know. I feel tired all the time, but he comes often, and he just needs me. I take his mind off things."

Noah and Jane looked at each other.

"Do you talk much?"

"Not really," I said, and I saw how Noah's gaze lowered to his hands. "We're more about touches, and I'm happy. I never felt my body so raw, and I don't know how long it'll last, and I want each moment of it."

"So you don't think it's a long term?" Noah asked.

"I don't know, okay?" I was getting defensive.

"We care about you, but as long as you're happy, we're happy too. Just know that we're here for you," Jane said and squeezed my hand. My eyes blurred for a moment, and I blinked it away.

I was happy. I was. Was I?

But it was so different from shining Noah by my side. He was glowing. The man from the gallery asked him to move in with him, and last week Noah accidentally blurted out that he loved him. Noah said he never saw anyone so happy. The man almost crushed him with his hugs, kissing Noah, saying that he loved him back. So, so much.

There was no love between me and Jason, I knew it. There was something different. It was as though I was addicted to him, and I knew that comparing him to drugs in my mind was not normal. But still, I needed the pill of him every day, the bliss was worth it, making me happy.

I lied to myself.

Happy and healthy drug addicts just didn't exist.

※

A few weeks later, Jane sent me a link to a news website.

"Found a familiar name there," the note said.

I opened it early in the morning. The article was about how the law now protected criminals. How law could be twisted to protect not people, but companies.

The story was about the blood money of Simon Rocherfield, a major player in the firearms industry who owned a few legal casinos as a side business. And how money protected his deeds, how he bought the best defense to cover his not-so-legal business brunches and his multiple sex assault accusations. And how a small legal company in New York helped him stay afloat: The company was owned by Jason Dillon.

The room swayed around me. I heard it all before. History was repeating itself. I grabbed the edge of the table so as not to fall. But I could not be upright anymore; I dropped to my knees and crawled onto the sofa.

It was not possible. These were just dreams—realistic, but dreams. They had nothing to do with my life now. I was not Sophia. Jason was not Daniel. I could make myself believe in it, but the green eyes, the same piercing shade. He made sure to always wear lenses now when he was with me, and I started forgetting the true color.

Even if my dreams were a figment of my imagination, some kind of premonition, they didn't end well. I felt a pain in my palms and looked down to see my nails leaving blood red marks where I clutched myself. I flexed my fingers. Still, I was shaking. I remembered how Sophia was beaten and only a vacant gaze from those green eyes. How he cheated, the click of a gun. That blinding pain in my chest when I opened my eyes from that dream when I saw Sophia for the last time. I gasped as an echo of that pain sliced my ribcage.

I should end things with him, I should cut myself off. It should be easy, I thought, we were connected by sex only, and in such a big city he could find my replacement easily.

But I was so mistaken.

Thirty-Two

Oh, he felt something had changed. That day a bunch of blood red roses were delivered to my office, the stems so long, the thorns so sharp, the flower buds so velvety rich.

There was a card saying: "Meet me at Muse today at 7."

Muse was the restaurant I loved, hidden in the heart of the city. Cozy Scandinavian design mixed with the lightest deserts, it was one place Jason showed me that I liked. He preferred fancier spots, darker places with perfect kitchens and deifying stuff.

The flowers were so unnaturally big on my office table that they drew envious glances from female coworkers, but Noah and Jane looked skeptically at them.

"He definitely wants something from you," Noah said.

"But he already has everything," I said.

All I could give I already gave, all my body. But I had one thing left—my heart.

I went to Muse straight from my office. My earlier resolve to finish things as soon as possible dimmed when I saw him standing to greet me. His smile, his beautiful hands that caressed me so many times. He was so handsome in his casual business attire; a gray shirt hugged his muscles and fair pants with a black leather belt. He kissed me when he saw me, his hand on my waist.

"There's going to be a corporate party at my company, our biggest clients are also invited. We're renting a venue, nothing major, just to thank the team for their hard work. To relax, to drink, and I want you to go with me," he said, tracing a finger up my wrist to my elbow, sending tingles.

"When will it be?"

"It's in a week," he said. "I want you to be there."

I took a swig of my wine, his eyes following my every move.

"Okay," I blurted, my resolve melting more. His hand was still on my elbow, but the light hold slowly turned into a cage.

He smiled. "This is a casual party, so no fancy dresses."

Jason released my arm and took a menu.

After dinner, he insisted on taking me home, and he climbed out of the cab along with me.

He opened the door to my apartment building; Jason stood behind me when I opened the lock. In the apartment, he went to my cabinet with bottles and poured me a glass of chocolate liquor.

"You were quiet today," he said, handing me the glass.

"I'm sorry, I just . . ." I could not say anything. I looked around my tiny apartment; I realized that I should feel safe here, but with him taking so much space, I felt shaken. He came here rarely, and he took me to bed immediately.

But now, he placed a glass in my hand.

"Drink," he said, and I gulped it, the alcohol stinging my throat, making me warm.

Jason came closer. "You're tense today, what happened?" he murmured, closing his hands around me.

"I'm just tired," I said.

"I'll help you relax." He found my lips, and my body started responding to him as usual, even as my mind was going blank when his hand lowered between my legs.

When he brought me down on the couch, when he unzipped my pants, when he took off my panties, when he lowered his lips there, when he made me breathless, when I came shuddering, I hated myself for being so open for him, for allowing him to take me when he wanted, for my body that was so responsive to his touch.

I was still trembling from the sweet sensation when he kissed my thighs, when he lifted to my face, when I tasted myself on his lips.

"Now you're relaxed," he whispered and stood. "I need to go, get some rest, my love."

In a moment, my front door closed, leaving the echoing silence in my apartment, and me half naked on the sofa, still breathing hard.

Thirty-Three

I spent the weekend at Jane's, saying to Jason that I got my period, and since each one of our meetings ended with me being naked, he agreed for me to spend some time away.

"I need to break up with him," I said to Jane.

She was sitting on the floor, when I was laying on her sofa. She steeled herself and looked at me.

"Why?"

"From the start it was all about sex, and we had a lot of it: raw, crazy, lustful. We never actually talked; you know. And now, I feel like there's nothing of me except my body, he plays with it, he takes it, and he keeps saying that he owns me."

"Does he abuse you?" Jane asked, her eyes wide.

"No, never. But with him I feel like I'm caged," I said. What I didn't say was that I felt an invisible hand on my throat, tightening with each meeting.

"It doesn't sound normal, Cassie. When are you going to talk to him?"

"There's going to be a party at his company next week, and he'll spend time getting it ready, so after that I think."

Jane nodded. "I worry about you," she said and squeezed my

hand. "Do you think he'll let you go? Could he become violent?"

"I hope not," I said.

"You need to let me know exactly when you decide to do it, so Noah and I can be close."

My eyes stung. "Thanks."

Jane hugged me, and I found myself breaking in her arms.

"It's a mess," I said, taking a shaky breath.

"He's gorgeous, Cassie, and you've never felt somebody wanting you so much, lusting after you, and you fell for it. It's human behavior, now let's get you out of it."

A wave of gratitude swept me, and I clutched my friend tighter.

I didn't see Jason until the evening of his event.

I wore a black casual dress and heels that hugged my ankle, my hair down, with blood red lipstick. Just a little more, I kept telling myself. The last week without him in my life made me breathe lighter; I felt like my old self, not corrupted by his need.

He met me at the building entrance. His company had rented a penthouse apartment, and New York lights were scattered at our feet, the view taking my breath away.

Jason kissed me on the cheek and took my hand. A waiter placed a drink in my hand noiselessly and disappeared. Jason paraded me to group after group of people, a string of names, smiles, curious gazes. And then we stopped in front of a tall man with a heavy-set jaw. He looked me up and down and I felt shivers down my spine.

"Simon Rocherfield," he said, taking my hand in his, shaking it just a little harder than necessary.

The important client, Jason had said, and I remembered the name from the news article.

I noticed how his eyes fell to my legs, slowly dragging up, assessing. I smiled, but my hands started shaking. I gripped my glass tighter to hide it.

Thankfully, someone distracted Simon, and he turned his icy gaze to another person.

Jason turned us to another group of people, three men and two women. He kept saying names when a woman with black curly hair turned to us.

My heart stopped beating when I looked into her eyes. The color of night, the stars shining in the darkness. Pale skin, full lips, locks of silky raven hair framing her face.

From a distance, I heard the shattering of glass, and in a fog, I realized that I had dropped my tumbler, the commotion of people around, the waiter rushing to my side. But it was all so far away, because I was looking into the warm night, because the woman was smiling at me, so familiar, so heartbreaking.

"I need fresh air," I whispered to Jason, breaking the spell, looking away, and I turned around and rushed to an open door to the patio.

The cool evening breeze on top of the world licked my cheeks, and when I stopped near the enclosure, I squeezed my eyes shut. I took a deep breath, my heart crazy in my chest.

"I found you." I heard a raspy voice by my side.

I opened my eyes—there she stood. Her eyes were partially hidden by a curly fringe and she was wearing a black pantsuit with white pointed-toe heels.

"You recognized me, didn't you? Do you remember?" she asked.

"I don't know what you're talking about," I whispered, my eyes on her face. She turned her head to the side, and I gasped when I saw more of him in her: William.

My head started spinning and I gripped the banister.

"My name's Rachel," the woman said.

I just stood quiet, looking at her.

"You look so much like her," Rachel whispered. And when I didn't say anything again, my voice trapped somewhere inside, her lips moved, making it almost impossible to catch what she was saying. "Sophia."

My trembling hand went up to my lips.

"I need to go," I said, stepping around her. I needed to leave this madness. My life overlapped with the one from my dreams from high school, which froze everything inside. And this woman knew Sophia's name. And her eyes.

Something warm touched my wrist, and I looked down to see her fingers around my hand. The short dark blue matte nails on my skin.

"Wait, please." And there was something in the way Rachel looked at me. She released my hand and fumbled in her pocket, retrieving a business card. "Call me, I need, I . . ." she was lost for words. "Please."

I took the card and without glancing back I stepped inside the room full of people. My heels clicked on the floor, echoing two times slower than my heart. I found Jason standing with Simon, the man's hand loosely on his shoulder. The sight made my stomach churn.

I touched Jason's shoulder. "Can I speak with you for a minute?"

He was still laughing at Simon's joke when his hand circled around my waist, leading me to a quiet corner.

"I don't feel well," I said, "I think I ate something bad at work. I need to go home."

Jason looked at me.

"You're pale." I was more than pale, cold sweat dripped down my spine, I hugged myself with clammy hands.

"Do you need any help getting home?" he asked, but I saw how he was looking back at the crowd of people, longing to be there.

"No, no, I'm okay."

He nodded.

"Oh, wait, I'll be out for a week with Simon, he has a case in Texas we need to work on," Jason said.

"Okay, sure. And if it's food poisoning, I'll be out for a couple of days too," I said, such a wave of relief washing over me.

He guided me to the exit.

"I'll call you," he said and disappeared into the crowd.

Don't, I thought.

I looked around the hall again, everyone lost in conversation, so loud, laughing, smiling. And only one pale face turned to me, Rachel, worry written all over her face.

I turned away and went to the elevator.

Outside of the building I hailed a cab, the city blurring outside, the fog in my head.

The first thing I did when I was back home was that I got rid of those heels, my legs hurting. Discarding every piece of clothing on the way to the shower, I breathed out only when the hot trickle of water warmed my shaking body.

It was all clicking into place with a clear quality. I was Sophia. Or she was me. Or we were one. Daniel definitely was Jason. I gasped when I understood that Noah was Elena, Sophia's maid and friend from Riga. Alexander, Daniel's boss, was Simon. And Will, the man who saved Sophia's drowning soul, whom she fell in love with so swiftly, so lightly, in this life, Will was a woman, Rachel. His handsome features melted into her beauty. I turned the knob to make the water even hotter so it seared my skin.

I dried myself with a towel and wrapped a soft bathrobe around my pink skin. I shuffled to the sofa and dropped on it, draping the hood over my head, curling up. I closed my eyes and listened to my breaths.

Some kind of magic made me remember my previous life. Sophia was trapped from the moment she gave herself to Daniel, and she didn't want to live in the world without William so she took her life. She didn't finish anything. And now here I was, walking into the same trap, meeting Will too late and him being a woman here. What did it all mean?

One thing I knew for sure, I had to break up with Jason. I needed to run away and as soon as possible. Because if I lingered, this life might turn into an even bigger nightmare than the previous one.

I stood and fished my phone from the bag. *Rachel Maier* was written on a white business card, attorney, and her number. I sent a message to her.

"*I need to talk to you.*"

A reply pinged almost instantly.

"*Tomorrow, at 7, Williamstone bar.*"

The name made me laugh. I typed "*Ok*" and started to wonder if I was going crazy.

Thirty-Four

The next day, I didn't tell anyone that I was going to meet Rachel, I was distracted all day, and Jane and Noah looked at me with worry.

When I stepped into the bar, I saw her. She wore a black jacket, cropped pants, white sneakers, and her curly hair glinted in the warm bar light. She was sitting alone by a small table in the corner.

When our eyes met, I was thrown back into that old kitchen, and a warm feeling spread down my spine. But that was not me; I shook my head and tried to discard the memory.

I stopped by her table and lowered myself on the chair. I noticed that she was only a couple of years older than me in her early thirties. She looked at me silently, but I saw light crackling in her eyes; as Sophia was harmonized with Will when she was living with him, I had memorized every expression and look. Now I saw hidden light under the mask of calmness.

"How the hell did it all happen?" I asked, anger dripping in my words. "I didn't ask for all this. I didn't ask to remember. You know, normally people don't know their previous life."

Rachel grinned. "What are you going to drink?"

"What?"

"We're in a bar, what are you going to drink?" she tried to hide her smile.

"Vodka martini," I said, "I need something strong."

She nodded and went to a counter to order it, saying nothing more.

In a few minutes, she placed the glass before me, and I took a huge gulp. She sipped her Manhattan.

"Better?" she asked.

I took one more mouthful of cocktail, the vodka firing my mouth and throat, surprisingly clearing my head.

"Yes."

"Good. Now, tell me how much do you remember? And how did it come to you?" Rachel said.

I shook my head. "No, you go first, I don't want to sound even more nuts than I do already."

She laughed, and I couldn't stop my lips from twitching; it was as though I was attuned to her movements, to her reactions. I pressed my lips into a thin line, but she noticed it.

"This whole situation is nuts. Even if we wanted to find something sane in it, I'm sure we wouldn't manage." She sipped her cocktail and lowered it on the coaster.

"Back in 2010 I was in a major car accident, the driver on the opposite lane veered into my car—supposedly he was texting—which careened my car into the tree. Thankfully my speed wasn't high, and the impact wasn't extremely strong, but it broke my right hand and leg, and I hit my head pretty hard," Rachel said, looking down, swirling the dark contains of her glass.

"I was in the hospital for a couple of weeks, and there I started seeing things." She looked up at me. "It was like I had memories of not my life, of a childhood of a man who lived almost one hundred years ago. I could see every detail: his education, his path. And then the swelling in my head because of the car crash started getting bigger, doctors were worried, and I was on a lot of medication, half asleep. And during that time, I almost lived Will's life. I remember him seeing Sophia for the first time, I felt everything he felt. The protection, the injustice, and when he saw her beaten after that encounter with—"

"Thom," I said.

She nodded. "Yes, Thom. I guessed where it all was going, I felt how he cared, how she stayed close, how he hugged her, how she leaned in. Doctors said I was crying a lot in my dreams, tears silently falling down my cheeks. I didn't see yet how it all ended, but I felt the impending danger of something terrible, and how Will fell in love with a fierce girl in the next room."

I was looking at her, the way her head tilted, her hand movements, the set of her spine, I saw it all before. She was so like him, but much gentler, feminine.

"As I was hooked to monitors, doctors said my heart skipped a few beats and was beating erratically one day, they could not explain what was happening to me. That was the day Will and Sophia kissed." She smiled at me, and I felt tears stinging my eyes. I blinked them away.

"So much hope, and I knew there was no way they both would be free. They were careless, they were so in love, and then Daniel came. And that shot stopped Will's and my heart. Here in this life it resumed beating, in that life it didn't. But the pain was here," she placed a hand to her chest.

"And I knew that was the end of them. They had just a few moments of happiness to be snatched away so violently. But those were violent days. I remember that moment, when I opened my eyes here, I was so overwhelmed by the thought that Sophia was left there with that monster, that she did not deserve it."

I felt a tear rolling down my cheek.

"Later, I tried to find any information of what happened to Sophia, but it was as though someone erased Will and Sophia from all the papers. I only found a record of how Sophia came to

America and then nothing. No mention of either of them. Daniel died at the age of 65 in his apartment in New York," Rachel said, and took a sip from her glass.

"So, after William was shot, I never had those dreams again. The swelling in my head subsided, my heart rate stabilized, and some time later I was back home healing. I remembered everything I saw, but I decided it was some kind of drug delirium, vivid dreams. I went back to my studies, I finished university, I moved to New York, I was looking for a job. And one day I had an interview in a small law firm, I'm still surprised how I didn't faint there. Two people were interviewing me, the HR manager and . . . Daniel. The moment I saw the man, I knew it was him," Rachel said and ran a hand through her raven hair.

"No need to say that I failed that interview spectacularly, I tried not to stare at him while all the memories rushed back, when the man in front of me was the one who killed William. I vomited in the bathroom after the interview, all my body was slick with sweat, shaking. But when I got home, I realized one thing: If Daniel was here, Sophia should be with him. And I needed to see her. So I begged them to give me another chance at the interview, claiming that I had severe food poisoning that day, and it played well that the HR manager saw me retching in the bathroom. So, this time I prepared, I knew what they would ask, I dressed immaculately, I was perfect for the job, and they hired me. It was four years ago." She looked at me, pausing, her gaze reaching deep down inside me. She shook her head, curls swaying. "Sorry, I still can't believe you're here. Anyway, soon I realized Sophia was not with him yet. I saw strings of girls he took to social events, a new girl every time. And I was afraid that maybe I missed you, that maybe I saw Sophia and didn't recognize her. But every time the next girl came, I knew it wasn't you, because according to the story once Daniel met Sophia he held her close, never letting her go. I decided to wait. And seven months after I started working for him, Simon came, and Jason started working with him. Well, you saw Simon, did he remind you of anyone?"

"He's Alexander, the same cold stare, the chilling power," I said.

"Yes, and in this life he does almost the same as in the previous one."

I gripped the edge of the table. "Drugs?"

"Yes, and casinos, weapons," she said.

I paled. "And Jason helps him to stay clean in the face of law," I murmured.

"Yes, taxes, off-shore companies, everything."

"And you help him?" I looked at Rachel.

"I needed to find you, and after Simon came it only proved that you would appear by Jason's side sooner or later."

"What's your role in his company?" I asked.

"Jason couldn't be helping only Simon, he needed something good to boast about, so he created a small legal department to help people who actually needed help but couldn't afford it. I'm the head of that department, but anyway, it's all sponsored by blood money. I walk the same path as William: He was a doctor, but he saved criminals. I help people, and it may all seem well and generous, but from time to time Jason asks those people for reciprocal help. They never leave his office free; they're always indebted."

She leaned back on her chair and covered her eyes with her hands. "It's all the same," she breathed out. "Do you remember what happened with Sophia after Daniel shot Will?"

Rachel didn't know. And I saw how she leaned closer to hear, the body tense, eyes pleading.

"Sophia talked to Daniel, realizing that she had lost. She shot herself with the same gun, in the same kitchen, minutes after Daniel shot Will."

Rachel looked at me frozen, and then she covered her mouth

to hide the sob, her face crumpling with pain, tears falling down her cheeks. She dropped her head in her hands and her body trembled.

"She didn't want to live without him," I whispered, and Rachel looked up at me, eyes red.

An ancient pain opened in my chest when I looked at her, when I saw how she hurt. And I didn't realize that I moved closer, that I took Rachel's hand, and when we both looked at our entwined hands, I hugged her. She smelled like forest, in this megapolis, she smelled like woods, and having my arms around her, the pain subsided.

"They didn't deserve it," I whispered.

We were silent, and moments later I moved back into my seat. Rachel was calmer now, she was looking at me, the warm summer night in her eyes, stars playing around. And then she smiled, and I smiled back. And I couldn't remember the last time I was so warm inside.

"Now's your turn," she said, taking a sip from her glass. "Tell me the story of how you remembered."

And I told how I started having a double life in school, one by day, one by night. How it messed with my perception, how I struggled.

"I can't imagine how it was for you," Rachel said. "I was knocked out with so many drugs lying in the hospital, I was mostly unconscious when I saw Will's life. And you were seeing all of it while living your daily life."

"Yeah, and it messed with me pretty badly. But Sophia's life was so much more interesting than mine, there was so much intensity, traveling from Riga to New York. All the lust, the ignorance. And I saw how Daniel became obsessed with Sophia, and I saw how wrong it was, how he owned her. And then Will came, and I spent a lot of time daydreaming about him," I said and blushed. "And then it all ended with two shots of a gun."

Rachel looked at me for a very long moment. "I'm sorry," she said.

My glass was empty already. "One more?" I asked, and she nodded.

I stood and fought my way through the crowded bar, many more people had filled the place compared to when I arrived.

When I returned with two glasses, Rachel smiled at me, and that smile took my breath away.

"How did you meet Jason?" she asked.

I told her the story of the art gallery, and how on the first date we kissed, and on the second date I was under him. I was blushing violently.

"I became so greedy, I wanted more, no one made me feel like he did. Every encounter was sweet with a small drip of poison," I said. "Anyway, I'm going to break up with him when he's back from Texas."

I saw how Rachel paled.

"You need to be extremely careful," she said.

"I'm just a toy," I waved my hand. "He'll find another one easily."

"No," Rachel moved closer. "You're not just a toy, all things we remember aside, yesterday he introduced you to everyone, he never did this before. He was showing you off, like look what I have here. He wants to keep you."

It stung, talking about me like an object, but with Jason's possessiveness I knew it was true.

"We need to think. Last time they rushed, and they both ended up dead," Rachel said, looking at my hands.

"Everything's going to be fine," I laughed. "You're dramatizing it too much."

"Cassie, I worked for them for four years. Do you know how much money Simon uses to cover his sexual assaults? Do you know how many young women came to the office so Jason could negotiate the price for them forgetting Simon's behavior? And he charmed them, they took money and went away. Simon doesn't see women as human beings, they're just things to him. And Jason isn't so far away from him as you think he might be. And even now, do you think they're just working in Texas? I'm sure lots of naked bodies are involved."

That was like a slap. I remembered how Daniel was unfaithful to Sophia, but I never actually thought that Jason could be the same.

"I don't care who he shags, I'm breaking up with him."

Rachel was silent again.

"Okay, maybe this time it'll be easier. You're not in love with another man, and me being a woman makes everything uncomplicated."

Something shadowy clouded the night of her eyes and I wanted to touch her cheek. But I moved my hand under the table, resting it in my lap.

"Do you have a boyfriend?" I asked.

"No," she smiled. "I work a lot. I try to help as many people as possible with the money Simon gives. At least something good comes from all this nightmare."

She took a sip of her cocktail.

"What do you do for a living?" she asked.

"I work in a digital marketing company. I help brands grow online and on social media."

"Far from the numbers provided by Ben, hah?"

"Yeah, I guess so," I said and smiled. "I have two close friends, Jane and Noah, we all work together."

"Did you tell them about your dreams?"

"No, of course not, I didn't tell anyone. It's too impossible."

"Yes, me neither," she said.

The music started blaring around, as though everything was muted and suddenly I was back, the voices around.

"We should be going," Rachel said.

I looked at her and I realized I didn't want to let go of her yet. But she stood already and picked her bag. Already, a couple was eyeing our table.

Outside was much quieter, the pulsing of music almost nonexistent.

"Can I see you again?" I blurted.

She was looking at the road, but after those words she turned to me.

"Do you want to?" she asked, a mix of hope swirling the edges of her words. She tried to hide it, but the softest smile played on her lips.

"Yes." And I touched her wrist, just for a second. She looked down and beamed.

"I'm going away for a few days, my dad's having an operation, when I'm back I'd love to see you," she said.

"Is it serious, the operation?" I asked.

"Not really, but it needs to be done, hopefully he'll be up and running soon. I just want to be there," Rachel said. "Meanwhile, please, please, don't do anything stupid. Wait till I'm back."

I nodded.

Minutes later, I watched from my Uber how she was climbing into a different car, waving and she was gone. I rested my head on the headrest and closed my eyes. The stars appeared under my closed lids.

Thirty-Five

"I didn't know you knew Rachel," Jason said when he called the next day.

Everything grew cold inside me.

"My secretary was at the same bar as you two yesterday. Williamstone, wasn't it? She said you two had a pleasant chat, like you knew each other for a long time," he said.

"I . . ." I was lost for words. "Yes, we met previously. And when I met her at your party, she suggested we hang out."

That was so lame, I hoped he didn't press for details.

"Oh, okay. She's a saint in our company," he laughed coldly. "I think it's because she's gay she's so devoted to what she's doing."

"What?"

"She's a lesbian, Cassandra, didn't you know?"

I was silent, something clicking in place. The rough cold wall supported my weight when I leaned into it, standing in my office's smoke room.

"With a body like hers, you would think she'd make some man lucky, but I saw her with a woman a few years ago in

Central Park, her hands on her waist, so I guess Rachel's going to make some woman lucky," he laughed.

I chimed in, sounding flat.

"Anyway, I'll return home early. And I missed you," he purred. "Come over tomorrow evening, I have a surprise for you."

My throat closed, but a resolve pulsed in my mind. Even though Rachel asked me not to do anything while she's away, I needed to break the connection as soon as possible. "Yes, I'll be there."

"Perfect, see you soon, babe."

And he hung up.

Good, I would end everything. I would cut myself from him.

Thirty-Six

The next day, when Jason opened the door, he was wearing white shirt and soft pants, his fair hair a sexy mess on his head. I couldn't say a word before his lips crushed into mine, he pulled me close and his hand started roaming my body; in a second, he unhooked my bra. I hated how my body reacted to his touch, I felt the slow burning fire in the pit of my stomach. But he released me and led me into the living room.

"Please wait here," he said and disappeared into the adjoined room. I fastened my bra, my heart pounding.

He came back, a long dark green velvety box in his hand, a jewelry box. Jason put it in front of me, but I turned to him.

"I need to talk to you," I said.

His expression darkened for a moment and was back to smiling again.

"Sure."

"I'm leaving, Jason. I don't want this anymore, us. You know everything's based on sex between us, and I'm sure you could get this kind of sex or even better from any other woman."

And now the smile disappeared.

"Cassandra, I want you, not any other woman, you. You

make me feel powerful, and I know you enjoy it too, I know you weren't faking. So why do you want to make it stop?"

"Jason, relationships are not only about sex, they're about closeness, about being together, not only the animal rawness of bodies crushing together. And we didn't have anything but it," I said.

"Okay, I see, you want to be closer to me." He leaned back, a hand resting on the armchair. "We can fix it, move in with me."

"No, that's not what I'm saying." I imagined living here and an icy chill ran down my spine. "We're over, Jason."

He stood abruptly and sat by my side on the sofa, our thighs touching. I could not read his face. The years working in court made him a perfect actor.

"I want you to have my gift anyway," he said and placed a box in my lap. "Please open it."

"No, thank you. I need to go." I made a move to stand, but he placed a hand on my waist, pinning me down.

He opened the box; a necklace was there, a big pendant with a green emerald encrusted in the middle.

"The white gold's going to look perfect on your pale skin," he said. "I want you to have it as the last gift from me."

"I can't, Jason," I said, and he looked hurt, and this time I stood as his hand released me.

"Cassandra," he whispered, the pain on his face. "Have a glass of wine with me before you go. Please, I want to know why. I want you to be happy, but I must know. What went wrong?"

But I stepped to the door to leave this place.

"Please," he said quietly, something resembling hurt was written all over his face.

"Okay," I said, and he smiled, jumping up.

"Please wait here, I'll be back in a minute."

I sat on the couch, and my phone vibrated in my purse. Jane was asking if everything was fine; I did tell her that I would break up with Jason today.

He appeared in the doorway, two glasses in his hands, swirling of dark red.

He sat back in the armchair and placed a glass in front of me.

"You're the most beautiful woman I've ever met, and I want you to be happy," he said and clinked my glass, he took a swig from his, and I took a small sip from mine.

It was sweet, warming me. And I drank more, I needed some courage to stand and leave now.

In a few moments, the room swayed, my limbs getting heavier. Jason moved closer and took a glass from my hand.

"What's happening?" I asked, and tried to stand, but I couldn't feel my legs anymore, Jason caught me mid fall and rested me back on the couch. "What is . . ." and my tongue betrayed me also.

I felt his hand on the back of my head, and Jason's face was in front of me.

"Cassie, dear, you're not going anywhere, you're not leaving me, no one leaves me till I say so. You think you're so sophisticated, having a place of your own, a job, friends, but it all won't matter soon, because I own you now," he said, and my eyelids closed, the heaviest blanket pulling me down, "You're mine, Cassandra."

And everything went black.

I opened my eyes in his bedroom. The sun was shining outside, and my head pounded to the beat of my heart. The parched dry tongue barely moved in my mouth, my limbs still partially frozen. The panic clouded my mind for a moment, but I managed to push it away.

I moved the blanket and looked at myself. I was wearing his white shirt and my panties. There was no bra, and something sharp scraped my chest as I moved. With a shaking hand, I tugged on the hem of the shirt, and there, laying on my chest, was the necklace.

"I said it would suit you," Jason said standing in the doorway. "It laid so beautifully between your naked breasts, sexy," he chuckled and sat on the edge of the bed.

He was wearing his glasses again, the piercing green of his eyes matching the emerald on my neck.

I tried to stand, but my body was still so weak, my hands filled with lead. Jason caught my hand and placed it down on the blanket. He touched my face, stroking my cheek, dragging his fingers down my neck, my breasts, my belly, tracing my panties.

An image crossed my mind, and I almost retched on the white sheets.

"Did you touch me when I was unconscious?" I whispered, my dry throat making barely a sound.

"No, of course not," he laughed, "It's not my style, darling, I like when a woman responds to my touch. But I've heard stories from men who enjoy this kind of fetish."

"What did you give me?"

"Oh, it's a bit of this and that. You'd have been out after that first sip, but hungry as you always are, you drank more. It'll make you uncomfortable for a few days, which gives us plenty of time to talk."

I moved my hand again, my fingers didn't respond, a numbness filling my limbs. I tried to sit, but the strongest dizziness in my head swiped me back on the pillow. I turned my head to the nightstand, a dazzling pain slicing my skull.

"Where's my purse?" I croaked.

"You mean your phone? I took care of it; it's turned off in my safe now. But I wouldn't need to worry looking at how you barely can move."

Jane, I thought. She knew I was here, and since I clearly was out for a night, she would be worried.

Green eyes studied my face.

"You have loyal friends, you know," he said, as if reading my mind, steel notes in his calm voice. "Your phone kept vibrating, and when you were out it was so easy to unlock it. You never hid the passcode from me. I texted Jane from your phone saying that you decided to postpone breaking up with me, and you'll spend the weekend at my place. It was easy to mimic your texting style."

I closed my eyes.

He stood from the bed and walked out of the room. He was right, I could barely move, my hands hardly shifted, fingers frozen, and my legs still slept. I touched my thigh; I could only feel the echo of it.

I should have feared this man, but I knew Daniel, I knew Jason, he would not hurt me, he would only keep me prisoner, he would keep me with him.

Jason returned to the room.

"Cassie, you need to drink." He held a glass of water with a straw to my lips. I looked at him; the wall of green gazed back. I turned my head away.

"Even like this, barely in control of your movements you're the most beautiful thing I've ever seen," he sighed. "Drink it, it's just water, I promise. I don't need to knock you out again. And we'd need to talk, you need your voice back."

I scowled at him.

"Finally, some kind of emotion on that perfect face of yours," he smiled warmly. "You think you hate me, but you don't. You can't hate a person who takes you to the moon."

He stroked my cheek, and I opened my mouth to say something, but no sound came. My throat was scraping dry.

"Drink," he said and guided the straw to my lips.

I swallowed the liquid, one, two, three times. I felt a sliver of power rushing back.

"Good girl." He placed the glass on the nightstand. "Now we need to talk."

"Let me go," I said, my voice surprisingly stronger.

"Yes, that's the thing I wanted to talk to you about. I'll let you go, you're free to leave the place as soon as you're strong enough to walk. But before that, I need you to know one thing, and I wish we never came to this point, I wish you just loved me, you would move in with me, I would have you all to myself, you would marry me, we would be happy. With you by my side, I feel that I can do everything, but you decided to break it all."

And there was sadness on his face again, but I didn't believe him for a moment; he had proved himself to be a perfect actor. Jason lifted his hand and there was a remote control in his hand, he pointed it to the massive TV mounted on the wall.

A picture of this same room was on the screen, empty. I jerked my head to the corner of the dark wood panels where the image was coming from, and there, almost impossible to see, was hidden the smallest camera.

My heart pounded. The figures appeared on the screen: I was in Jason's bathrobe, he was in pants. He kissed me, and I leaned on him, my hands in his hair, his fingers stroking my neck. Jason paused the video.

"Look at this, you're happy, we're perfect together." And he unpaused.

His hand moved to unfasten the robe, and I was naked under it. I remembered this day clearly. I watched as he traced my skin, as his hand moved between my legs, as he turned me around pressing my back to his chest. And how I died in waves of pleasure on the screen.

My face in a pure image of ecstasy, Jason's hands holding me. And the next moment, I was on my knees, taking him in my mouth, and then minutes later, he was taking me from behind. Jason switched on the sound, and I heard myself moaning, pleading for more. My breasts were moving with his thrusts, and I crashed as I came, loud, panting, sweaty.

"You're beautiful, Cassandra," he murmured. "And I want

you to be mine only, because I know, only I could make you feel like this." He gestured to the screen. "But if you insist on leaving me, I'd need to make you a woman of the world."

A dread started creeping somewhere deep inside my head.

"First, I'll send this video to all your coworkers. Of course, I'll cut myself from it, only beautiful close ups of you'll go to the final version, how you eat me, how someone rides you."

I could not breathe, there was no air in this bedroom. I clutched the sheets, all the blood draining from my face.

"You wouldn't," I managed to say.

"It's your choice, Cassie. Either you stay with me, or you go and live freely." He put the two last words in imaginary quotes. "Did you know that every employee of your company is listed on the website with their email next to it? It's so easy I could do it myself, but as you know I'm a busy man, and I'd hire a search engine marketing company to help me. Did you know there are teams that specialize in distributing fake information? I would ruin your online presence. It's kind of funny, don't you think? I'll hurt you with the same methods as your daily job. And they'll do it constantly, they won't stop."

"No." I was breathing hard, but I knew it all was possible. And even if I could remove some of these fakes, I wouldn't be able to fight the whole bunch of people who'd spread dirt on my name online, day by day.

"And you're a smart girl, you know where it would lead. They'll fire you, and with the internet screaming with all the things that you did and did not, no one will hire you again. Everyone's checking online presence before hiring a person. And oh, you'll be the star of porn websites, I have so many videos of you here in this bedroom and all around the apartment. The shower, the kitchen, right by the entrance door, so many places I made you high."

I was trembling violently.

"Cassie." Jason stepped closer, he put a cold hand on my

forehead. "I wish none of this happened. Do you think I want everyone to see this footage? Do you think I want to share?" He lowered his lips to my cheek, the stubble scraping, he kissed a corner of my mouth, and then he found my ear. "I want you to be mine only."

"The team will follow all your movements, if you change your name, they'll change their tactics. They won't leave you alone, you can't run from them. How do I know? They destroyed a couple of influential people already. If you think about the Internet, it takes up so much space in our lives, but it could also hurt badly. So, this is one way your life can go if you leave this apartment tomorrow. The other way is much brighter. You leave this apartment to pack your things, I'll help you move here. All your life stays the same, your job, your friends, you live in the heart of the city, you have money, you have me."

Jason took my hands in his, and through the fog of numbness I felt how cold his hands were.

"I'll care for you, Cassandra, I promise. I'll remove all cameras, you will have the perfect clothes, the perfect life," he said and twirled a lock of my hair between his fingers.

"And do you think that after all of this I'd sleep with you?" I spat.

"I'll give you time to recover, to think about your life and behavior, to think about how grateful you should be, and then you'll crawl to my bed, you'll beg me to touch you."

"Never," I growled.

And I saw the fire burning in his eyes, the hunger.

"You can't believe how you turn me on with all resistance." He shook his head and stood. "Can't you see that you can have me? I'll do as you say, I'll serve you as long as you're mine."

"Liar. You can go and sleep with any other woman. How many have been there since the day we met?"

He stopped and turned to me.

"There's no point in lying: few," he said.

And his calmness was maddening; there was no pain, just a confirmation of what I knew already.

"I'm a man, Cassandra, with needs, and I take them when they give. But never have I met anyone who makes me feel like you do, I'm so obsessed with you to the point that sometimes I can't think straight. I need to know where you are and what you're doing. Thankfully, there are people who do it."

"Did they follow me?" I whispered, a downing sensation freezing everything inside.

"Sometimes, yes."

I tried to sit, my body shaking.

"Jason," I said, "do you remember?"

He looked confused. "What?"

"Do you remember Daniel?" I asked, but he looked puzzled. "Does the name of Sophia ring the bell?"

Something darkened in his eyes.

"I've never met any Sophias. But the name, I . . ." He looked down and rubbed his chest. "It stirred something. Who's she?"

"No one, it's from a story I read once," I said, and he looked confused.

"Do you film every woman that you bring here?" I asked, switching the topic.

"None of them I take to the bedroom, this room," he waved his hand, "it's only for you and me."

"I don't believe you, prove it," I said and pointed to a screen.

"I'm not sure it's such a good idea," he said.

"I want to see you with another woman," I said. "Now."

He shrugged and switched to a living room view and played back. And there he was, a beautiful woman clutching him as he took her, her eyes shut, the mouth slightly open.

"Sound," I growled.

And he turned it on. Jason watched me closely as my eyes were glued to the screen. The woman was naked, a pale beautiful body wrapped around Jason, her long blond hair spilled on the sofa. She had perfect form: Jason's hands on her full breasts, she moved her body to the rhythm, she was loud, she was losing it. And I watched as this beautiful woman came shuddering under Jason.

"You can have her, why me?" I asked, the room was filling with her moans. "She's more beautiful, she has the perfect body, she enjoys you."

He never took his eyes off me. "From the moment I saw you, I knew that I must have you." So simple.

And I knew, I looked down at my hands, I knew I had no choice, same as Sophia. I was trapped, sewn to the man who wanted to own me. But I would fight, and from the looks of it, I would sink fighting.

"I need to think about your suggestion," I lied.

"Of course, you have one week. If in a week from the day you leave this apartment you don't come back, all these videos leak online, and the marketing team starts working. By the way, you gave me an idea of this online strategy, you help people and brands grow, so there must be people who help destroy them. And it's untraceable, Cassie, they accept payment with bitcoins; it's a clean job."

Jason sat on the bed again, I tried to bend my legs closer to be as far from him as possible, but the drugs were still in my system, still numbing me. My knees only moved a few inches, I could not control them. He pushed back the blanket and touched the sole of my left foot. I didn't feel a thing. He traced his fingers higher, brushing my calves.

I jerked the blanket back with my trembling hands, clutching the fabric awkwardly with numb fingers.

"Don't touch me," I growled, the words sharp.

Jason smiled. "I'll be waiting for you in a week." He stood, his piercing green eyes lowered from my face to my neck, to the blanket I was clutching close. He chuckled and walked out of the room.

I breathed out and closed my eyes with a hand, pressing fingers to the sockets till I saw stars. And then I remembered the camera, and that he was watching. I dropped back to the pillow and pulled the blanket up, burying myself, covering my head, hiding from the camera lens. The camera that filmed me when I was most vulnerable, when I was most out of control, most open. And he hid them well, all around the apartment. And I knew that there was no one to blame but me for the lust and greed, for some kind of twisted magic that brought me back to Daniel in this life.

I laid there for hours, my limbs numb, my mind drowning in the fog of unnatural green till I drifted away.

Thirty-Seven

I opened my eyes to the white of the sheet and pulled it back immediately. I could tell it was still early in the morning, the light only barely touching the city outside the window. I flexed my fingers and almost laughed when I could feel them, move them. I lifted my legs, touched my toes; I was back in control of my body. And then I rushed to the bathroom, grabbing the towel to cover myself when I lowered on the toilet. Jason said that he was filming me in the shower too, and the big glass wall was just a few steps away.

I looked at it and remembered being pressed to the glass when he was behind. Bile rose to my throat, and I tried to push it away. I found my clothes on the chair in the bedroom and stepped right in the corner under the camera to change, standing in the blind spot.

The necklace was still on my neck, and I almost broke the chain when I tugged it through my head, it tangled in my hair, but finally landed in my palm. The green of the stone was the same as Jason's eyes, watching.

I dropped the necklace on the pillow on my way out of the room.

The apartment was silent as a tomb, I wanted to wreck it, to break every valuable thing he had there, but it would only add evidence to the camera. And I knew that the truly valuable items he had he stored in a big safe in his office.

My purse and my phone were on the kitchen table, the phone still switched off. I grabbed them and rushed to the door, my heart beating fiercely when I paused with my hand on the cool handle. What if it's locked?

But it went down under my touch, opening.

Outside, I hailed a cab, hugging myself from the morning chill. As the driver veered through the streets of the city I loved, I drank in every corner, saying a silent goodbye.

My apartment was the same, teeny-tiny, but I had decorated everything, I made it my home, my island of calm in the wild loud life of New York. I looked around at the same white walls, the same artworks, the vintage decorations, and my eyes landed in the corner where photos of my family, of Jane and Noah, of all of us laughing, were pinned.

And I fell to my knees and took the pillow from the sofa. I pressed it to my mouth, and I screamed till my throat was raw, till my lungs were empty, because I knew what I had to do.

Then, finally sitting back on the floor, I turned on my phone. It started vibrating in my hand from the string of messages.

Jane and Noah wanted to know if everything was okay, to call them. And a few messages from Rachel.

Rachel.

I closed my eyes, and saw her smile, how it warmed me, saw her eyes, how the stars shone just for me. And I knew that I had to protect her, to keep her out of this mess.

I thought about it, and I don't want to see you anymore. The past is the past, and I don't want it. Goodbye.

I stared at the message I just typed, my chest aching, till it blurred from the tears that fell on the screen.

I hit Send.

I cried silently as I blocked her number from contacting me, as I switched the settings of my social media accounts so only my friends could contact me. I would need to delete these accounts soon anyway.

And I felt that in this moment the world was crumbling, that my life I loved so much was coming to an end, ripping from my heart, and I tried hard to push the image of a beautiful woman with raven curls from my mind.

I texted Jane and Noah, asking them to come to my place.

Just thirty minutes later, the doorbell chimed. I shuffled to open the door, my left hand clutched to my chest, because the things I was going to tell them would break me even more.

Jane rushed through the threshold and flung her hands around me, pressing me close.

"I was worried," she said. "There was something strange in that message, and then your phone was off."

Noah stood silently watching us.

"What's happening?"

They didn't need my invitation to come in, they just walked inside and sat on the uncomfortable high chairs by the counter that divided the small kitchen space from the living room.

"Cassie?" Noah said and looked nervously at me.

I took a deep breath and leaned on the fridge.

"I need to leave the city and to quit my job, soon."

Jane gasped. "What, why?" she asked, her voice deepening. "What did he do?"

"What the hell, Cassie?" Noah said, standing up.

I sat on the third chair in front of them and tugged Noah back.

"Well, I messed up badly. Going out with Jason was a mistake, meeting him was . . ." I scratched my neck, trying to find words to describe my dreams. "It was meant to be, I'd say, but falling for him, tangling with him, it was my mistake. I was charmed, and never had I felt so important, so wanted, I was a goddess between the sheets. And the more time I spent with him, the more he needed me. And not in a beautiful loving way, no, in a cold possessive way. He wants to own me, for me to live with him in his cage. And I don't want it, I can't. He wants my body, my freedom, my soul."

Their eyes were huge, two pairs of shining saucers.

"And I tried to break up with him," I said.

"Jason won't let you go, he's the kind of a man who doesn't take no for an answer," Noah said, shaking his head.

I nodded. "His apartment's filled with small cameras, and he filmed us having sex. He has all these videos of me naked, splayed on the bed, in different positions."

"Sick bastard," Jane said, finding my hand, squeezing it.

"And well, he gave me a choice. I have a week to think, if in a week I don't come to live with him, all these videos will go to our colleagues' emails. He'll hire a goddamn team to spread filth about me online, the videos landing on major porn sites. And they won't stop."

Noah's eyes were filled with anger.

"There must be a way to stop him," he said. "We can go to the police."

I shook my head. "There won't be any traces leading to him. He said that the marketing team gets paid with bitcoins. Probably he found them somewhere on the dark web. And when it all unfurls, I don't want to be here, I don't want to talk to the police after they saw the videos of me crashing in sweaty delirium. Our whole office would see me with his cock in my mouth."

Jane flinched. "What are you going to do?"

"I won't go back to him. I'll run back to my parents, to my

old room and bury myself under the covers. I'll quit my job, leave my apartment, I'll erase my online profiles and lay low. When the wave hits, I want to be as far from New York as possible. Later, I'll work freelance. Because no one will ever hire me to work in an office, I simply won't pass the checks with all the new information spread online."

Big shiny tears were rolling down Jane's cheeks, Noah's face was pale, they both held my hands. And looking at them, I tried with all my might to stay calm to not turn into sobbing goo right here.

"He takes New York from me, he destroys my career, my life. I'm sure with his inflated ego he thinks I'd choose him. But no, I'm choosing freedom, severed as it will be."

Noah pressed his manicured fingers to his eyes, and a soft sob escaped his lips.

"I'm so sorry, Cassie. This is so unfair. This shouldn't be happening. What can we do?"

I stood and crossed the counter; I hugged them both, the warm bodies shaking.

"Nothing," I whispered. "I'm going to sink so low."

"We're going with you," Jane said, her voice wet from the tears that choked her. "We'll be by your side when all hell erupts."

And now I was crying. The three of us, a sobbing mess, and I could not say no. Because I would need my friends when the blow landed. And when the wet tears were running down my skin, burning, when my heart was aching, the eyes the color of the night appeared in my mind, with the face I already missed so badly, the raven curls, the full lips. And I wanted to see her one more time, but no, I would protect her. I would keep her away. Because the last time she stayed with me, with Sophia, it ended with a bullet in her heart.

Minutes later, the three of us moved to the sofa and I lay in the crook of Jane's arm. Noah's head rested in her lap. We stayed silent for a long time.

"What are you going to do next?" Jane asked, her voice chiming in the eerie silence in the room plunged into the shadows of the early evening.

"Tomorrow, I'll take sick leave from work and pack; thankfully, my lease runs out at the end of this month, and I'll let the landlord know that I'm going to move out. The next day, I'm going to the office, I'll come up with some kind of emergency that needs me back in Tallahassee, and I'll quit."

"They're going to suggest you work remotely, Fred would be furious at you for leaving the project," Noah said.

Fred was my boss and my mentor; he raised me as a professional. He was always strict, but his help and guidance made me want to learn all the time, to improve. And this project we were working on was the first project where I was a manager, and after a few blunders, it was growing. It was one more thing Jason was taking from me: the respect and trust of my coworkers. Making me leave now, when the project I nurtured from the beginning was so close to success.

"I can't take the remote job offer, I wish I could, but still being connected to the company will ruin me. Fred will look at me like I'm filth," I said.

It hurt. I worked so hard to earn his respect, to prove that I was good at my job. Now the video of me would land in his inbox, and after it, he wouldn't be looking at me the same. I hated it so, so much. And a hot flash of pure hatred rolled over me towards Jason.

The warm hand pressed to my forehead. Jane.

"I'm so sorry this is happening, I wish there was a way to stop it," she murmured.

"Yes," I echoed.

Noah took my hand and squeezed it tight.

Thirty-Eight

That night was awful, I could not close my eyes, because all I saw in the shadows of the night were glimpses of the footage. I sat on a high chair in the kitchen, where only hours ago I was talking to Jane and Noah. The mint tea was warming my hands when everything in my body was slowly freezing. I dropped my head in my hands and took a shuddering breath.

Rachel.

I tried not to think about her, I tried to focus on my busy days ahead, of packing, of fleeing.

But my thoughts went back to her face, to her smile. Even though I saw her only twice in this life, the powerful connection Sophia and Will had in the previous one tugged the hidden strings of my heart.

I found her social media pages, and even if I blocked her, I still could see her profiles. Just a few photos on neglected pages, and I sat there silently, between the noise of a night in New York, the city that never slept, and I looked at the close-up portrait of her. And I smiled, lightly touching the screen. I remembered how Sophia felt with Will's hands around her, protecting.

How blind I had decided to be when I knew that this kind of

closeness was possible, when I remembered the light, just to fall into the trap of darkness.

I shuffled to my bed, the cold floor chilling my soles. I connected my phone to the charger and turned off the auto lock on the screen. I tried to stop the cold tremor of my body that started at Jason's apartment, but it was still there, even as wool socks now itched my toes, my icy hands never found warmth. I draped the blanket closer to my chin and turned to the left side, the dimmed screen of the phone showing a picture of woman with raven curls, those eyes the color the night when you stand in the field, somewhere far away from any city, and where you see the sky with all the stars.

Finally, sleep covered my mind.

A few hours later, I opened my eyes to the same picture and smiled at her, but the smile faded fast from my lips, a dull ache reminding me of reality.

I called the office, saying that I had food poisoning and that I would do my best to be in the office tomorrow.

I tried not to think when I pulled out of the closet the pack of flattened cardboard boxes. I was numb, packing my clothes first, moving to the kitchen and then the bathroom. The apartment was small, but box after box was filling. I barely breathed, my hands working, the hollow in my chest growing bigger with each second.

I was holding a set of towels when the doorbell chimed. My heart beating fast, I stepped closer when I heard Jane's voice through the door. I unlocked it.

"What are you . . ." I said, but my voice died in my chest.

Between Jane and Noah stood Rachel. Her eyes instantly connected with mine and I froze. My left hand flew to my mouth, but the right did something surprising. It stretched in

Rachel's direction, close to her hand, and in a moment, I was in her arms, no space between us, my fingers lost in the silk of her hair, my face in the crook of her shoulder. I inhaled the fresh smell of the forest, and my nose touched the skin of her neck. Her hand was holding gently the back of my head, the other pressed to my waist.

And in her arms, the tremor stopped, and I sighed slightly.

"I'm here," she whispered, and I opened my eyes.

Jane stood open-mouthed while Noah grinned wildly.

"You shouldn't be here," I said quietly, taking a step back. But my hand was still in hers, and I felt the warmth pulsing.

"So, it seems that you know each other," Jane said, her voice unnaturally high pitched, trying not to look at our connected hands.

"It's a long story," I said.

"We've heard a part of it," Noah said.

"Noah and I were heading to lunch, exiting the building, and this woman," Jane said and pointed to Rachel, "stopped us and started asking about you. Of course we didn't say anything, then she started telling a crazy story of dreams..."

"Sophia?" Noah whispered.

And the way he titled his head I saw a glimpse of Elena, there and gone in a flash.

"Yes, it's the name from the story," Jane said impatiently, missing the moment completely.

"Do you remember?" I asked, all eyes on Noah.

He slowly shook his head. "Remember what?"

Jane glanced at her smart watch and gasped.

"We should be back in the office. But you," she pointed at me, "you owe us the whole story. We'll be back in the evening."

Her demeanor changed when she looked at Rachel.

"Please help her," Jane whispered and turned around, rushing away.

Noah stood there, a faraway look in his eyes. "I want to know in the evening what I don't remember," he said quietly.

He shook his head and squeezed my shoulder. "See you soon, Cassie."

And they were gone.

I turned to Rachel, and I could not believe she was standing there. She brushed a thumb over my hand and smiled.

"Can I come in?" she said.

I tried to pull myself back to reality from the warmth of the night.

"Yes, sorry, please," I said and opened the door wider.

She walked inside and I watched her from behind, pressing myself to a closed door. Rachel was wearing a cropped pantsuit with white sneakers and a white shirt. She stopped in the middle of the living room and looked at all the boxes.

"What did he do?" she asked, her voice like liquid steel.

She turned to me, and I fought the urge to rush to her, to touch her porcelain skin. So I just circled around her and gestured for her to sit on the sofa. I moved the boxes from it and sat by her side, our knees touching. The shame blocked my lungs, it was difficult to breathe, but it all cleared when she took my hand in hers again, when our fingers entangled together.

And I told her everything. She squeezed my hand tighter, and her nostrils flared, but still she listened to me without interrupting.

"Why did you cut me off?" she asked at the end.

"Because I want you to be safe," I whispered and looked into her dark eyes.

Rachel moved back, a look of wonder on her face. Then she stood and paced the room.

"Even if you run, Jason will find you. He'll bring you back, he'll come up with more ways to blackmail you. And after he releases the videos, you'll be vulnerable, which he would see as more of a challenge, he won't let you go. He'll threaten the wellbeing of your family, of your friends, till he has you."

I clutched the soft edge of the sofa, breathing hard. She was right.

"What should I do?" I asked, my sight blurring from the tears.

Rachel stopped and turned to me.

"Are you sure you don't want to be with him?" she asked.

Her eyes darkened, a hint of fear flashed on her face.

"No, of course no! I want to break free from his dark spider web."

Rachel nodded, relief lightening her features. "I know how to help you," she said. "Jason wants to have you, but one thing he'll place above any of his wishes is saving his head. A few weeks after I joined his company, he was installing cameras all over the office. But one place was soundproof and camera less—his room. He is obsessed with filming evidence. And I was inspired by his method, and, with all the commotion of office reconstruction, I managed to install a small camera in his office, hidden in a place he never looked," she said and inhaled shakily. "And, Cassie, the things I have heard and seen through that camera made my fingers curl. He discussed everything with Simon in detail, the amount of drugs, money laundering, and girls. How many young women came to Jason's room after Simon hurt them, the poor souls didn't know how to fight, and how Jason smooth talked them into taking money and never mentioning Simon again. Simon's a devil, and Jason's his advocate."

My heart was beating fast.

"And I saved all the talks. I knew sooner or later I'd need to have leverage against him," Rachel said. "Or you'll need it. And I was right." She smiled widely.

"But he can hurt you when he finds out," I said, shaking my head. "No, no, Rachel, it's too dangerous for you. I'll take the hit, I'll disappear, but you need to stay safe," I said, standing up and walking to the window.

I was standing there, looking outside, my fingers curled in fists, nails digging into the skin.

"I can't live in the world without you," I whispered, "You know I can't. Sophia took her life shortly after Will's heart stopped beating. Now that I know you exist, even if I'm miles away, I need you to be safe."

I heard cautious steps behind me, and I felt her standing right next to me. She touched my fists with warm fingertips.

"I was looking for you for so long," she said, and I felt a soft touch on the back of my wrist. "You must trust me, Cassie. The previous time Will was careless, he didn't prepare for a fight, he was blinded by his newfound feelings. This time, I had time to collect all the needed information to strike back. We'll finish it, he'll let you go, or all three of us will sink."

I turned to her. The dark eyes fixed on me, power kindling in them.

"One of his people saw us talking in the bar. Afterwards, Jason told me you're gay," I said.

Her hands dropped to her sides as she looked directly at me.

"I was influenced powerfully by the previous life I had, it's not a secret," she said.

"But I'm not," I said, looking away, "gay."

She nodded, "I know. Do you want me to stay away?"

I shook my head. "I just can't understand how I'm so . . ." I tried to find the right words, "pulled to you."

"I guess it's our history. When I saw that Daniel was a man in this life, I realized that Sophia would be a woman. For me, it meant two things: one good and one really bad. Good, it was suitable since I was attracted to women, bad, that you would be straight and have no interest in me. So I decided that being a friend would be enough."

She sat on the sofa, her eyes crinkling, a warm smile on her lips. And in a moment, I was back, I was Sophia, and she was Will, and the light shone between them. But I was in a different body, and he was too. My skin ached in different places, and I swayed lightly.

"Come here," she whispered, and I sat by her side, too close.

"I'll talk to Jason tomorrow, you'll be free, Cassie. He'll let you go. If something happens to me, the files will leak online and to the police, same if something happens to you. You'll be safe," she said.

"I'm going with you," I said.

"No," she almost growled. "No way, he's dangerous."

"Yes, he is. That's why I can't let you go by yourself, you're too fragile."

She snorted. "I'm not."

"The last time you were not and look how it ended."

"The last time we were not prepared! Now everything's different, we have the power to fight, not to flee," Rachel said.

"I'm going with you," I said again. "We'll face him together, tomorrow it'll all end, one way or another."

She was silent for a long time, looking down at her lap.

"Fine, but if anything happens to you, I'm going right after you, and our lives will play all over again," she said, fire playing behind her features.

I curled by her side, her hand on my shoulders.

"I'm afraid," she said. "Just a little."

"I'm terrified," I laughed, but saying this made me realize that it sounded worse than I actually felt.

We stayed on that sofa till the evening shadows poured into the room. We just laid there, my head on her shoulder, her cheek pressing the top of my head, her hands on my shoulders, our hearts beating faster than usual.

"You're going to lose your job," I said.

"Yes, but I have enough savings to stay afloat till I find a new job. And it shouldn't be difficult after the immaculate references Jason's company will provide," she chuckled.

"I hope everything works out," I whispered and buried my face in her neck. The soft smell of the forest hit my nose, and I inhaled deeply.

The doorbell rang and I twitched.

"These are probably your friends," she said.

I completely forgot that they were coming, my mind was elsewhere, on tomorrow's plans, but mostly fixed on the woman who laughed just now.

"Good luck explaining everything," she said and grinned.

I opened the door and a tornado of Jane whirled inside. She turned to me.

"You can't drop this weird information about dreams and expect me to go back to work, I barely waited till the end of the workday." She stomped into my kitchen and took out one glass and filled it full to the brim with wine from my fridge.

"Oh," she noticed Rachel and her disheveled suit. "You're still here," Jane murmured, but there was no menace in her voice, just a vague interest. "I don't want to know what you were doing here."

"She's lying." Noah walked in after Jane and took out three more glasses and poured some wine. "Jane's dying to know what's happening," he said and took a huge sip from his glass, motioning for me and Rachel to take ours. "So do I."

Rachel looked at all of us with amusement.

"Let's get comfortable," I said weakly, pointing to the living room.

Noah darted to his usual spot by the left wing of the sofa, groaning when he leaned on his favorite pillow. Jane sat on the low pouf, folding her legs, Rachel sat on the other side of the sofa, earning a smile from Noah. I lowered myself into the armchair.

I took a deep breath and looked around. Three pairs of eyes

shone at me, one crackling with a faint delight, and I barely managed to stop myself from sticking a tongue at her. Rachel was enjoying this so much.

"So," Noah said.

"I don't know where to start," I said and looked at my hands. This conversation would be so weird.

"Start from the beginning," Jane said.

I took a deep breath. "When I was in high school, I started having these dreams about a girl named Sophia who lived in Riga."

"Where's that?" Jane asked.

"Latvia," Noah and I said simultaneously, which made him pale.

"I saw the world through her eyes," I said and told in as many details as possible the story of Sophia, Daniil and Will.

"But as time went by, I started to forget about the life I saw; I moved here, I met you guys, none of it was similar. I didn't want to face the truth when Jason said that I was his, like Daniel kept repeating to Sophia. Everything clicked in place when I met Rachel," I said and dropped my head into my hands.

Rachel leaned closer and I felt her touch on my shoulder, I lifted my eyes to hers and squeezed her hand gently.

"So what, are you together now?" Jane asked, her gaze on our hands.

"Give them a break," Noah said, standing up and walking to the window.

Everyone was silent, the curious look at Jane's face turned to worry as she watched Noah.

"Noah?" I whispered. "Are you okay?"

He turned to look at me.

"Yes, it's just so weird to hear about your previous life, and you say that I was a woman named Elena who was a maid in Riga," he said and shook his head.

"I'm not sure," I said, "I'm only sure about Rachel and

Jason, because I never told anyone and Rachel has the same story, and I felt her and Jason, he has the same eyes, uses the same words. So I'm not sure about you being Elena."

"The thing's that I'm sure." He dropped his head and looked at the floor. "When I was in my early years of university, I dreamt about a city I have never seen in my real life, I could not identify it. I dreamt about walking the streets, and I dreamt about a man, his kind eyes, he was between rows of fruits and vegetables."

"Grocery store," I said quietly.

Noah jerked his head up. "What did you say?"

"Elena met a man who worked in the grocery store when Sophia was leaving for America."

His face became even paler. "Right. It took some time for me to Google the name of the city I was seeing in my dreams. I walked numerous streets of European cities on Google maps till I finally stumbled upon Riga. And that man, I saw him young, I saw him older, I saw his arms around me, and I never felt so at peace as when I dreamed about him. Till I met David," he said. Of course, the gallery manager. Noah added, "The strangest things kept happening as if I knew him already, but still I was afraid of the feeling. I almost pushed him away. And now, after everything you said, everything has clicked in place. The thing I didn't want to acknowledge was that he's the man from my dreams."

"Guys, you do know that it's not normal to remember your previous lives?" Jane said. "Cassie, Noah, you know I love you. Rachel, I need to know you more, but since you have a history with Cassie, and I have a feeling much more to come, there won't be a problem."

Rachel smiled so widely, the light sparks playing in her dark eyes.

"But why do you think you all remember it? I've never had dreams like those. I rarely dream at all," Jane said.

"Maybe that's the clue? I was an avid dreamer before I walked the streets of Riga, I even played with lucid dreaming," Noah said.

"You know, me too, I always loved seeing dreams. Before I dreamt of Sophia, I had a dream journal and I practiced remembering my dreams," I said.

Rachel shook her head. "I almost never remember my dreams."

"But you saw everything when you were out from the car accident. Maybe the shock of a hit made you remember."

"I thought so too, but at that time I thought I was going crazy, and I tried to bury everything deep down till I met Jason, and then I knew these were not just dreams," Rachel said.

We all went silent, everyone deep in their thoughts.

"I'm not sure I'd like to remember my previous life," Jane said slowly. "Noah's nice and settled with David, but look at you two," she gestured to me and Rachel. "This Daniel, Jason, he killed a man, just shot him, and Sophia held the warm body of a man she loved, to the moment his heart stopped beating, and then she went and put a bullet in her heart. Cassie, I saw how you withered away with Jason, a huge contrast to how Noah bloomed after he met David, and then you say that you need to leave the city, your old life, because the sick bastard blackmailed you. And how you can't hide the glances you give another woman, how two of you move in unison, how from the moment I saw you together today one or another part of your bodies is touching. And now it seems that two of my friends are gay."

"I'm not gay!" I cried, blushing violently. For the first time in my life, I felt that even the tips of my ears burned. I could not bring myself to look at Rachel.

"Of course, love," Jane cooed at me. "But when I see how Rachel watches over you, and how your body language is so attuned to her, even if you're not aware of it, it makes me wonder about my previous life and people I knew. But your lives had so much drama, and, well, it all transferred to this life. Now I'm afraid of every bad dream I have because it could be a memory, which leads to something in this life," she said and scratched her temple, taking a gulp of wine, "God, I need something stronger."

"Tequila?" I asked.

"Maybe later," she said and looked at the three of us. "And now I'm a bit jealous. You all were connected, but where was I in that life?"

"I think Sophia would have met you later in life, but since she decided to go early there was not a chance," Rachel said.

Noah nodded and I leaned back into the armchair, closed my eyes and breathed out. The events of today, all the revelations, it all took a toll on me.

"Do you think these videos will be enough to threaten Jason into letting Cassie go?" Noah asked quietly.

"They must be, there are so many details, enough to bury Simon and Jason with him. And I'm sure he wouldn't be reckless enough. He could not have Cassie while staying in jail anyway," Rachel said.

My heart was beating so fast in my ribcage, fear pounding in my veins. What if these videos were not enough? What if he had something more on me? What if he hurt Rachel? I was breathing hard when warm fingers touched my cheek, and I opened my eyes. Rachel's face was close, worry in her eyes.

"Everything's going to be alright. He won't hurt you," she said.

"He can hurt *you*," I whispered.

"No, he can't, trust me," she said and kissed my forehead, bringing me back to the room from the place of fear.

Noah was beaming. He stood from the sofa and turned to Jane.

"We need to go," he said.

Jane was sitting on her pouf, her mouth hanging open again. She rushed to her feet and took my wrist.

"I need to talk to you for a second," she said.

Jane led me to my tiny bedroom and closed the door behind her.

"Why didn't you tell me that you were gay?" she whispered.

"Because I'm not gay!"

"Bisexual?"

I shrugged. I did not know.

"You're so into Rachel, you should have seen your face, how it changes every time you look at her, and how she looks at you, so much trust and light. Wow. You have to tell me later how it works between women."

I groaned. "It's not like that!"

"Yeah, okay," she laughed and winked. "When you're ready."

I stomped out of the bedroom, my cheeks burning, while Jane trailed me, giggling.

Rachel and Noah stood by the window, talking. Noah, who rarely trusted people, who always was so cautious, stood so relaxed, so at ease with Rachel. This time, Jane walked to Noah and said that they needed to go.

In the doorway, Jane turned to Rachel and threw her arms around her.

"Thanks for saving Cassie," she said.

And it would have been the perfect moment if Jane didn't add, "And you know, you smell delicious," still holding Rachel in her arms, "maybe I should find myself a girlfriend?"

Noah and I let out a groan, he unpeeled Jane from Rachel, and dragged her out of the door.

"Good luck tomorrow, keep us updated," he said, and they disappeared in the hallway.

Rachel closed the door and turned to me.

"That was interesting," she said.

"They liked you."

Rachel smiled, and I was again lost in the night full of stars. She walked closer to me, and I stood there, watching. What Jane said was right, I wanted to touch Rachel every second of being in her presence, to feel her silk skin under my fingertips. Rachel lowered her gaze to my lips, and I gasped lightly when she touched my elbow.

"You need to rest," she said and led me to the bedroom.

My heart hammered when she lowered herself on my bed, gently tugging me towards her. I fit perfectly into the crook of her arms, laying there, my pulse beating in anticipation, but she did not move, her chin pressing to the top of my head.

"You need to calm down," she chuckled. "I can practically read your thoughts, how loud they are. And your heartbeat betrays you."

She put a palm to my neck, feeling the pulse. My heart seemed to pick up even more speed, fluttering under the touch. Rachel lifted her hand and put it on my shoulder, snuggling me into her.

And I felt myself calming, fitting with her like a puzzle. The steady rise and fall of her chest was like a meditation to me, and I listened to it, and I dreamed of the clear night sky as I stood on the edge of a forest.

I opened my eyes to a touch on my cheek. Rachel squatted in front of me, her face level to mine.

"I need to go home to prepare the videos," she said.

I nodded and started to sit up, but she pressed me gently back into the covers.

"I'm going with you," I said.

"It's two in the morning," she laughed. "I'll meet you by your building entrance at 10 AM, okay?"

I nodded, taking my phone from the nightstand and

opening the Alarm app. I was not sure I would be sleeping anymore today, but just in case.

Rachel stood, and I saw her movements in the dim light from the window. Her hands shook slightly, a hard expression on her face. This time she could not stop me from leaping from the bed; in a few steps, I was by her side, cupping her chin, turning her eyes to me.

"Thank you," I whispered, "for fighting for me."

Rachel moved closer, and I glanced down to her lips, just for a moment, and looked away fast, blushing. But she smiled and touched my shoulder lightly. I let out a shuddering breath and stepped back.

"I'm sorry," I whispered.

Rachel kissed my cheek and walked to the door. She turned to me, her hand on the handle.

"Finally, I found you."

The soft click of the door was much quieter than my thundering heart.

Thirty-Nine

I managed to sleep for a few more hours, and after six in the morning, I was sitting by the kitchen table, trying to calm my trembling hands.

In ten minutes, I was sitting in my dark jeans, a black T-shirt, and my hair was up in a ponytail, wearing no make-up. My phone pinged with worried texts from Jane and Noah, and by 7 AM I was pacing the tiny space of my apartment. I called Rachel.

"Can I come, please?" I asked. I didn't know where she lived. I realized that I did not know much about her at all, and it was the strangest thing about trust. But I would die for her, and in some ways, I already had as Sophia.

"Are you okay? Is everything alright?" She sounded worried.

"Yes, I just can't sit here anymore. I . . ." *need you.* I didn't finish this sentence, but it was as though she knew the end anyway.

"I'll text you the address."

I was already by the door when I copied the address she sent to Uber. She lived only fifteen minutes away, but with thousands of people between us, we had never met before.

Twenty minutes later, I stood by her doorway. She was

wearing black sports leggings, a shirt with Donald Duck and white fluffy socks. She pulled me into her the moment she saw me, and I was back in the forest again, the songs of the night birds in my ears.

She took my hand and let me inside. The apartment was small, but so light: massive paintings decorated the white walls, her initials on the corner of each one. An oriental rug was spread in the middle of the living room and a vintage coffee table held two laptops and a battered old iPad. A cable ran from an iPad to the Mac.

"All the information's backed up hundreds of times, the copies are given to the people I trust, and hard copies are hidden in safe places," Rachel said.

I nodded and lowered myself to a small couch.

"Do you want coffee?" she asked.

"Yes, please."

My eyes were glued to the paintings on the wall; the bold strokes of oil paint showed a crowded bar and women in vintage dresses. The old New York, the golden age, was long gone. Smaller paintings showed the streets of the city. But the biggest canvas was of a field littered with flowers, the colors so vivid. The field stopped at the foot of green hills. I stood enchanted by nature, and I could almost feel the soft breeze caressing my arms.

Rachel stood by my side, the smell of coffee wafting with her.

"Where is it?" I asked.

"My parents have a ranch in North Carolina, far away from any civilization. I go there often," she said, a warmth sipping in every word.

"Did you paint it there?"

She nodded.

And, for a moment, I forgot that just in a few hours I would be standing in front of the monster who wanted to own me, a glitch in his twisted mind making him want to possess my body, my soul.

I was in the middle of the flowery field, and the woman who found me was standing close. The calmness of her gaze steadied me. And under this canvas I turned to this same woman, and I pressed my lips to hers. A little sigh escaped her lips as she met me, as she tried to fight the urgency in my movements, her hands roaming my neck, the back of my head, sending prickles down my core. I was lost in the raven curls, in the night sky, in the sweetness of her tongue. There was no air between us, memories of other people who we were, other bodies, all blending in the thread of hope for the future we might have.

A door of light opened in my chest as I hugged her, as we breathed hard, as we stood lost in each other, daring to hope.

So many words were left unsaid between us as we looked into each other's eyes. Rachel traced my brow with her fingertips, a mix of emotions swirled on her face.

"Sorry," I whispered.

"For what?" she arched her eyebrow.

"For kissing you."

She chuckled. The dark eyes watched me under the curly fringe. "I can take it."

※

Two hours later, we were sitting in a car which slowly crawled through the New York traffic. My leg twitched and I tried to look out of the window, but every time my eyes went back to Rachel's face. She sat there, a wall of calm, her hand holding mine. After what seemed like the twentieth time of me glancing in her direction, she lifted my hand and kissed the back of my palm.

"Everything's going to be alright," she said.

I smiled, but my knee kept moving in a staccato rhythm.

I caught the eye of the driver who glanced at us from the rearview mirror, and how he rolled his eyes when he saw our hands clasped together. But there was no menace in his gaze. And at first, I could not understand his reaction, but then it dawned on me that I was with a woman and that we looked like a couple. I was smiling when I dropped my head on Rachel's shoulder and when she draped her hand around me, pulling me closer. A few moments of peace before the world erupted to hell.

My knees almost buckled when I entered the hallway of Jason's building, the mirror in the elevator showed my pale face and almost bloodless lips. The fear gripped my body. We knew that he would be home. Rachel said he had a late meeting today, and he never came to the office before a meeting.

I rang the bell; my hands were shaking so much I had to hide them in my pockets.

Jason opened the door. He was wearing a gray shirt that hugged his body, the muscles on his arms rippling under the fabric and his favorite sports pants which hung loosely on his sculpted torso. A sly smile spread on his face as he looked me up and down, his eyes stopping at my breasts. I almost ran.

"You're early, dear. But come in, come in," he said and gestured to me to go inside.

Rachel stepped out of the shadows; she had been standing out of the door camera's reach.

"You brought a friend," he said, a smile slightly faltering, but staying the same. The acting part turned on.

Jason turned and walked inside, the door opened after him. Rachel went next, her fingers brushing mine before she disappeared inside. I grabbed the door frame to steady myself and took a deep breath. This would be over soon, I thought. Never again would I come back to this place.

I lifted my head and went after them into the kitchen.

"I'm not coming back to you," I said.

He merely shrugged. "It's your choice, we discussed the consequences."

And in that moment, I did not care that he would use my videos against me, that I would need to leave New York and my job, I just wanted not to be here, to be somewhere away. A flowery field came to my mind.

"We have a counteroffer for you," Rachel said, her voice calm.

"She did tell you everything, right?" Jason asked. "You know, that's the strange thing about you two. I'm sure you have never met each other before, I checked. And just after a couple of times together you act like you're best friends." He ran his hand through his hair, his smile turning darker, crueler. "Or even more . . . Do you like girls, Cassandra? You could have told me, I'd have supplied you with women, the three of us could play nicely. That pretty face of yours between the woman's legs while I took you."

"Enough," Rachel barked as I was clutching the marble countertop to find my strength. "You made her an offer, and I have an offer for you."

She took an old iPad from her bag and opened the video app on it. The gallery of the same office room.

"Where should we start?" she asked. "This one's nice."

She tapped something and turned the screen to Jason.

Familiar voices filled the room: Jason and Simon. They were discussing the batch of cocaine that would need to be distributed.

Jason's smile was still in place, but it was turning into a grimace with every sentence uttered in the silence of the kitchen.

"Let's hear more," Rachel said and paused this one just to play the next.

In this conversation, they talked about ways of distributing the powder to younger kids. They talked about elite schools and how the experiment they held in Baltimore was a success.

"They buy our stuff like crazy," Simon said.

"I told you it was a good idea to target children of rich people," Jason replied.

And it went on and on.

In the next video, there were two people in the office again—Jason and a young girl. Her dove-like neck was lowered down, her angelic face red with tears. She was barely a teenager, the features of a child still so pronounced in her. Her hands were pressing to her stomach.

I jerked my face to Jason as I listened to him sweet talk her into an abortion and staying silent. I remembered Rachel said that Simon liked young women, but this one was just a kid. My face was turning hot as I listened to the veiled threats, as he gave her an envelope of money. The acrid bile rose to my throat as I saw the man on the video, as I remembered his hands on me, these same hands that paid off the girl who was violated.

There was no more smile on Jason's face as he watched the video. His skin grew paler and beads of sweat glistened on his forehead.

"Bitch," he growled, "you filmed my office."

"Yes, everything's on the tape, everything," Rachel said. "So the offer is this: You have intimate videos of Cassandra you wanted to share with the world, I have videos of you and Simon I want to share with the police. As long as those videos of yours stay hidden, shared with no one, the videos I have will stay in a secure place. You need to let her go, Jason. Never to cross paths with Cassie again, stay away. As long as she never sees you again and those videos are secure, we're even."

"And you have to let Rachel go from your job without a fuss. She'll quit and you'll send her away with immaculate references," I said.

The vein on Jason's neck pulsed very quickly. I almost missed the moment when he moved; in the blink of an eye he rushed to Rachel, his hand clasping her neck.

"Why would I do it?" Jason growled, his face inches from Rachel's, the skin on her face turning red, mouth trying to take a breath. "I could destroy that iPad; I could destroy you both here and it all would be over before my morning meeting."

I had seen it all before in different ways: the hand clasped around the neck, the threats, Will's body on the floor, a red stain growing under him.

My icy hand wrapped around a metal handle of a kitchen knife from the stand by my side and I gripped it hard when the blade stopped at Jason's neck. He wheezed.

"Let her go," I said calmly.

He didn't stir, I moved my hand a little, burying the edge in his skin, nothing but a cut yet, but the small trickle of blood marked the hem of his shirt.

"The story of the three of us goes a long way back," I said. "It can repeat again."

"No," Rachel croaked, the white of her eyes veiled by a red web already.

I pressed the knife a bit harder, slicing the skin deeper. Still he held his grip.

"You wouldn't do it," Jason said.

There was fear in Rachel's eyes now, her gaze on the knife I held. Her body tensed, and then she wriggled her hand and punched Jason in the solar plexus.

His fingers relaxed for a second, and Rachel moved. Her first move should have been to flee, to move out of his way, but her hand went to the knife; she yanked it from my hand, clasping her fingers around it and throwing it on the floor, far away from us.

"You're wrong, Jason," Rachel rasped, her left hand going to her neck, red already, the other taking my hand.

Jason was bent in half, trying to take a breath.

"The thing is, she would have done it, she would have sliced you open," she said.

He lifted his head, finally a trickle of air going into his lungs.

The cut of his neck oozed blood, but not much, staining his shirt.

And I stood there, my hand gripped hard between Rachel's fingers, but all I wanted was to hurt him, to destroy. I wanted to lunge for the knife, I wanted to bury it in his neck, the murderous violence buzzed in my veins. He wanted to take everything from me, and he had taken it before.

Jason looked at me, his hands still on the middle of his chest as though protecting the sensitive part. But what he saw in me made his eyes go wider, a sliver of fear on his face. I looked at the knife laying a few steps away, and I imagined it burying in his flesh, the warm rivers of his blood on my fingers. I looked back at him, and my lips curled, the images from my crazed imagination showing me the revenge. When our eyes met again, the dread made his jaw go slack. He took a step back, gripping the countertop with a shaking hand.

But everything stopped when someone grabbed my face hard, and all I saw was night again, the stars.

"Stop it, Cassie, it's not you," Rachel begged.

"I'll kill him," I said simply. The images of his blood on my hands making me smile again. "He took Will from me."

"I'm here!" she cried.

"He wanted to take my life from me," I growled.

"Look at me," she said and lowered my face to hers. "Cassie, really, look at me. Now *you* want to take his life. He does not deserve it, and I won't allow it. I can't lose you."

In the corner of my eye, I saw Jason crouched in the corner; it was still difficult for him to take a breath.

The red wave of anger finally loosened its grip, making me focus on the woman in front of me.

"You're hurt," I said and touched her neck gingerly, the dark print on her skin.

"Oh, thank god," she whispered and ran her fingers over my

cheek, pressing her forehead to mine for a second. "Let's get out of here."

She turned to Jason who looked at us with confusion soaked in dread.

"What's the story between the three of us?" he asked quietly.

"You killed a person I loved in order to have me; you didn't have me in the end," I said.

"What?"

"It doesn't matter anymore," Rachel said. "It's good if you don't remember it."

"You both are insane," he cried.

And now a smile spread on Rachel's face. "Agree to the deal and you'll never have to see us again, delete those videos of Cassie and go back to your life. Forget about us, about this nightmare."

He stood there silent. "If those videos you have stay hidden, I agree."

"Deal," Rachel said and tugged me to the exit, my body stiff.

One leg in front of another, the tsunami of fury was not so far away. I turned back to the kitchen entrance. And that wave was coming again, I saw that child from the video clutching her belly, the talk of drugs, and I saw red again. I wanted to lunge at him, to scrape his handsome face with my nails, to destroy that smirk from his face, to claw his skin, to hurt.

His eyes were on me.

"I hope I never see you again," I spat.

Forty

Now all I saw was gray. In the elevator, Rachel touched my hands, my fingers twisted into fists, nails digging in my skin. She wrapped her hands around my fists and leaned closer.

"You're free," she whispered.

I nodded. This did not feel like freedom. This was a red wall of fury.

She guided me out of the building, grabbing an Uber back to her apartment. All the way, she glanced in my direction, the blankness of my face turning the night in her eyes to a small storm.

Rachel opened the door, and I stepped inside. I walked after her to the kitchen. It was so light and stylish, the boho style all over her place. But it all was tinted with gray and blotches of red in front of my eyes. The air stopped being enough for me to exist and I leaned on the table, my clammy fingers leaving prints. I looked down.

"How could you?" I said, my voice trembling.

She walked around the table and stood right there; I only had to lift my head and I would be face to face with her. She was silent.

"How could you watch all he was doing and stay silent? How many girls were there like that one from the video? She was a kid!" I screamed. "And the drugs, Rachel, the drugs were distributed in schools! How could you stay and watch? How could you work there?"

Now I lifted my head to her, those marks on her neck grew darker, the eyes still red from the suffocation. But she met my eyes, not flinching.

"I had to find you," she said. "It's pure selfishness, I put my need of finding you in front of everything, in front of those horrors. I could have stopped them, put them both in jail, but Jason would never have met you, and I would not have found you. And now, after all's done, after you're free, I wouldn't have done otherwise, I'd have walked the same path: filmed, gathered evidence, and stood aside. Because it's enough, it was enough for me to see your eyes, how you looked at me, to set you free. The thing is, I'll always put you in front of everybody, I don't care about the world as long as you're safe, about the kids, the drugs. I protected you and always will, because I'm selfish."

"It's all the same, isn't it? Will was patching criminals up, helping them. And still Sophia fell in love with him," I said. At those words, Rachel lowered her gaze, the palm of her hand going to her heart, covering it. "But they would have run, they would have left the horrors of Daniel and Alexander behind. This time we managed to run."

"We?" Rachel asked.

I blinked at her, not understanding the question. And then it dawned on me: the lowered gaze, a hand clutching her heart, as if trying to protect it from the break. I crossed the table and pulled her in my hands.

"Is there a we?" she whispered. "Still?"

I pressed her tighter, feeling the light tremor in her body. "Of course." And I kissed the top of her head.

"Who am I to be mad at you when you just stood aside?" I asked, my voice trembling. "We're doing it again. Sophia did nothing to stop the mob; she helped them! Oh, how she enjoyed being needed, working with Ben, counting that blood money. At least Will helped people, not good people, but still. And in this life, you tried to help people who needed it, using blood money. And I landed in the bed of the criminal. And today, Rachel, I would have done it. I would have killed him. And who am I now?"

The roles were reversing now; Rachel held me while I clutched the edge of her shirt.

"I wanted to feel his blood on my fingers, I wanted to slice and punch and make him suffer. Look what I have become," I said and dropped my head on her shoulder. "I'm a monster," I whispered.

"No, no," Rachel said. "He's still playing with your mind. The monster is Jason. He did so many bad things, hurt so many people, that it's only natural for you to want to make him bleed."

She took my hand in hers and led me to the sofa. I lowered my head to her lap.

"You're the light, Cassie," she whispered and tugged the band from my hair, spilling it all over her lap, running her fingers through it. I closed my eyes and focused on her touch, the soft strokes on my skin.

After minutes or hours or days, I relaxed. She brushed my cheek and whispered, "You're free."

I nodded lightly.

But something was not right; claws still gripped my heart.

※

I went home, and in an hour, Jane and Noah were crushing me between them. Their faces were alight, smiles so true.

"He just let you go? No struggle?" Noah said, his brow shooting up.

"I guess he didn't want to have anything to do with me anymore. I kind of went off the rails," I said, my throat bobbing.

"What did you do?"

"He wanted to hurt Rachel, he grabbed her throat, started squeezing, I grabbed the knife."

Jane's face went pale. I looked down and closed my eyes.

"I didn't know I had it in me, and it would be so easy, just a flick of my wrist and his sharp kitchen knife would have cut him open," I said. "Rachel stopped me."

Noah draped his arms around me, snuggling me in.

"I feel the smell of another man from you," I noted.

"It's David," he just said.

I smiled to myself, burying my nose in his shoulder.

"Is it over?" Jane asked.

I stepped out of the hug and lowered myself to the floor, grabbing a pillow.

"I guess so," I replied.

Jane sat on the armchair, folding her legs, Noah in his usual spot. They looked at each other and then at me.

"I'm going back to work tomorrow, the usual life's back," I said.

"Cassie, what's wrong? You don't seem to be awfully happy to be free from the chains of a man who blackmailed you," Jane probed.

I put my head into my hands.

"I'm just tired, so, so tired," I whispered.

Jane stood.

"I'll get a bath running. Noah, prepare the bedroom and her clothes," she said.

And bless them both, they started running around me, the apartment a blur of movement. They dimmed the lights, Jane lit candles in the bathroom, soft music played from my portable speaker.

"You need to rest," Noah said and helped me stand up from the floor. "Get some sleep and we'll see you tomorrow."

"I'd recommend that you take a bath with Rachel, but I see that you're too tired," Jane said, and I blushed violently.

She laughed and planted a kiss on my cheek. Noah shook his head, but he was smiling.

In a few moments, they closed the door behind them, saying that I needed to get into the water while it was still hot.

My clothes fell in heaps on the bathroom floor, my hair up in a bun. I tested the water; it was searing hot. Good. I lowered my body into the pink foam. Jane loved bath bombs and shared this love with everyone in a vicinity of two miles around her.

The bathtub was so tiny, I had to scrunch my knees up. I lowered my head on the folded towel and closed my eyes. The hot water pricked my skin, and only now I noticed the cold knot in my chest. It eased a little in the steamy room.

I thought about Noah and Jane, two of them always with me, about Rachel and her dark eyes, I thought about myself, that I was really free. The fear on Jason's face upon seeing the records proved that he would not move.

And it seemed everything was fine, perfect even. But as seconds trickled by and the water turned colder, a thought formed in my mind. And I knew what I had to do.

Forty-One

The next day, I walked to my office, the sun shone from the glass skyscrapers, and the warmth of a late spring warmed my skin. The city moved around me: so many people, so much concrete, so many lives. How many of them stayed true to themselves? How many stood true to their closest?

Did that cab driver smile today? Or was he deep in his problems? This woman had dark circles under her eyes. The elderly man with a cane stood and watched the edge of the Central Park, and I wanted to stand with him and just look.

I texted Rachel, asking if I could see her after work and wished her luck today because I knew she would have to go to Jason's office for the last time.

She replied, "Sure. Meet me at my apartment at seven? He's not in the office today."

I smiled and did my job that whole day. I looked into the faces of my colleagues and imagined how they would change if they saw the videos of me Jason had threatened to share. And I realized that seeing porn of a colleague would be only mildly interesting amongst their full lives.

Noah and Jane looked after my every step; they saw

something was off. And as much as I tried to sound cheerful, they stood closer.

"You have to stop pretending, Cassie, you're the worst actor in the history of humanity," Jane said.

Noah nodded. "Tell us."

"I need to talk to Rachel first," I said.

"From the look of it, it won't be about you wanting to see her naked. Did you two have sex already?" Jane asked, looking intrigued.

Noah and I groaned.

"What?" she asked. "Did you?"

"No!"

"But you want it, do you?"

"My mind's elsewhere," I said. But after her words it was exactly where Jane painted it: my imagination pictured Rachel naked. And now a familiar sense stirred at the bottom of my core.

"Hah, it worked," Jane laughed and punched Noah with an elbow. "Do you see how her cheeks are growing red?"

Noah looked at me and also laughed. "You're right," he said.

I covered my face with my hands, but their laughter pulled a smile from me, and in a few seconds, I was laughing along, a genuine sound escaping my lips. And I realized how long it had been since I laughed that hard.

Rachel opened the door and my breath lost deep in my chest. She was wearing black leggings and a sleeveless shirt, the fabric hugging her chest tightly, and since there definitely was no bra, I could see her nipples peaking.

My resolve to talk to her went in a different direction.

"You're using Sophia's methods on me," I said.

Her eyes studied my face, a mischief playing on her lips.

"They're working, aren't they?" She smiled and took my hand, leading me inside.

I tried to look away when she turned and put a glass of wine in my hand.

"Today was my last working day," she said and clinked my glass.

I took a gulp of wine, my eyes roaming her body, the glow of her skin, the rise and fall of her chest. God, give me the strength, I thought.

"I need to talk to you," I said and took one more gulp. "But honestly, all I want to do is undress you."

She laughed and walked to me, pressing her body close and gently stroking my back. I wanted to touch her lips, but she moved her face and murmured in my ear.

"Let me get dressed," she said and bit my earlobe lightly.

She disappeared into the bedroom. I stood there, my heart like a bird in my chest from the light caress, and I fought with all I had not to rush after her.

Rachel walked back, a huge hoodie covering her upper body.

"I'm all ears," she said and took her glass back.

"Just for the record, I'd much prefer you to be without this hoodie and that top and leggings. Not that I don't like them, but . . ." I mumbled and Rachel laughed, so light, the song of it going right into my chest and staying there.

"You don't know what you're talking about," she said and took my hand in hers, our fingers entwining in a familiar pattern. I brushed her knuckles and took a deep breath.

"I can't go on like this," I said. "Jason must be stopped along with Simon. The man's pure evil. I can't stop thinking about that poor girl. She was just a child and already knocked up by a man thrice her age. She was like a little lamb, already faced with something she was too young to see. This is wrong, Rachel. And there are more on those videos, more outrageous things they're doing. And drugs. Anyway, I'm ready to face the consequences of my actions, be as it may, Jason can share my videos, but I'm going to the police."

"You just can't let it go, can you?" she asked.

I shook my head.

"No. And I'm sorry."

"You know, in his previous life, Daniel died from a heart attack, but do you know where? It was the most expensive building in New York, he stayed in the city and got richer and richer. No one stopped them and they went on spreading their filth throughout the country," she said and looked at me. "I think even if Sophia and Will managed to run away, Sophia would have looked back, she would have returned, she would have said the same words you're saying now, that it should be stopped. And it's crazy, but I agree."

"They are going to question you too, because you worked there. Jason would drag us both with them," I said.

Rachel shook her head and smiled sadly. "No, he won't drag you into all of this."

That sounded ridiculous. "Why are you saying that?"

"Because Daniel never married."

"That doesn't mean anything," I said.

"It means everything. Cassie, he loved Sophia in his dark and twisted, adulterous way. She was the one who believed in a boy from Moscow with the wildest dreams, who took him seriously. And even if Jason doesn't remember about it in this life, he feels the connection. What did you see in his face yesterday?"

"Fear."

"And?" Rachel looked at me, the clear night of her eyes studying me.

When I kept silent, she continued. "It was hurt and disbelief. According to his plans, you should've come back to him and stayed with him, because even in this life he was slowly falling in love with you, and when he saw that you wanted to leave him, in his awful way he started threatening you, and in his rage, he would have shared those videos. But if you chose to stay with him, he'd never ever hurt you intentionally. Daniel loved Sophia; Jason remembers the feeling. So no, he won't drag you down with him."

"But he'll drag *you*," I said quietly.

"Don't worry about me, I did nothing wrong, I just did my job. All clear and official."

I pressed my forehead to her shoulder. Rachel rubbed the back of my neck.

"We can send the videos anonymously," I said.

"No, Jason would know who did it anyway, he could spin us into the tale. If we go to the police and tell everything as it is, show the videos, we're protected. But he can still do what he threatened to do. He can send videos, because we're going to break the deal."

"I know. It's okay, it's only my naked body and reputation against all they're doing, and I'm willing to take a fall just to stop them."

Rachel closed her hands around me, and I rubbed the tip of my nose on her neck.

"Are you sure?" she asked.

"Yes."

I lifted my face a few inches and touched the base of her neck with my lips. She tensed as I slowly went up, my lips touching the skin under her ear, her jaw.

She did not lower her head, she did not move, and I stopped. I pushed away from the sofa, her hands falling to her sides.

"Why are you doing this? Why are you toying with me?" I asked, as tears threatened to fill my eyes. "I can't understand; when we kissed, it was the most sensitive thing I ever felt, but it was only once. You're fighting, keeping me at a distance. But all your actions show that you care—what about that top today? You wanted to see the hunger in my eyes? You don't need to play games with me to see it. I'm open, Rachel, and I want you, and

I'm this close to falling in love with you, but you keep pushing me just to pull me back."

"Don't say that," she said, so much pain in her eyes. "This is your mind playing tricks with you. You want Will, and I'm not him anymore, I don't have his body, I'm not a man! And you can't possibly love a woman. You can't be attracted to me!"

"I said that I'm almost in love with you, and you're saying I can't be attracted to you," I said, shaking my head. "I remember Will's devotion, his care, his love, not his body. And now I see everything he was to Sophia in you, but you're so much more. How you protect me, how you look at me, and in that same moment, how you fight me. Why are you doing this? Why are you pushing me away?"

"Because you're not gay, Cassie! Because the more I kiss you, the more difficult it would be when you're gone. You're saying you're *almost* in love with me. Do you know why there's this word, *almost*? Because I'm a woman in this damn life. It would be so easy if I had been a man again. I would scoop you up and make love to you right here. But I can't do it because we're two women, and I was a lesbian from the moment I felt any attraction, but you're straight, Cassie. All I want to do is touch you, smell you, make you smile, I want you to be happy. There was no word *almost* from the moment I met you. Because I knew you, and I would do everything for you to stay safe. And now every time you're close, you end up in my arms. And I try to protect my heart from breaking into a million pieces, because of that *almost* word, because I'm a woman, and we can't be lovers."

Hot tears ran down my face.

"You're wrong, so, so wrong," I said.

"Please don't cry," she whispered.

I lowered my head. "Please kiss me," I said, my lips barely moving, because I hurt, because my chest was cracking. "Please." I was not looking at her, but I knew if she would reject me now I would break, something physically would die in me. "Please."

And her lips were on top of mine. She pressed me against the wall, her body blending into mine. And she was hollow in the places a man would be hard, she was full in the places a man would be flat. I did not care a bit. I grinded my hips into hers while our tongues met. I pushed my hand under her hoodie, under the top.

"Cassie," she whispered.

But I pushed my hand higher till my fingers found the flesh of her breast, till I cupped it, brushing my fingers around her nipple, touching it. A soft moan escaped her lips, and she pressed me tighter to the wall.

"You can't throw that *almost* word in my face," I whispered, inches between us. "I'm crazy about you, I want you, and that *almost* exists only as a last wall against your resistance. We're meant to be together, Rachel, you and me. I don't care that you're a woman, because I love you."

And we fell to the floor, our lips crashing, our hands roaming each other's body. I pulled the hoodie over her head, the raven curls falling on her eyes, spilling on the floor. I kissed her neck, my hand under her top, touching, squeezing. I kissed her nipple through the fabric of the top, sucking it, leaving a wet stain. I lowered my hand to the skin under her navel, barely touching as I moved lower.

"Wait," she whispered. The hot breath on my lips, the sweet fog in her eyes. "I'm on my period," she said, avoiding my eyes.

I almost laughed but stopped when I looked at her; she was so vulnerable, so open, breathing hard.

"I don't care," I said and touched the skin right on the edge of her leggings. A jolt of lightning went down my core.

"No, please," she was looking at me. "I want it to be perfect. Not today."

I nodded. "Okay. But you need to know, there's nothing I

ever wanted more than to taste you, and don't you dare say that I'm not a lesbian, I'm not. But I'm so into you."

I lifted her top, revealing the peaked breasts, the dark skin around her nipples so smooth as I ran my tongue over it. Her fingers were lost in my hair, and my body ached for her touch, but it was not about me. Rachel arched her back when I kissed every inch of her exposed skin. I was so wet when she brushed her fingers between my legs, rubbing the seam against my hot skin. I gasped when she moved it faster, the silk of my panties and jeans a wall between her fingers and me. I pushed against her touch, and I was losing it. She covered my lips while I gasped, when she held my trembling body.

I breathed hard, my eyes on the woman I loved, one hand lost in her hair, another on her breast, her heart hammering under my touch.

"Like a teenager," I whispered, my voice rasping, the blush covering my cheeks.

"It was a little preview," she said and pressed her lips to mine, biting the tip of my tongue.

Forty-Two

We stood in front of the gray building. The city roared behind us, the doors in front of us opened and closed as people went in and out of the police department. We both looked up at the sign, our hands together as they were often now. My heart was pounding, but I knew that this was right. We needed to end this string of lives, of lust, of possession, of business that goes from life to life, the business of destroying so many souls.

I turned to Rachel and studied the edges of her face for a second, till she turned her face to me. The radiant smile took me to a place of safety.

"You sure?" she asked.

"Yes."

She squeezed my hand and took a step forward; she opened the door for me, and as I was stepping inside, she nodded slightly. We could do it. We would.

It took us an hour to hop from one officer to another till we were asked to wait in a room which suspiciously looked like one from the movies, just a table and four chairs. There was no mirror, but the steady light of a red camera light watched us from the corner of the room.

Our hands were clasped under the table as we waited.

Finally, the door opened, and a woman in her fifties stepped in. She wore a gray suit, and her lips were pressed in the thinnest line, the deep wrinkles lining her forehead and skin around her eyes. She squinted at both of us, reading our faces in milliseconds.

"My name's Alma Brown," the woman said. "I'm a NYPD detective."

Alma sat in front of us and clasped her hands on the table. "You said to an officer that you had information to share regarding the drug spread."

My throat was dry, and I was afraid to utter a word, hands slightly shaking. Rachel looked at me and nodded, she started to tell the story. A few beats later, the words finally came to me.

We told about how we met at the office party in Jason's office. I rewound back to where and how I met Jason. How he blackmailed me into staying with him and his obsession with cameras. We slightly changed the story to how Rachel got access to the videos from Jason's office. We did not say that she installed them, only said that there was a glitch in the system which gave her access to records. And how what she saw opened Rachel's eyes to the true identity of Jason's company. As Rachel and I got close, I shared with her that Jason blackmailed me, and we decided to use the videos against Jason. It worked, but I realized how much more important what they were doing was compared to videos of me. So, here we were.

Alma listened quietly, from time to time asking questions. In the end, she leaned back on her chair and looked from me to Rachel and back.

"This sounds like a perfect coincidence: You meeting Rachel, realizing you're attracted to her, at the same time as she was the only person who could have helped you to blackmail

Jason in return," Alma said, her steel voice accompanied by the rise of her brow.

The story of our past lives we left to ourselves, and it was the only explanation we could give for this concern.

"I'm lucky, I guess," I said.

Alma grunted. At least she did not question the nature of the cameras in Jason's office and the system glitch.

"Do you have these videos with you?" she asked.

Rachel nodded and pulled up that same old iPad, the back panel scratched.

We showed the video with the girl, Alma's face a mask of stone. But when Jason and Simon were discussing the school in Baltimore with rich kids, a dull fire played on the otherwise calm face of the detective.

She took the iPad and scrolled down, swiping from one video to another, stopping on the video of them discussing names and places I had never heard of.

Alma paused the record and turned off the iPad.

"This is valuable information you collected here," she said and covered the screen with her hand. "But I don't believe Jason to be that stupid as to install a camera in his own office, where information like that is discussed. And certainly he's not a man to put some lousy protection on the video storage. How did you retrieve these records?"

We knew that our story could be revealed sooner or later, but it was too soon.

Rachel did not skip a beat.

"I installed the camera in his office. A few years ago Jason hired a company to install cameras all over the corridors and kitchen. Every room had a small lens recording every move. Every room but Jason's. The office was a mess when the workers installed them, wires all over the walls and ceiling. I knew Jason was not all clean, and a quick Google search revealed the smallest camera. I used the time before the system started recording and hid it in his office."

Alma was looking at Rachel, her gaze freezing the air in the bleak room.

"Now, this sounds like it could be true. Ten minutes ago, the story was different. Why did you lie?"

"To protect Rachel," I blurted out.

"This also sounds like it's true," Alma said, finally her face crumbling to a smile. "Girls, don't lie to the police, we see it. And even if that move of installing the camera in your boss's office sounds weird, I can believe in it. Are there copies of these records?"

"Yes," Rachel said.

"Can you leave this iPad for the investigation? Is everything on it?" Alma asked.

"No, there's more. Five terabytes of videos on the different hard drives and in cloud storage."

Alma nodded. "We suspected that Simon Rocherfield was connected to the web of the drug distribution, and with these," she pointed to an iPad, "we finally have all the evidence to take him."

"What's going to happen to Jason?" I asked.

Rachel slowly turned her head to me and found my eyes.

"He'd be charged as an accomplice," Alma said. "And about those videos of you, do you really think he'll share them?"

"Yes, but it's okay, I've made my choice," I said.

Alma laughed, but her eyes warmed for the first time since she walked in here. "If he doesn't know that you're here now, and if he did not do it yet, it could easily be prevented. I need all the videos from his office from you, but even the ones I saw here are enough for the arrest."

"They're stored online, I can share the access here," Rachel said.

"Perfect," Alma said and gave the iPad to Rachel. She tapped her fingers, and the cloud storage app revealed the list of numerous files with dates.

The detective opened a few videos and nodded.

"Rachel, you'll be questioned as the person who installed the camera and your motives, because you worked there and because you concealed this information from police," Alma said.

My heart skipped a beat, and suddenly I was suffocating in the small room.

"What?" I whispered as I clutched her hand, she squeezed back.

"I know, detective," Rachel said.

She sat there, the dark hair fell on her eyes, her face pale, but her spine was iron straight. The tips of her fingers grew cold against my skin, and I wanted to take her far, far away from here. How could I believe in fighting for justice when Rachel was so deep in this? She knew and I did not, she knew that they would question her and charge her. The smallest noise escaped my lips as I turned to her.

"If you have nothing to hide and all you did was conceal it from the police till now, you don't need to worry," Alma said and moved closer to us. "You were afraid for your job, but now you're here, and that's all that matters. Do you have anywhere safe to go to leave the city?"

"Yes," Rachel said.

"Good, it'd be safer if you can leave New York for a few weeks till the dust settles," Alma said and stood. "We'll be in contact. And Rachel, you worked in a different department, you realized what Jason was doing and wanted to collect evidence; hence, you installed the camera, and you collected it till now, is that correct?"

Rachel nodded.

"Is that correct?" Alma asked again, her voice more authoritative than before.

Rachel turned her face slightly to the camera in the corner of the room. "Yes, I was working in a department helping people who had no means to protect themselves. Once I overheard what Jason and Simon were discussing, I knew if I went to the police I would have nothing but my words to prove it. I installed the camera, and I stored all the videos till now. Now I realized I had enough evidence to prove Simon is guilty and came here."

Alma smiled. "That sounds right. Now, girls, leave the city for a few weeks. I'll be in touch."

She took the iPad and walked out of the room.

I took Rachel's hand, and we stepped through the corridors of the police department. Once outside, I hailed a cab, and it took us to Rachel's apartment building.

She was quiet all the way as I held her both hands in mine.

"We did it," she whispered as we stood in front of the entrance. "We did it."

"Let's go inside," I said and pulled her in. She fumbled with the keys as her hands were shaking, and finally the lock clicked open, and we were in the safety of her flat.

I touched her face, putting my hands on the back of her neck. Her eyes searched my expression, and I went to my knees, hugging her waist as tears finally choked me.

"I'm so, so sorry," I said as I pressed my forehead into her belly. She ran her fingers on the top of my head, tangling in my hair.

"Now, you're free," she said.

"I'll protect you," I said. "I'm so sorry."

"They'll question me, but that's all," Rachel said and lowered to my level, dropping to her knees. "We're free, Cassie."

"They can charge you."

"They won't, and Alma knew it. Look at me," Rachel said, and I listened. "It's almost over."

And she kissed me, the salt of my tears between our lips.

"Now you kiss me," I laughed weakly.

"Because you love me," she said simply.

"I do," I said and kissed her back, hoping with all my mind that all she was saying was true. That it was almost over, that we could be free, that the police wouldn't hurt Rachel.

I kissed her cheek, her forehead, her neck, I stopped at the base of her throat and inhaled, the smell of forest took me over.

"Where are we going?" I asked.

She moved in my hands and as I followed her pointed finger, my gaze landed on the painting of the field.

"Perfect," I said and rested my head back on her shoulder as we lay there on the floor in each other's arms.

Fred looked at me from under his bushy eyebrows.

"Do you really think that it's wise to go remote on the final stage of your project?" he asked.

"It won't matter," I said. "I'll attend all meetings online. I'm going to stay in contact with the team. But you know, it doesn't matter where I'm sitting—here or in another part of the States—as long as I do my job, and you taught me well. Trust me, I won't fail you."

He looked at me and grunted. "Okay, if nothing changes in your schedule, as long as you do what you do now and are present in all meetings online, you can go. Let's test this remote working thing."

I almost hugged him.

Now, I had to talk to Jane and Noah. I waited till lunch time, and we perched on our usual spot with takeout boxes. They already knew about the police and how it went.

"The detective suggested that Rachel and I leave the city for a couple of weeks. She thinks it might be safer if we were out of town," I said.

Jane froze with her plastic fork of salad in midair, Noah looked at me for a second and lowered his gaze. But we all knew why it should be done, they could backlash, Simon could find out who had given them up to the police.

"It makes sense," Noah said and put a hand on my shoulder. "We're going to miss you."

Jane's eyes watered and she almost knocked me over when she hugged me.

I loved them both so much, my people who I wanted to stay close with, whom I wanted to protect.

"I'll be back in the blink of an eye," I said and laughed.

"You better be," Jane sniffed and tried to smile.

"A little vacation with your new girlfriend," Noah sang, and I blushed. "How's it going between you two?"

"I still can't believe Cassie has a girlfriend," Jane said and this time she really smiled.

"It's easy and natural," I said.

"Oh, wipe that dreamy look from your face!" Jane said teasingly.

And we all laughed. "I love you, guys," I said.

They looked at each other and smiled. "We love you."

The sun of an early summer played with the tops of the trees in Central Park. I looked around at the calm oasis of the bustling city and the monstrous buildings of New York, the streets so full of life. I dropped my head on Jane's shoulder and closed my eyes.

Forty-Three

Rachel's parents were a lively couple living in a big farmhouse and deep into the cheese-making business. They sold a townhouse in New York and moved here ten years ago. They were always busy and so in tune with each other. I saw them more like a unit, not two separate people. They welcomed me warmly, and they did not pry about why we needed to come on such short notice. Rachel's dad, George, just threw the keys to her and hugged her. The keys were to a tiny house on the outskirts of the farmland, hidden in the trees. Joan, Rachel's mom, had the same raven hair but shorter than her daughter's. She was wearing overalls and a red checkered shirt and those eyes, lighter than Rachel's, but still so dark crinkled at me.

"Welcome to the family," she said and draped her arms around me.

The Tiny house, as Rachel called it, had only one bedroom and one bathroom. I shot Rachel a look, my eyebrow going up, she just shrugged and winked. The Internet reception was surprisingly good in the Tiny house, and we put two desks for us to work on weekdays.

The image from the painting was in front of my eyes. The vast field of blooming flowers which stopped right before the hills started. My hand was in Rachel's, and the most serene expression bloomed on her face: She was smiling at the nature around. The birds were chirping, and the smell of green grass and flowers was almost unbearable to my city lungs.

Rachel draped a blanket on the bed of lush green grass and tugged me down. We had nothing with us but a bottle of champagne and a few sandwiches. She poured two plastic glasses, and we clinked.

"You know, there's no one around for miles," Rachel said as she covered my hand with hers.

"Really?"

"Yes, and I wanted to try one thing," she murmured and touched my lips.

She tasted of champagne and something sweet as she found my tongue, as her hand went down my shirt. A small jolt went down my core when her fingers touched my belly, going up. The thin fabric of my bra was everything between my skin and her fingers.

"I want to see you," she said, a caress to my ear as she pulled off my shirt. With a flick of her wrist, she unclicked my bra; it landed in the grass.

I had never seen such hunger as I saw in that moment in her eyes, her hand was shaking as she brushed the swell of my breast, as she closed her lips around my nipple. She kissed me, her tongue flicking over it, she sucked, and my hips started moving involuntarily. Rachel lowered me onto the blanket and kissed me down, unbuttoning my shorts till all I was wearing was my silk black panties. She moved her finger between my legs, and I gasped. I was melting under her touch, but I pulled her to me, dragging her shirt up as my fingers roamed her breasts.

Rachel went down on me, her raven hair spilled on her face when she kissed me between my legs. I begged her not to stop, I pleaded for more, my hands pressing her into me. Every inch of my body electricized as it moved under her lips and tongue and fingers. It shook violently as I was climaxing, as I repeated her name over and over again, as the wall of blinding light hit me, hard.

I was dazed when she found my lips, as I tasted myself on her. Our naked bodies touched, and I looked down, her breasts were close to mine, the image so impossibly real, her nipples grazing mine, and I flipped her on her back.

The darkness of night looked back at me, the need, the want mixed with a tinge of shyness. I needed to see her, to feel her with my lips. I trapped her nipple between my teeth, so lightly, and lowered my hand to her leggings, I went down right to the core, nothing between me and her. She was so hot there and so, so wet. Her lips parted as Rachel watched me as I took my fingers out from her leggings, as I put them in my mouth and sucked.

"Oh god," she whispered.

And it triggered something in me, something wild and raw. My hands shook violently as I helped her out of the leggings, as she spread her legs in front of me, I saw her. And again her eyes locked with mine, just for a second, before I rubbed my fingers over her, and she closed them, taking a shuddering breath.

And in that field, I tasted woman for the first time in my life, and it was easy, and it was natural, and she was crashing under my touch, her fingers lost in my hair as her hips thrust against me, as she was losing it, her moans taken by the summer breeze and carried to the hills. I had never seen anything so beautiful, so raw and open as Rachel in those seconds as she crumbled to pieces. The sweat was glistening on her skin as she arched her back, as with the final cry, she came.

I cradled her in my arms, pressing her into me, the sun warming our naked bodies.

"You're so beautiful," I whispered, kissing her neck.
"I love you," was all she replied.

Forty-Four

Everything changed after that first day in the field. As there were no more walls between us, I found myself so deeply in love with the woman by my side, I could not imagine my life without her in it. Now, I finally understood why Sophia did what she did; she just stepped after the man she loved, stepped into the nothingness to chase him. That love was rooted, it stretched through lives, and we wondered if there were lives before Sophia and Will, the ones we did not remember. I mourned the life the two of them could have had, and how it was cut short, probably triggering the memories in this one.

After a week of staying in Tiny house, Rachel drove us to Asheville, just a thirty-minute drive from the farm. And walking the streets of that city, my heart stayed there.

As we stopped in front of the brightly colored art shops in the River Arts District, I entwined my fingers with hers.

"Can you imagine living here?" I asked.

She turned to me.

"Actually, I can," Rachel said and pulled me into the nearest shop.

That same night, lying in the tangled sheets of the bedroom

of the Tiny house, my head in the crook of her shoulder, slowly tracing the silky skin of her belly, I looked up at her.

"Rachel?"

Her hands were around me. "Yes."

"I love it here. I love the mountains around, I love nature, the trees, the sky, I could actually see the blue of the sky here!" I said. "And today, that city was something so warm, so inviting, so different from New York."

I propped myself on my elbow, looking into her dark eyes. She was smiling.

"Do you . . ." Rachel asked and paused to kiss my jaw, sending tingling lights down my core, "Would you like to live in Asheville?"

She trailed her fingers down my waist, my hip.

"I think I would," I said and laughed, catching her fingers, and kissing the tips of them. "What about you? What do you think?"

"I think we should go to a real estate office tomorrow," she said.

"Really?"

"Really. As much as I love New York, I'm a bit tired of the rhythm of life, of all the crowds, and those tiny boxes we all live in. And the drama, Cassie! All that previous life remembering, it's a bit energy draining," she said and laughed when I tickled her. "I'm unemployed now, I can do whatever I want. And opening a small practice here in Asheville sounds like a good idea."

I was beaming; we were standing on the edge of something new and so different.

"I could work remotely," I said, "We could find a house on the edge of the forest, we could hear the birds in the mornings, but..."

"But what about Jane and Noah?" Rachel asked after I stopped, after my smile dimmed.

I loved my guys so much I needed them close. The separation would tear a piece of my heart and shred it into a million chunks.

"They'll understand," I said and dropped my head on the pillow. In a second, a worried face was in front of me.

"We don't have to decide anything, you can talk to them first, and anyway, you love New York. Do you think you could leave it?" she asked.

The thing was I could. And I wanted to. As much as I loved the Big Apple, I felt it did its thing; it led me to Jane, Noah, and this woman in front of me, and now it was time to move on. I felt free here; even now, the room was filled with the noise of the forest outside. I took a deep breath.

"I want a life with you," I said, "I want it outside of the city. There are too many memories there, but I want to build new ones, happy ones." My hand was lost in the dark curls as Rachel lowered her lips to mine, just a graze before she kissed my shoulder, lowering the strap of my top.

※

I opened my eyes to the sound of falling water in the shower, the empty place to my right still warm. I stood by the door and watched her through the transparent curtain. The talk of the previous night was still rolling in my thoughts, and as scared I was, I knew it was something I wanted to do.

She peered from the curtain, the wet hair plastered to her face.

"Come here," she said quietly.

The crumpled nightgown landed on the tile as I stepped out of it and into the hot stream. Rachel took shower gel and poured it on my chest, the liquid sliding down between my breasts. She caught it and rubbed my belly, my arms, my thighs. I found her lips, the softness crashing into me.

"You don't have to change anything," she whispered. "We can go back to New York, back to your life, we'll rent a bigger apartment."

"No," I said and rubbed the tender skin between her legs.

Rachel moaned and I caught it with my lips.

Forty-Five

TEN MONTHS LATER

We did not know what the word *pandemic* meant before. Just a word amongst thousands from the vocabulary. But this word changed everything in the spring of 2020. When the world closed down, the panic, the loss of loved ones all over the world.

It had only been a month since Rachel and I rented a house on the edge of the forest, when the world found out about it. The office in New York I had begged to allow me to work remotely now switched to a complete work from home schedule.

Zoom calls with kids crying in the background, cats sitting on the edge of screens, it would have been funny if we were not so scared. After a month of isolating in New York, I asked Jane to visit us. Rachel, the hostess of the house, prepared a room with huge windows looking at the old oak tree. Once Jane drove to Asheville, she never drove back. That old oak did something to the dark circles under her eyes, the work laptop sitting just in front of the tree.

Her lease ran out in May 2020, and we drove Jane to New

York to pack her things and move her into the house just down the street from ours. For the price of a small apartment in New York, in Asheville she could rent herself a house—small, but so like her. Something shifted in her in those months when the world was going crazy, she became grounded, started oil painting, hiking, and on one of her solo hikes, she met Matthew, a quiet web developer who moved to Asheville from scorching California.

She did not mean to stay in Asheville, but the new reality of empty streets with so many people staying at home in those tiny apartments, Jane was withering there. Here, she soaked in nature, and tender blushes of love highlighted her cheeks.

Before we moved to North Carolina, Rachel had a hearing about Jason and working in his company. As Alma had said, they did not press the issue of why she installed the camera in his office. I saw Jason only once during that hearing, and when he looked at me, there was only pain in his eyes, not anger but disappointment and sadness. He was charged along with Simon. All this time sitting in the courtroom, I was praying to all the gods who could listen about Rachel, she needed to be safe. And in the end, when Jason turned to me one last time, I silently begged him to let me go.

And a few days later, we packed all our lives in a rented truck and drove to our new home on the edge of the forest. Did I miss New York? It was a bittersweet sensation of parting with a friend, but we both knew I was just on the verge of a new part of my life.

My parents visited us a few weeks after we moved. They loved Rachel on the spot, not questioning her gender, accepting her to the family immediately. My Dad said that there was a new glint in my eyes, and my mom found a close friend in Rachel's mother. They talked for hours, sometimes leaving us to explore art galleries and roam coffee shops by themselves. She invited all of us to visit Tallahassee.

In February, I got a call from Lorraine. We had drifted apart a little after I moved to New York, mostly it was my fault. I dove into my new sophisticated job and big city life, while she stayed there in a cozy cocoon of her life with Paula. We talked from time to time, sharing major events. And only a week ago, I messaged her to say I moved to Asheville; I tried calling, but she never replied. And now her voice was trembling as she talked about Paula getting pregnant; after a few rounds of unsuccessful IVF, it happened. They had wanted to have a baby for years, and now, it was happening.

Lorraine asked why I moved, and I invited her and Paula to visit us.

"I moved in with my partner, Richard," I said, and Rachel, who was standing right by my side, almost dropped the plate she was holding.

Lorraine drove to us in a week for an extended weekend, and, oh sweet lies, it was so worth it. She rushed to my side and threw her hands around me in a hug while Paula hovered on the steps.

"Where's Richard?" Lorraine asked.

"Um, it's not Richard, it's Rachel," I said as she stepped outside, our fingers finding each other as they did now all the time.

The expression Lorraine had was a mix of puzzlement, shock, and a long, long pause. Paula laughed and stretched her hand to Rachel.

"What? Are you . . ." Lorraine said slowly, looking at me. "She's a woman."

"I know."

"But you're not gay, are you?"

"No," I said, kissing the top of Rachel's head.

Paula was smiling widely, standing a few feet away. Rachel stepped to her and took a bag from her hands.

"Let's give these two a minute," she said.

Paula nodded, and they disappeared inside. Lorraine was silent, and then she hugged me again.

"Are you happy?" she whispered in my ear.

"Yes," I replied.

And I was.

Epilogue

We sat in a circle on sports mats, a few feet apart from each other, six people in our backyard. Jane's back was pressed to the oak, Matthew sat by her side, their knees touching,

Noah and David drove from New York. With the pandemic, David lost his job, and with Noah working remotely like the rest of us did, there was no reason to stay in New York. Tomorrow was a big day; they would go house hunting.

And just like that, the people I cared most about moved closer to me. We were back together.

❦

It was dark and quiet in the house when everyone left.

"Rachel?"

"I'm here," she said, the voice coming from the porch.

She turned to me when I opened the screen door, her hair glistening from the moonlight shining directly on the porch.

"What are you doing here?" I asked and walked to her, draping my hands around her.

"Listen," she said, turning to the forest.

Somewhere deep in the forest an owl was hooting, the movement of the leaves and branches, twigs swinging, the life of the night forest just a few steps away.

And we stood there, listening, our bodies pressed together, the story of dreams, previous lives, coming to an end. Under the night sky that was so familiar, the color of the eyes of a person I remembered, of the man who died, but now blooming with the shining stars in Rachel's eyes.

"I will always find you," Rachel said. A soft breeze wrapped around her words and took them into the forest night.

Acknowledgments

This book was inspired by my numerous trips to Riga, the city that enchanted my mind.

I want to thank Jean Lowd and the team at Creative James Media for believing in me and my books from the very beginning. Thank you for your support, I truly value it.

Special gratitude goes to my family. My Grandmother is a great believer in my books. My Mom has a special stand for my books in her house, and everyone who visits her inevitably sees it. Thank you, Mom, for making me blush.

I'm grateful to my friends who read my books and who couldn't because of the language barrier. My heart swells for the encouragement and your belief.

Often, my mind slips away into an imaginary land, and there is a person who tolerates those blank stares. Thank you.

And of course to the readers, reviewers and people who believe in my art—thank you so much for taking time in this crazy world to read my books. I'm immensely grateful for each of you.

About the Author

Laura May is the pen name of a Ukrainian-American author. She travels around the world, but her hometown, Kyiv, always calls her back.

For the latest updates on Laura May and her books, visit LauraMayAuthor.com, and you can also follow her on Instagram at Instagram.com/LauraMayAuthor

I See You in My Dreams is the second book by Laura May published by Creative James Media.

Spread the Love

Dear Reader,

Thank you so much for reading this book!

Would you like to receive exclusive discounts, special deals, and advanced reader copies? Join my newsletter today:

LauraMayAuthor.com/newsletter

If you enjoyed the book, I would be immensely grateful if you could leave a review on Goodreads, Amazon or any other online store where you bought the book. The reviews help other readers to find and make a decision to read the story.

Your support is extremely valuable to me. Thank you for being a part of the adventure!

Printed in the USA
CPSIA information can be obtained
at www.ICGtesting.com
LVHW020415080324
773861LV00005B/430